Adèle and Co

DORNFORD YATES

Adèle and Co

WARD LOCK LIMITED
LONDON

Designed by Humphrey Stone
Text set in Intertype Baskerville
Printed by The Compton Press Ltd.
Bound by Leighton Straker Ltd.

TO
THE VILLA MARYLAND, PAU,
WHICH, WITH ITS ENGLISH GARDEN,
MADE ME A HOME WORTH HAVING
FOR SEVENTEEN YEARS

Contents

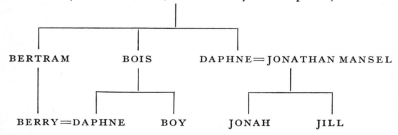

BERTRAM PLEYDELL
(of White Ladies, in the County of Hampshire)

BERTRAM   BOIS   DAPHNE═JONATHAN MANSEL

BERRY═DAPHNE   BOY   JONAH   JILL

CHAPTER I

We Sup with the Devil

I afterwards found that it was six o'clock in the morning when first I opened my eyes.

I immediately shut them again, not because of what I saw—though that was enough to make any man cover his face—but because the impression that a red-hot skewer had been suddenly passed through my head was overwhelming. I can describe the pain in no other way.

Almost at once, however, the emotions of curiosity, horror and alarm furiously demanded the truth, and, after bracing myself, I opened my eyes again.

To my infinite relief I almost immediately discovered that it was not the opening of my eyes, but their movement which caused the torment which I have sought to describe, and, without more ado, I proceeded to look about me, cautiously moving my head, like some mechanical doll, but keeping my eyes as still as those of statuary.

In my time I have looked upon many disorderly scenes, but I have never witnessed any spectacle which was quite so dissolute or suggested half so vividly one of those full-dress debauches to which the more genial of the Roman Emperors so much delighted to subscribe.

As rooms go, the *salon* was small, and the large, oval table, still bearing the remains of supper, occupied much of the space. All the lights were still burning—to no account, for the brave May sunshine was streaming into the room and sending a shining rebuke on all depravity. Borne on the sweet, fresh air, the morning cry of Paris came through the open windows which gave to the Place Vendôme, and the grateful swish of water declared that that famous pleasance was being washed for the day.

On my right, my sister Daphne had sunk as low as she could in a straight-backed chair. Her right hand was touching the floor, and her head had fallen forward and sideways until it was almost resting upon one arm of her chair. Though the posture was

9

scarcely graceful, nothing could diminish her beauty of figure and face. Her breathing was regular, but she was sleeping like the dead.

On my left lay my cousin Jill, Duchess of Padua. She had slipped from her chair, which had plainly abetted her movement and let her weight move it back. With one slim leg drawn up, she was lying flat on her back, exactly as though she had lately come out of the surf and were taking her ease on the sand in a bathing-dress. Her golden hair had fallen back from her brow, and, though she was now a mother, she looked like a child of fourteen.

Beside her, her husband, Piers, was hanging out of his chair and over his wife. His right arm was dangling free, for the arm of his chair had caught him beneath the arm-pit and held him up. His body was slack and crumpled, his head was down, and he made me think of a candle for which the heat of summer has been too much.

Beyond him, looking stouter than ever, Casca de Palk was still sitting square in his seat : but his head was down on the table—to be exact, in the dish which was resting upon his plate. The *foie gras* the former contained had melted before the touch of his countenance and was rising like a brown tide about his nostrils and bubbling gently before the breath of his lips.

On the opposite side of the table, my wife, Adèle Pleydell, was drooping as droops a flower whose stem has been snapped. Her fair arms were stretched before her upon the cloth, and her head was sunk between them like that of some suppliant. Her face was wholly hidden, and all I could see of her head was a hint of her dark brown hair. Had she been petitioning Zeus, I cannot believe that she would have gone empty away. Her shoulders must have found favour in his appreciative sight.

Against her reclined Berry Pleydell, my brother-in-law. His head lolled upon her shoulder, his body was supported by hers, and his arms and legs were sprawling like those of a sawdust doll. I regret to record that he looked especially shameless and more than anyone present sounded the Roman note.

On the floor, a little apart, lay my cousin, Jonathan Mansel, brother to Jill. He had fallen flat on his face, and his right arm was stretched before him towards the wall. His fingers were actually resting against the skirting-board. His posture suggested effort—some frantic attempt which had failed.

To crown this degrading scene, champagne was, or had been,

everywhere. Two glasses lay broken on the floor, and where each had fallen a patch of carpet was stained to a darker red. My wife's glass had fallen on the table to drench the cloth. Two bathroom tumblers stood on the mantelpiece : one was half full of wine, and cigarette-ends were fouling the other's dregs. Two bottles stood in a corner close to the door, and a third lolled in an ice-pail a foot away : a fourth bottle lay on its side between Berry's feet.

All this I saw and considered as though I had stumbled upon some battlefield. I was stupefied, shocked and dismayed. I found the time out of joint and deplored the snares and temptations of Vanity Fair. I felt much more than uneasy and I simply loathed three flies which were ceaselessly circling and darting beneath the red silk basin which hid the electric light. And that was as far as I could get. Reason why, I could not. My head . . .

Without thinking, I moved my eyes, and again that skewer of agony seared my brain.

Now whether that set my wits working I cannot tell, but in that instant the mists of confusion parted and three things struck me three several, staggering blows.

The first was that we had been drugged : the second, that two of our party were not in the room : and the third, that Daphne, Adèle and Jill were wearing no jewels.

My sister's emerald bracelets that came from Prague, her diamond and emerald necklace and diamond rings; the Duchess of Padua's pearls—historic gems which appear in a portrait by Velasquez that hangs at Rome, my wife's pearl necklace and rings and diamond watch—the lot were gone.

Dazedly I got to my feet and stepped to where Jonah was lying with his hand to the wall.

"Wake up," I cried, and shook him. "Jonah, wake up. We've been stung."

My cousin moved. Then he rolled on to his back and opened his eyes.

"Listen," I cried. "The Plazas have done it on us. They've made us tight, and there's not a jewel in the room."

Jonah sat up slowly and put a hand to his head.

"Half a moment," he said. "I must walk before I can run."

I left him and turned to Berry, who proved less easy to rouse.

I set him upright in his chair and shook him with all my might :

I lifted his head and bellowed into his ear : but both these assaults were vain : he continued to breathe stertorously. It was then that I thought of the ice-pails. . . .

The water was refreshingly cold and I put my face into a bucket and then brought it up to Jonah who did the same. Then I returned to Berry and sluiced a quart of the water over his head and neck.

For a moment I thought that even this measure had failed. Then he gave a little shiver and opened his eyes.

"Wake up," I cried. "Wake up. There's the devil and all to pay. The Plazas—"

His scream of torment snapped the sentence in two. He had, of course, moved his eyes. But it saved a lot of trouble, for no trumpet that ever was blown could have sounded so frenzied a note.

In an instant all was confusion.

Daphne started to her feet and stood swaying slightly and holding to the back of her chair : Piers gave a startled cry and then went down on his knees by the side of his wife : Adèle sat back in her chair, looking dazedly round, with a hand to her head : and Casca de Palk lifted up such a face as I had never imagined in all my dreams.

From his nose to the nape of his neck, one side of his head was coated with rich, brown grease. This was unevenly applied and gave to his face fantastic and dreadful contours for which no distortion could account. Out of the havoc an eye, like that of a toad, glared stupidly up into mine. For some unaccountable reason its owner was as yet unconscious of his unspeakable state.

Jonah was speaking.

"What's happened is this. The Plazas were crooks. They soused our wine last night and they've cleaned us out. When I felt myself going, I tried to get to the bell. That's the last thing I remember."

There was a moment's silence. Then—

"Thank God for that," groaned Berry. "I'm not in the mood for reminiscence, and I never did like your voice. Oh, and if anyone moves my eyes, I'll split his skull."

He drew in his breath venomously.

My sister was regarding her arms.

"My bracelets," she breathed. I saw her hands fly to her throat. Then she stooped to Piers on her left. "Jill's pearls," she cried.

"Are they gone?"

"Yes," said Piers, quietly enough.

De Palk clasped his head in his hands. Then he started, stared at his palms and let out a squeal of dismay.

"*Mon Dieu*," he screamed. "They 'ave serve me the dirty turn."

Berry regarded him earnestly. Then he covered his eyes.

"Good Lord," he said, "it's alive. I've been trying to wave it away. 'Love-in-a-Mist' by Epstein. If Rima could see him she'd wrap herself round him and bark."

If it was unfeeling to laugh, the punishment fitted the crime. At the first contraction of the muscles, the concentrated essence of anguish leaped in the top of one's head.

The general bubbles of mirth died into cries of pain.

"I can't believe it," wailed Daphne. "D'you mean to say that those people—that nice-looking man is a thief?"

"There's no other answer," said I painfully. "You can't suggest that this is a practical joke."

"But how did they do it?" said Adèle.

"Dope the wine? I don't know. But there weren't any servants up, and—and didn't he freeze the champagne?"

"It is true," screamed de Palk.

"O-o-oh," said Berry, wincing. "Someone explain to that siren that if he wants to play trains he must go and do it outside."

But Casca was not to be hushed.

"It is true," he raved. "It was Plaza has shown us the quick way to cool the wine. Oh, *mon Dieu,* we 'ave to walk straight into his mouth."

This was a fact.

We had come in to supper, to find the wine in waiting, but not upon ice. In some annoyance we had thrust it into the pails. Count Plaza had said he would cool it in double-quick time, and calling for salt, had added this to the water and started to twirl a bottle with all his might. In a word, he had made himself useful, and we had let him be.

"That's right," said Jonah. "Casca's got it in one. Plaza laced the liquor, and because it was Madame's birthday we all of us drank her health."

A bitter silence succeeded this simple statement of how the trick had been done.

13

At length—

"But we must do something," said Adèle. "We can't sit here and—"

"I do wish you wouldn't talk," said Berry weakly. "Every word you say is like being trepanned."

"Rot," said his wife. "You're no worse than anyone else. What about Jill's pearls?"

"They can have them," said Berry generously. "And my cuff-links, too." He glanced at his wrist. "Oh, they've got them. Never mind. D'you think they've taken the aspirin, just out of spite?"

"The beastly sweeps," cried Jill. "What harm have we ever done them? And they weren't my pearls. They were Piers'—his family jewels."

"Then why worry?" said Berry. "Now those cuff-links—"

Another squeal from de Palk lost us the argument.

"The greedy treachers!" he howled. "They 'ave stole my beautiful case. The cigarette-case *en platine* my brother 'as 'ad of the King. Were not the pearls enough? And Madame Pleydell's bracelets? And Madame Adèle's little watch? But, *mon Dieu*, what gluttony!"

This was a point of view which only a Frenchman could have seen, and despite the pain in my head I began to laugh.

"I expect they thought it was silver," said Berry, provocatively.

De Palk made a noise like that made by the dregs of a bath as they enter the waste, and it took the united efforts of Daphne and Adèle first to reduce him to coherence and then to make him believe that Berry's sense of decency does not exist.

Jonah was speaking.

"They've got five and a quarter hours' start. Why give them six? If you girls will get to bed, we'll send for a manager first and then for the police."

This counsel was common sense, and, since our rooms were *en suite*, it was easy enough to persuade my sister and wife and cousin to make themselves scarce. Five minutes later a manager came to the room.

The scenes which followed may as well be imagined as set down. Managers, porters, waiters and plain-clothes men came and went and were summoned and dismissed and reappeared until I felt that I was moving upon some fantastic screen. The telephone was

used and abused : statements were taken right and left : all manner of orders were issued, and if I described the Plazas, I described them a hundred times. Casca de Palk sat by the open window, cleansed but collarless, continuously reviling all "treachers",
arguing explosively with the detectives and calling God to witness
that the shooting pains in his head were not to be borne. Piers and
Jonah and I did what we could to compile an exhaustive list of
the property gone—by no means a simple task, for, as was to be
expected, the Plazas had been through the bedrooms before they
left, and the effort to recollect possessions which were no longer
there to speak for themselves, called for a concentration which no
one was fit to afford. Berry, wearing orange-coloured pyjamas and
a green felt hat of Daphne's which he had made sopping wet,
strolled to and fro, smoking, now goading de Palk to frenzy by
some idiotic advice, now criticizing our description of some of the
stolen goods, and now confusing the detectives by deliberately
referring to the Plazas as "the Count and Countess de Palk". The
effect of these "mistakes" upon Casca will go into no words that I
know, and though in the end even Jonah threw in his hand and
laughed till he cried, such devilry was inconvenient and at last
Piers and I intervened and fairly drove its author out of the room.

Not until past midday was some sort of order restored. Then
Casca de Palk took his leave, and the rest of us went to such rest as
our physical and mental conditions allowed us to take.

We had, it seemed, done what we could. The authorities had
been informed and would get to work. That we could ourselves
do no more seemed painfully probable. What was as clear as paint
was that until our heads stopped aching we could think to no
purpose at all.

We had been in Paris five days and had been proposing to stay
for another fifteen. The visit was annual. Three years ago we
had all met in this way, sharing the same suite of rooms in the
same hotel and all returning to England about the middle of June.
Paris can be very charming when summer is coming in, and our
stay had proved so pleasant in every way that we had determined
to make it an institution with which no other engagement should
interfere. When I say "we", I except Casca de Palk. Casca was of
Paris, but we had known him for years and while we stayed in his

city he was continually with us in all we did.

Regular habits suit a thief down to the ground. I have no doubt that our ways had been studied for years, for the blow had been timed with a nicety which only a considerable patience could have brought forth. At no other time in the year were we all assembled together within a hotel. The Duke and Duchess of Padua came from Rome : Jonah from London : and the rest of us from the New Forest, where we live. Privacy, servants, safes—for once in the year we put off these protections without a thought. In a word, we stepped out of our ground. What was so very unfortunate was that we took our jewels with us. At no other time in the year did Daphne, Adèle and Jill wear so consistently the precious stones they possessed. For all that, we were not careless. On the morning after a night on which they had been displayed, the Padua pearls and other important gems went into a mighty safe on the mezzanine floor. But if we took ordinary care we were robbed by no ordinary thieves. And there was the rub.

The Plazas we had met on the train six days before. That that is a damning confession I frankly admit, but it is always the obvious which one never perceives.

When we entered the train at Calais, they were already sitting in seats which we had reserved. No one, I think, could have argued that this was their fault, for they had been issued with tickets which bore the same numbers as ours. Flatly declining to break our party in two, they had instantly seized their baggage and made their way out of the coach, and though we had followed and begged that the Countess, at least, would return till other seats had been found, they would not accept this proposal and presently entered a carriage which was not reserved. Such courtesy is devastating. We naturally worried about it for the rest of the day. And when, twenty-four hours later, we saw them at lunch at the *Ritz*, Daphne had naturally voiced the distress we had felt. The rest, I suppose, was easy—from their point of view. Before two minutes had passed we were all introduced and were exchanging such small talk as the moment seemed to demand. It at once emerged that the Count was an Austrian, though Madame Plaza was of American birth. Learning that my wife was from Philadelphia, the Countess mentioned the name of a rather exclusive school.

"But I was there," cried Adèle.

16

"How very strange," said the other. "So was I. Before your time, of course. You're younger than me."

This very compelling lie she had proved to the hilt and had then gone on to remember my wife's relations and friends. That she had made no mistake, Adèle is ready to swear, and since her manners were faultless, not one in a thousand would have perceived any reason for disbelief.

On the following afternoon Daphne, Adèle and Jill had gone to the Plazas' flat. This was a fine apartment, commanding the Arc de Triomphe and breathing good style. Plaza himself was out, but then and there his wife had delivered the master stroke. Daphne had asked them to lunch, but the lady had pleaded engagements they could not break. This was only a flying visit, and just for the moment their time was not their own. They must leave for Vienna on Thursday. On their return, however, if we were still in Paris . . . Then, *just as the girls were leaving,* the Countess had remembered the box—the box which the Count had reserved for a gala performance of *Faust* on Wednesday night.

"Now do pray use it," she said. "We had hoped, of course, to be there. We both love *Faust*. But now there is some reception to which we must go. So the box will be empty, unless you will use it instead."

"You're awfully kind," said Daphne, "but isn't there anyone else you'd like to—"

"Why should I? We'd like you to use it."

"Well, of course we'd love to, but—"

"Couldn't you come on?" said Adèle. "I mean, if you're not too tired."

Madame Plaza was more than doubtful, but in the end it was left that we might hope to see them on Wednesday night. Supper had been mentioned, of course, but it had not seemed likely that they would stay out so late. And when they had joined us that evening in time to see the last act, they had been hardly persuaded to come back to our hotel.

I have done no more than outline the game they played. It might not have been good enough for some people. The unhappy fact remains that it was quite good enough for us. From first to last we were fooled to the top of our bent.

How they had obtained reservations which coincided with ours was never satisfactorily explained, but that was because some clerk was holding his tongue. The flat, of course, was hired. No embassy had heard of Count Plaza, and Philadelphia knew no more of his wife. Whilst we were at the Opera, someone had telephoned to our hotel and, speaking with the night-porter, had charged him to see that our wine was not placed upon ice. The speaker had used Berry's name, and since the latter is notoriously particular about his liquor, the instructions had been accepted without a thought.

Indeed, as Berry observed, the "treachers" had paved our way with bad intentions and we had fairly waltzed down it—into the muck.

"Well we can't stay here," said Daphne. "For one thing I haven't the heart."

Twenty-four hours had gone by, and we were once more in the *salon*, more or less recovered, discussing our plight.

"I agree," said Adèle. "We came to play about Paris, and—somebody's pinched our ball."

"You can buy a new one," said Berry. "All the stuff was insured, and the quartier Vendôme is just the place to refit."

"I don't want a new one," said my sister. "I want my old ball back. A week ago I longed for half the jewels in the rue de la Paix. But now my desire has gone. I never knew the value I set upon what I had."

"That's right," said Adèle. "We shall replace them, of course. But it won't be the same. Mine were bought gradually. Each one was a precious extravagance which Boy and I couldn't afford. And how can Jill's pearls be replaced?"

"They can't," said Piers gloomily. "There'll be a row about that."

"Rot," said Berry. "If somebody steals an heirloom it's not your fault. You showed reasonable care. So did I and Boy and Jonah. It's the women that let us in."

A pregnant silence succeeded this monstrous charge. Then—

" 'The women?' " said Daphne shakily. "What do you mean?"

"What I say," said her husband shortly. "Who picked up the Plazas? Who walked bung up to their table an' gave them a face full of teeth?"

"How dare you?" cried Daphne furiously. "And you know I spoke for us all. It was you who said, 'Ask them to dinner,' and slimed round that awful woman and——"

"That's right," said Berry. "Be rude. That's what I get for entertaining your friends."

"They weren't my friends," shrieked Daphne.

"Well, Adèle's then," said Berry. "Who sat around in their flat and lapped them up? Who came back and said they were diplomats?" He raised his eyes to heaven and covered his face. "Diplomats! Give me strength."

"You thought they were, too," cried Jill. "You know you did. And when they hung back, you pressed them to come to supper and said we'd be all alone."

My brother-in-law frowned.

"I had no option," he said stiffly. "My hand was forced—as usual. And now I'll tell you something. I never liked the man."

The *suggestio falsi* was received with a storm of disapproval to which its author listened with a pitying smile. As it died down——

"If that's the case," said I, "why didn't you give us the tip?"

"Why argue with the brute?" said Daphne. "It's a wicked lie, and he knows it. Oh, and if you were so suspicious, why did you drink the wine?"

Her husband shrugged his shoulders.

"One can't be stand-offish," he said. "You were all sloshing it down, and if I had drunk water——"

"Pity you didn't," said Jonah. "That would have made us think. Never mind. The highest you can put it is that we are guilty of contributory negligence. All of us—equally. I tell you frankly, I never gave the Plazas a thought."

"Nor did anyone else," said I. "They were very civil, and we were civil back. Where we tore it right up was in letting a perfect stranger fix our wine."

"But we did it together," cried Piers. "He asked me to give him the salt, and I stood by his side. I saw him open the bottle and I could have sworn he never put anything in."

"Sleight of hand," said Jonah. "He opened the bottle five minutes before it was used."

"He said it'd cool quicker open."

"And then he left you to serve it and came and sat down. But what an artist. Never mind. What do we do?"

"We'd better go home," said Daphne. "We'd better pack up

and go to White Ladies at once."

"We can't do that," said I. "The painters are in."

This was a fact. The house would not be ready for three or four weeks.

"Let's go to Irikli," said Jill. "It's lovely now."

Irikli belonged to the Duke of Padua. When I say that it added to the beauty for which the Lake of Como is justly famed, I am stating no more than the truth.

"Yes, let's," said Piers. "I'll go on and get it ready, and——"

"Why go away?" said Jonah, filling his pipe. "We've taken a nasty shock, but why clear out of the ring?"

For the first time since the outrage my heart leaped up, for though I had not said so, I would have given the world for a smack at the thieves. Compensation was all very well—so far as it went. So far as I was concerned, it went a very short way. What I wanted was satisfaction. I wanted to see the Plazas stand in the dock. And I had a desperate feeling that nothing the police could do would ever bring this about.

I think I may be forgiven—this crime was a dirty crime. War had been made upon women from first to last. The men of the party had practically been ignored, but Daphne, Adèle and Jill had been insulted and robbed. Compared with theirs, our losses were scarcely worth setting down. The attack had been made upon them—for what they had. They had been fooled : they had been drugged : they had been robbed : and the five grown men who should have been their protectors had been of no more use than a pack of drunken servants that prefer their own amusement to the common duty they owe.

"Jonah," said I, "I'm with you, but what can we do? For only one thing, we were bound to call in the police : and when the police came in, the matter went out of our hands."

"Don't you believe it," said Jonah. "The police'll go their own way : if we like to go ours, there's no reason why we should collide." He flung himself into a chair and crossed his legs. "You see, the point is this. For a month or six weeks the Plazas won't try to leave France. If they tried to leave France, they'd be taken—the nets are spread. And they're damned fine nets—that's where the French police excel. Where they fail is that the bird must go to the net. In England it's different : but there the net isn't so fine. You can't have it every way."

"You seem to know a lot about it," said Berry.

"Hearsay," said Jonah shortly. "What do you think?"

"I don't," said my brother-in-law. "I face the facts instead. What if the Plazas are in France? What if they've hidden the stuff under somebody's bed? Hell of a lot of beds in France, you know."

"I agree," said Jonah. "We can't look under them all. And if we could it would be silly. The stuff's not under a bed. It's in a safe-deposit."

"That's common sense," said I. "But where do we start?"

"There you can search me," said Jonah. "But if we leave the country, we throw up the sponge." He paused to set a match to his pipe. "There's the Villiers' place near Dieppe. They'd be only too glad to let it for June and July."

"But Jonah, dear," purred Daphne, "d'you think we've the slightest chance? I mean, if the police can't get them, what can we do?"

"We can look about," said my cousin. "You never know."

"Well, I protest," said Berry. "The thing's absurd. And I know what 'look about' means. You don't get me standing outside any cafés with a false nose on and singing 'Abide with me'."

"But don't you want to get the Plazas?" said Adèle uncertainly.

"I want quite a lot of things, but I'm not such a fool as to waste my life trying to jump when they're out of my reach. We are seven: with Casca, eight. How the devil are we to comb France? You might as well try to empty the Welsh Harp with a stomach-pump on a rainy night."

"Must you be vulgar?" said his wife.

"Yes," said Berry, "I must. Futility always arouses what baser instincts I have. As a boy I was corporally reproved for my definition of algebra. I said it was like——"

A shriek of protest smothered the impious revival just in time. Still, what Berry had said was much to the point. With nothing whatever to go on, what could we do?

"If you think there's a chance," said Piers, "I'll come in blind."

"So will we all," said Adèle. "If you think there's a chance."

"Which means that you don't," said Jonah and got to his feet.

"There's always a chance," said Berry. "Plaza might lose his

21

memory and stop me to ask who he was. And he might do it near Dieppe. So let's take the villa—in case. It's only nine miles from the town, so we shan't need a car. I can walk in and get the bread —easily. And if it's wet I can always take the string-bag."

Jill was shaking with laughter, and one of Adèle's slim hands went up to her mouth.

"I fully admit," said Jonah, "the force of the point you make." He leaned against the wall and folded his arms. "On the face of it, it is futile for us to make any attempt to recover the jewels or to bring the thieves to book. Quite futile. And futility breaks the heart. . . . If I press you enough, you'll stay—I'm sure of that. You'll do it 'to make me pleasure', as Casca would say. But that's no use to me. You've got to work hard—as I shall. Stand out in the rain and go hungry and lose your sleep. And you won't do that—no one would—when you know in your hearts that it's futile . . . beating the air. And so I must prove that it *won't* be beating the air . . . that what we do *won't* be futile, but ordinary common sense."

Everyone sat very still. Jonathan Mansel was not the man to waste words. If he said . . .

"I don't want to do it," he continued. "I'd rather you trusted me. But I'm up against human nature, and so I must prove my case. But before I do it, I want you to give me your word that the proof I'm going to give you will not go beyond this room. More. That you'll never give it away by word or look or deed to a single soul."

A breathless silence succeeded my cousin's words.

Then—

"We swear," said Berry. "We give you our solemn oath." An excited, definite murmur indorsed the pledge. "Have you given this clue to the police?"

"It's not a clue," said Jonah. "It's a simple, downright proof that if we stay in France and use what wits we have we shan't be wasting our time. All the same, I've not told the police, because that would have been futile—you'll soon see why. And now hold on to something. I'm going to give you a shock. The Plazas deserve great credit. They played a most difficult game, and they played it devilish well. But I think you'll agree that so far as play-acting's concerned, the honours must go to Casca—Casca de Palk."

We Sup with the Devil

For a moment there was dead silence. Then a gasp of amazement greeted the staggering charge. For myself, I confess that I sat as though turned to stone.

"Oh Jonah," breathed Jill, "are you sure?"

Her brother stepped to the table and laid upon it two wads. These were of cotton wool, were stained a faint brown and fairly reeked of tobacco.

"These wads were in the fireplace when Boy woke me up. They were almost the first thing I saw. If you remember, I was lying close to the grate. No one employs them but Casca. They're made for the cigarette-tube we gave him last year. Now Casca had not been smoking when we went down."

"That's right," cried Piers. "When I took him the box, he refused. He said that one oughtn't to smoke just before a meal."

"It follows," continued my cousin, "that *Casca smoked quite a lot while we were asleep.*"

"But it may have been the Plazas," cried Adèle. "They may have pinched his tube, and——"

"If they did, they took the trouble to give it him back. He was using it yesterday morning, before he left the hotel."

With his words the telephone rang.

"Talk of the devil," said Jonah. "I'll lay a pony that's him."

"Act Two, Scene One," said Berry, and stepped to the instrument.

Before we could beg him to be cautious, he had the receiver off.

"Hullo," he cried, "hullo . . . Oh, is that you, Casca? We were just speaking of you. How's your head, old cock. . . . Oh, that's no good. . . . No, I've not finished yet, dear lady. *Ne coupez pas.* I'll tell you what I'll do when I've finished. I'll put the receiver back . . . No, Casca. That's no good. What you want is some leeches. Order in half a dozen, and I'll come and put them on. . . . But it's not the slightest trouble. I'd love to. Besides, they just dig themselves in. And once they're gorged, they come away in your hand . . . No, I've not finished yet, you vixen. *Ne coupez pas.* Why the devil . . . What? You don't want the leeches? Oh, well, perhaps you know best. Come and have lunch instead . . . Yes, something quite slight. A spot of *foie gras* and a gallon of half and half. Half stout and half milk. That'll do your head good. . . . Oh, nothing like it, my boy. Tunes up the system, you know, and makes the

23

liver think. . . . What's that? You won't take it? You know, mon
Casca, I don't believe you want to get well? Never mind. Don't be
late. We want you to meet some people we met on the train. . . .
Oh, no. Quite different to the Plazas. All the same, if I were you, I
should leave your cigarette-case at home. Just in case, you know.
No, I have *not*, you viper. *NE COUPEZ PAS*. *Didn't I say* . . .
Yes, Casca. Your cigarette-case. The platinum one your brother
had—I say, don't bring it, in case . . . What? You haven't got it to
bring? Why? . . . The Plazas took it? Oh, go on. . . . Well, why on
earth didn't you say so?"

A noise like a death-rattle was followed by a definite chunk.

My brother-in-law replaced his receiver with a sigh.

"He seems to have rung off," he said. "I can't think why."

Jonah smiled a grim smile.

"Good for you, brother," he said. "If we all do as well at
luncheon, we've nothing to fear."

I cannot pretent that we did. But we were as cordial as ever, and
the girls fairly spread themselves. Casca was very soon at the top
of his form. And before the meal was over he had accepted our
invitation to pay us a visit when we were installed near Dieppe.

CHAPTER II

Expert Evidence

"The Villiers' place" lay roughly ten miles from Dieppe. The house was large and stood in a pleasant park through which a curling drive ran down to the Rouen road. I had passed it a hundred times and marked its comfortable bulwarks and its spreading apron of pasture which the highway edged like a ribbon for half a mile. Indeed, for such as passed by, a mansion had been set among meadows with woods upon either side. No one, I think, would have dreamed of what lay behind; and I cannot forget the first time I stood on the terrace which ran the length of the villa towards the South. It was perched at the head of a valley some two miles long. Its sides were clothed with woodland which stood up on either hand to meet the sky : its floor was all green meadows, and right in the heart of these a wandering vein of silver argued a running stream. The dale was flooded with sunshine from end to end, and distance melted into a haze of heat : what wind there was passed by this sanctuary : only the song of birds bedecked the infinate silence, as stars the velvet of the night. As for privacy . . .

We knew the Villiers well, and three telegrams were enough to make the property ours for the next two months. All the same, until we had servants, we should have been well advised to stay in the place Vendôme. My sister's maid was on holiday : so was Jill's. But we had all been infected with Jonah's obvious impatience to get away, and since the caretaker's wife was ready to be our cook, we determined to take possession as soon as ever we could. Once we were there, we argued, servants would apply for such posts as had to be filled. Moreover, Jonah's man, Carson, was on his way from Town with my cousin's Rolls, and Piers had left for White Ladies to fetch the Lowland coupé which I had given Adèle.

It follows that on Monday morning we travelled down to Dieppe. Carson was there to meet us, and, after instructing him to buy some things in the town and bring them out with our luggage by motor-van, we took our seats in the car and made for the Rouen road. Twenty minutes later we sighted the Château de Nay.

"Yes, I think it's lovely," said Berry. "As battle-headquarters I don't think it could be improved. When do we lunch?"

"Well, we can't lunch yet," said Daphne. "We've nothing to eat. Would you like to walk to the village and get some things?"

Her husband regarded the heaven. The sun was blazing : there was not a cloud in the sky.

"No," he said. "I'll think I'll stay here—and make the beds."

"You needn't make mine," said I. "And I don't think I should make Jonah's. He's funny like that."

My brother-in-law frowned.

"Perhaps you're right," he said slowly. "It is rather menial work. Supervision's more in my line. Er, what about a bottle of beer?"

"No you don't," said Daphne. "Either you walk to the village, or pull your weight in the house. There's a bed that's got to be moved."

"How far is the village?" said her husband.

"Two miles and a half," said Adèle.

"Thanks very much," said Berry. "How big is the bed?"

When I explained that the bed must be taken to pieces, he picked up his hat.

Then he turned to his wife.

"Of course your staff-work," he said, "is enough to induce palsy. When you saw there was no manna, what did you let Jonah go for?"

My cousin was gone to Rouen, to make inquiries for someone he wished to find. And Carson with him.

"One can't think of everything," said Daphne. "You must get some bread and butter and slices of ham."

"Not real ham?" said her husband. "But how delicious. I know. Jean can go."

Jean was the caretaker.

"Jean's out raking up servants. You know what the French for slice is?"

Berry closed his eyes.

"Voulez-vous me donner dix tranches de jambon York?" he

said obediently.

Jill began to shake with laughter.

"That'll do for our lunch," said Daphne, "unless you should see any cheese. Meanwhile I'll talk to Anna and make out a list, and as soon as Jonah comes back you can go in again."

"I see," said Berry slowly. Again he looked at the sky. Then he stepped to the balustrade and felt the stone with his hand. "Marvellous weather, this is. Might be July. You know, I'm not at all sure I want any lunch."

"Well, we do," said Daphne shortly. "And what about drinks?" Her husband stared.

"Well, what's the beer done?" he said.

"The beer hasn't come," said Adèle.

"Not come?" screamed Berry. "Not come? Oh, don't be blasphemous."

"It's not Carson's fault," bubbled Jill. "The brewery's stuck, or something, and no one would let him have bottles to bring away. Jonah's going to bring some bottles from Rouen."

In a silence big with laughter Berry took a short walk with his hand to his head.

When he returned—

"I'd better have a hand-cart," he said.

Though the others protested, I was inclined to agree. I deeply suspected the water, which came from a well : Jonah might return before midnight, but then he might not : I was already more thirsty than those who have liquor to hand permit themselves to remain. After a short discussion, I went off in search of transport—of any kind.

There was, of course, no hand-cart : there was a garden-roller and there was the biggest and heaviest wheel-barrow that I have ever seen : of the two, the roller had it : no common man could have wheeled that barrow a furlong and been the same. Reference to the kitchen proved more fruitful : on being besought to obtain us something on wheels, the caretaker's wife produced a collapsible perambulator, which may once have looked a picture, but was now past its prime. Moth and rust had vied with each other in corruption. On being erected, however, the vehicle moved.

Standing at the head of the steps, Berry regarded his assistant with starting eyes.

"I don't want to seem fastidious," he said, "but is that the best you can do?"

"It's that or the roller," said I, brushing the dirt from my hands.

"I see," said my brother-in-law. "All right." He passed down the steps and set his hand to the rail. "I suppose you don't know any child that wants a lift. I mean, it seems almost selfish. . . ."

A moment later he was descending the drive.

As I turned to the house—

"But why," wailed Adèle, "why didn't he choose the bed?"

"Because he's thirsty," said I. "All the beer he brings back won't be in the pram."

The burden of the next three hours, I like to forget. I had no conception of the labour which precedes inhabitation of an ordinary furnished house. I unrolled carpets, I scaled and descended stairs, I fetched and carried bedding, until I felt faint. In the absence of Jean, I was forced to stoke the furnace and climb about under the tiles looking for taps. The electric plant was not working, and I had to pump for one hour to fill the tanks. And all this, with nothing to drink. At half past two I gave in and swallowed some milk.

At a quarter to three Jean returned from his tour, to say that three stout servants would report the following morning at seven o'clock. The tidings were politely received. By rights we should have been jubilant. Just at the moment, however, we were living for other things—the things my brother-in-law had been sent to get.

At three o'clock we met in my sister's room.

"He's gone to Rouen," said I. "You know what he is. Got a lift in a car for a monkey. When he's had a hell of a lunch at the best hotel, he'll buy the bread and the ham and hire a car back. And he'll pitch some tale of having been carried on past the village before he knew where he was."

"I refuse to believe it," said Daphne. "He'd never dare."

"Well, where is he, then?" said I. "He left here soon after eleven, and now it's three. I mean, five miles in four hours . . ."

A shuffle upon the terrace brought us pell-mell to the window to learn the truth.

We were just in time to see Berry cross the flags and come to the balustrade. That he was heavy-laden I cannot deny. On his back was a sack to the neck of which he was clinging as though it were full of gold. He reminded me of a gnome in a fairy-tale.

The balustrade he used as a porter's rest. Gingerly he lowered the sack till it rested upon the stone : then he turned round and lifted it down to the flags. Then he lay down on his back and closed his eyes.

All this in a pregnant silence we dared not break. His air was that of a saint from whom great tribulation has taken the urge to live.

My sister steadied herself and lifted her voice.

"Are you very done, old fellow?"

Her husband opened his eyes.

"Hush," he said. "There's illness in the house. At least, not in the house : on the terrace. Somebody's seriously ill. I don't think they're going to live." He closed his eyes again. "They'll have to be fed, of course. There's some stuff that looks like jelly irrigating the ham. You can sort that out, if you like and tempt them with that."

"To be frank," said I, "I made certain you'd wangle a lift."

"So did I," said Berry faintly. "I suppose the time was a bad one. Nothing but brakeless limousines seems to employ that road. Oh, and a tar-waggon : but I didn't like to stop that. And in the village they told me a short cut back. It's quite a good way, if you can find it. At least I suppose it is. I only found the first mile. I thought they said 'Turn to the left at the fourth dunghill,' but I think they must have meant the fifth."

So soon as I could speak—

"And the—the hand-cart?" I said.

Berry shuddered.

"Ugh," he said. "Was that real? I was hoping it was only a dream."

"You left here," said I, "with a pram."

Berry sat up.

"With a baby-carriage?" he said. "A thing like The Step Pyramid? That was black and smelt and had two detachable wheels?"

"Had it?" said I.

"Yes," said Berry, "it had. The way you get one off is to push it for half a mile. Then you walk slowly back looking for a small black nut by the side of the road. When you've wasted twenty minutes, you chuck the wheel over the hedge and proceed with three. This is just possible—I don't know why." He lay back and closed his eyes. "It takes about two miles to get the second one off."

We waited breathlessly.

At length—

"Go on," said Adèle tremulously.

"You can't," said Berry. "No one can. No man born of woman can push a pram on two wheels." He sat up with a jerk and flung out his hands. "You see the poisonous point, don't you? You see the snare—the stinking pit you've been at such pains to dig? If you wanted to destroy the swine, you might as well have done it at home. Instead of that, you've shoved it two statute miles, two sodden, soul-searing miles, up to its doom." He covered his face. "What breaks your heart is that you don't destroy it even then. You—you try to mend if first." He sighed profoundly. "I don't think they like being mended. I may be wrong. But without an anaesthetic it isn't a one-man job. It's while you're trying to mend it that you go out of your mind. You scream and seize it and——"

"Don't say you've broken it," said Daphne. "We shall have to pay the woman——"

"I didn't break it," screamed Berry. "The filthy thing was broken before I left the house. What I did was to reduce it to impotence, to smash its power for evil once for all." He sucked in his breath. "No one else will ever push it two miles. A break-down gang may get it off the kilometre stone it now surrounds, but no one will ever push it. They wouldn't know which way to go."

"Well, I call that wanton," said Daphne. "Some poor child . . ."

I put my arm round her waist and drew her into the room. There are times when she will not see danger. Already her husband was making a sizzling noise.

Of such were the first few hours which we passed at Nay. But Jonah returned at tea-time, and, with the Rolls to serve us, the position sensibly improved. That night we dined in Rouen and dined extremely well, and when my cousin announced that in coming to Nay we had done rather better than we knew, the trials of the day were forgotten as though they had never been.

"It's nothing very much," said Jonah, "but I've located a friend. A very knowledgeable fellow. He was in the Secret Service during the War. I hope to see him to-morrow. And I think Boy and Berry should meet him. So if you can let them off for a couple of hours . . ."

"And Piers," cried Jill. "Piers will be here to-morrow, and——"

"So he shall," said her brother. "But not just yet. Besides, he must go to bed. We shan't leave here before midnight. The man we're meeting doesn't keep office hours."

"I hope he's quite nice," said Berry. "I mean, Mother always told me——"

"He's good at his job," said Jonah. "So good that he was released to serve the Secret Service and help us to win the War."

There was an excited silence.

"When you say 'released'," began Berry. . . .

"I mean 'released'," said my cousin. "He was doing five years for robbery under arms."

The Wet Flag is a café which none of the guide-books to Rouen sees fit to recommend. It is convenient and quiet, and it stands in the heart of the town : the cooking is good, and its cellar is better than most. Indeed, it is well worth using—provided some regular patron will take you under his wing. Otherwise you will be un-welcome. *The Wet Flag* is more than a café : it is as good as a club.

No hush greeted our entry, and nobody stared : but before two minutes had passed I became acutely aware that our presence was under discussion by everyone in the place. It was a curious feeling which nothing could justify. The shrugged shoulders, the laughter, the confidential remarks might have related to any topic you please. In fact they related to us. The air was charged with resent-ment which was deliberately masked. I am not very sensitive, but only a full-blown idiot could have failed to perceive the atmos-phere of ill will. And I knew in my heart that if I were to get to my feet and step to the door, one or more of the company present would instantly do the same.

But if we were not at our ease, we had nothing to fear. We were three strong men, and Jonah and I were armed. Besides, we were there on business. We had an appointment with an habitué. Still, veiled suspicion is a very unpleasant thing. No one likes to be weighed and found wanting. But when one is weighed and found wanting by forty or fifty people all of whom live by defying the criminal law, it is much more than distasteful. It is almost embarrassing.

I crossed my legs and took a pull at my beer.

The place was clean and not unpleasantly hot. The floor was of some composition on which the waiters' feet made next to no sound, and while the room was well lit, the lights were carefully shaded, to spare the eyes. A woman sat at a desk beside the bar, but the host himself was playing the part of a waiter and wearing the long, white apron as well as his men. Of his guests a full third were women, none of them shabby and some of them very well dressed. By no means all were French, and half the men I could see were of English or American blood. I cannot pretend that they were a nice-looking lot. Shrewd, hard-bitten, tough, five out of six of them looked the rascals they were, but here and there was a face which no one would have suspected, and I cannot forget a gentle, mild-eyed old fellow who had the air of a prelate and was reading *La Vie Parisienne*. No one was dancing, although a space was kept clear, and the band, when it played, discoursed its music so softly that those who wished to converse could do so without an effort to make themselves heard.

"What would happen," said Berry, "if I got up and shouted 'I'm not a copper's nark'?"

"I can't imagine," said Jonah. "But I hope very much you won't. For one thing, the statement would be supererogatory."

"Then what's the trouble?" said Berry. "I feel that I'm misunderstood."

"So you are," said Jonah. "This crowd has an animal instinct. Whatever they don't understand, they at once suspect. If you were leading their life, you'd be the same."

"I see," said my brother-in-law. "Have they any other—er—animal instincts? You know. Lying in wait, or pulling down their prey, or—I mean, for instance, some animals don't like being watched while they're feeding. Of course it's very foolish, but . . ."

Right at the end of the room I saw a man get to his feet. Then he left his table and sauntered in our direction, stopping once or twice to speak for a moment with someone that caught his eye. One of these was a good-looking girl, very well dressed and wearing a small black hat. She would have done credit to any table I know. Then he passed on and up to where we were sitting close to the door.

"Well, Fluff," said Jonah. "How are you? These are two cousins of mine."

"Good evening," said Fluff politely.

"Good evening," said Berry and I.

"And now sit down," said Jonah, and pulled out a chair.

As he took a seat—

"Fancy you getting stung," said Fluff. "When I saw the fuss in the papers, I couldn't believe my eyes. You usedn't to drink with strangers once on a time."

"I'm sore," said Jonah, nodding. "I give you my word, I'm sore. We all are."

"I'll lay you are," said Fluff. "I'd like to 'ave had those pearls your sister wore. To think of them goin' like that to some amateur! Auntie Emma isn't half sick. One of his lot went up with those pearls from Rome. But when you met her at Paris, he turned it down."

"Well, who are the Plazas?" said Jonah.

"They're amateurs," said Fluff. "I don't know who they are any more than you." He sighed bitterly. "It's blood an' grief them jewels goin' off like that. Some dirty Jew'll get them for a song without words. Amateurs are outside the market. They can't never place their stuff."

His regret was ludicrous. I was halfway to laughter, and Jonah's lips were twitching for all his calm. Berry was suspiciously grave.

"What are you drinking?" said Jonah, with his hand to his mouth.

"Whiskey for me," said Fluff. "That beer's too small."

As I called a waiter, Berry took out his cigar-case and passed it to Fluff. With a nod of thanks, the latter withdrew a cigar.

"And you're no fool," he said. "What were you doing to let them sew you up?"

"My cousin's fault," said Berry. "I wasn't on duty that night."

The other grinned.

"I give you up," he said, and reached for a match. "Fancy pickin' them up on the train. You'll be playing chemmy next on board of some ship."

"Possibly," said Berry. "But we shan't be drinking champagne. Do you suffer from headaches at all?"

33

"Not that sort," said Fluff. "But I've heard that they're something cruel."

"Meiosis," said Berry shortly. "They're not of this world. Conceive a red-hot flat-iron being cooled in your brain. Are you sure you can't place the Plazas? I'd give six months of my life to stand them a drink."

"I wish I could," said Fluff. "They'd want a pick-me-up before I was through."

I glanced round the room. We were being regarded now—with friendly, if curious eyes. Everyone was looking to where we sat. The elderly prelate gave me a sad, sweet smile. The good-looking girl did more. Looking me full in the eyes, she smiled and lifted her glass. Slightly embarrassed, I gave the compliment back.

"Oh, you home-wrecker," said Berry. "Oh, you profligate——"

"That's Bermuda," said Fluff. "And I'll warrant you don't know why she loves you like that."

"I can't imagine," said I.

The other fingered his chin.

"A few years ago," he said, "the police took you off to a golf-links an' showed you a fair-haired crook."

"That's right," I cried. "The links at St. Jean-de-Luz. Her name was Eulalie."

"Very like," said Fluff. "We called her 'The Bank of England'. An' they asked you to recognize her, but you said 'No'."

"That wasn't very hard," said I. "Where is she now?"

"Got out an' married," said Fluff. "Lives in a hell of a place down Biarritz way." He turned to Jonah. "I think you've changed," he said. "First you go an' get stung, an' then you come an' sit here an' waste your time."

My cousin smiled.

"Don't be rude to yourself," he said. "I always liked talking to you. You say the Plazas won't work the oracle?"

"They can't," said Fluff. "That's what's been spoiling my rest. What sort of a chance does an amateur stand with a fence? A fence is a pro. You go an' pick up a parcel and see what you get." He drank abruptly. Then he set down his glass and pushed back his hat. "You've thrown away those jewels. That's what you've done. Some lazy, pot-bellied fence is going to pouch the lot for a couple of thousand pounds." He thrust his cigar between his teeth. "A couple of thousand—if that."

"A couple of thousand!" cried Berry. "But, man alive, the pearls alone were worth——"

"In open market," said Fluff. "That's a very different thing. But they don't like me at Christie's—I don't know why."

My cousin rubbed his nose.

"A couple of thousand," he said. "How much would you have got?"

Fluff appeared to consider.

"I know the pearls," he said. "Known 'em for years." He looked at Berry. "But I never see the bracelets your lady wore. Then there's her necklace and rings and other small stuff. Half a minute. I think Sweaty knows them cuffs. I'll see what he says."

He rose to his feet and strolled to the place he had left at the end of the room.

Berry watched his going like a man in a dream.

" 'Sweaty knows them cuffs'," he said. "What a very compelling thought. Sweaty. Supposing one winter's night Sweaty had had an urge to—to get to know them better . . . down at White Ladies . . . this winter, when George was ill. I'm damned if I'm going round that house any more."

Jonah shrugged his shoulders.

"If he'd dreamed they were there, he would have. I've told you a dozen times to keep them in Town."

"I shall always treasure," said I, "Fluff's point of view. He's a definite grievance against us. He considers we've let him down."

"You must remember," said Jonah, "that every decent burglar loathes and detests the fence. He can't do without him, and the fence exploits that fact. You'll be amazed when you hear what he says he'd have got. As for the Plazas . . . What Casca can do I don't know. I rather fancy he'd—er—take the fence in his stride."

Here Fluff returned to our table and took the seat he had left.

"Yes," he said, "Sweaty knows 'em. He says they were very fine. I'd have got fourteen thousand pounds for that little lot."

"Would you indeed?" said Jonah.

"I would that," said Fluff. "So you see what you've gone and done."

Jonah took his pipe from his mouth and frowned at the bowl.

"That's a healthy lump," he said. "But twenty thousand pounds is half as healthy again."

The other shot him a glance.

"That's mathematics," he said. "What if it is?"

"Twenty thousand pounds," said my cousin, "is what the under-writers offer for the recovery of the jewels."

Fluff looked him up and down.

"I told you you'd changed," he said. "There must have been things in that wine that troubled the brain. I'm not a ——— policeman."

"Neither are we," said Jonah. "But we're going after that stuff. And if you come in with us, you can have the reward."

With his eyes on my cousin's face, the other sat very still. Presently he leaned forward.

"You're goin' after them, are you? What do you know?"

"I know who took them," said Jonah. "I know who schooled the Plazas and held them up in his arms to reach the fruit."

"You told the police?"

"Now don't be rude," said Jonah. "You know as well as I do, I won't have that. I don't mind being chipped, but I stand no lip from you or anyone else. If you don't like the rules of the game, you needn't play."

So far from being abashed, Fluff seemed relieved.

"That's more like it," he said. "That's like what you used to be."

"You haven't changed, either," said Jonah. "You never respec-ted a dog till he showed his teeth. How many times have I told you?"

"As you were," said Fluff. "And it's my mistake. When I saw two Willies had stung you, I put you up on the shelf."

"Well, take me down," said Jonah. "Because a man slips up, it doesn't follow he's lost the use of his legs. And now about this business. I know who took the stuff and I know where he is. He's not a pro. He's something very special. It'll take us all we know to bring him down. More than we know, in fact. And that's why I'm offering you a chance to come in."

"He's not a pro.," said Fluff. "Are you sure of that?"

"Certain sure," said my cousin. "He's out of that little crowd that I used to call 'A.S.'"

" 'Above Suspicion'," cried Fluff, and slapped his thigh. "Gosh, I remember that book. I never see the inside, but I know you 'ad nine names down. What did you do with it? Burn it? We only got three."

"Yes, I burned it," said Jonah. "And to get three wasn't too bad. And now what about it? If we don't get home, there's nothing for anyone. But if we do, there's twenty thousand sovereigns into your lap. We pay expenses, of course. They shouldn't be high."

"It's a heap of money," said Fluff reverently.

"It'll take some making," said Jonah. "Be sure of that. And it's not a question of putting the man on his back. He hasn't the stuff in his pocket, and it's the stuff we want."

"Safe-deposit," said Fluff. "Sure as a gun."

"Exactly," said Jonah. "As long as it's there we've just about as much chance as a fish in a petrol-tank. We've got to make him withdraw it before we strike."

"Quite," said Fluff, nodding. "We don't want another Dufau."

Jonah turned to Berry and me.

"Dufau is the leading case on the folly of striking too soon. Cully Dufau got away with eighty thousand pounds worth of pearls. They took him, and he got twenty years. They weigh you out time in France."

"You're right," said Fluff warmly. "The ——s."

"But they never got the stuff," said Jonah. "Not one little pearl. While Dufau was doing his time, pearls came in. And when he came out, they were worth four times what they were when he put them away. He's getting on now, but he's got a villa near Grasse and a couple of cars."

"That's right," said Fluff. "An' a butler to 'old the door an' take off his boots. Still, twenty thousand's all right. I'd buy my father a pub. He's a good old crow, and he's always wanted a pub. The country's his ideal. A 'ouse of call in the country, an' a garden full o' roses an' cocks an' 'ens. I've heard him talkin' it over a thousand times."

This unsuspected piety warmed my heart. I began to like Fluff very much.

"Well, it's up to you," said Jonah.

There was a little silence. The band was playing—of all things —*The Eton Boating Song*. The strains of the famous valse swayed and rose and faded with all the tight-laced elegance of the Victorian age. In a flash I was skirting the ball-room I first adorned, shy, gloved, awkward, programme in hand. I saw the chaperons against the walls and the glassy eye of the matron whose charge I had contracted to claim. I heard the slow swish of the dresses and watched the uniform movement with which the floor was alive and I marked the frowns of disapproval which a girl with short hair provoked. I found myself wondering what they would have said to Bermuda. I am inclined to think there would have been a stampede.

"All right, I'll come in," said Fluff. He drained his glass. When I would have called for more whiskey, he shook his head. "And now who took them jewels? Don't say it's some high muck-a-muck."

"Not at all," said Jonah. "It's a very great friend of ours."

Fluff opened his eyes.

"What, not the Frenchy?" he said. "That lost a cigarette-case he had of the King?"

"That's the cove," said Jonah, and told his tale.

When he had done—

"Very hot," said Fluff. "An' I'm not surprised you didn't explain to the police. They'd have helped—I don't think. Never mind. You're right, of course. The Plazas played the hand, but he gave them the book o' words. An' we shan't land him by ticklin'."

"Never," said Jonah. "He'll want a hell of a fly. But we've got one thing in our favour, and that is time. He's not in any hurry. He's waited years for that stuff, and, now that he's got it, he's not going to rush to turn it into a cheque."

"That cuts both ways," said I. "So long as it lies in a vault, what on earth can we do? And he may keep it there for years."

"True," said Jonah. "But I'd rather it lay in a vault than went overseas. The moment it leaves the country we've lost the match. But as long as it lies in a vault, we've always a chance of making him get it out."

"I commend direct action," said Berry. "He's coming to stay with us. Let's tie him up and starve him until he hands us the key. When his stomach begins to argue, he'll listen to that."

"Too big a risk," said Jonah. "If it doesn't come off, we're beaten once for all. You can bet your life he's lodged the key at his Bank."

"What if he has? He can write to the Bank and tell them to give it to us. We can make it plain to him that water is what he lives on until we handle the jewels."

"That's no good," said Fluff. "You don't get me taking no papers into a Bank. Makes me go hot all over. What if he's signed 'em wrong. A cove like that'll put up a thousand bluffs. And you've *got* to call 'em, sonny. That's the snag. No, no. The Captain's right. We'll want a fly and a half for this old fish."

"I should very much like," said Jonah, "to have a look at his mail. Will you see what you can do in that way? He lives in a flat, and the postman leaves the letters down in the porter's lodge."

"That sounds all right," said Fluff. "Let's have the address. You'll have a room near, of course. The porter won't want to hold them for more than one post."

"That's right," said Jonah. "What about Friday next?"

"That ought to do," said Fluff.

"Aren't you banking a lot," said I, "on the porter's being a rogue? Supposing——"

"At fifty francs a letter?" said Fluff. "Where was you born?"

My cousin took out a note-book and wrote down de Palk's address. Below this he wrote down ours. Then he tore out the leaf and gave it to Fluff.

"To be destroyed," he said, "before you get into the train."

The other groaned.

" 'To be learned by 'eart,' " he quoted. "Who ever told me you'd changed?"

My cousin smiled.

"Where can I find you?" he said.

Fluff named a street in Paris of which I had never heard.

"Very good," said Jonah. "I'll let you know where to bring the letters along." He took some notes from his pocket and laid them down on the cloth. "And there's five thousand. Mind you pick him up before Friday. One never knows, and I want you to see his face."

Fluff folded the notes and slid them into his coat.

"Not 'alf what I do," he said.

The unexpected warmth of his words delighted the ear.

"We're off," cried Berry. "We're off."

"Not yet," said Jonah. "But I hope very much that we're coming up to the gate."

"You can never tell," said Fluff. "The mail may help, or it mayn't. But I've known the art of writin' put a rope round more than one neck."

"That'll do," said Jonah. "Why d'you want to see him so much?"

Fluff stared in reply.

"Because I love him, of course. 'His face is my fortune, sir,' she said."

"Put it away," said Jonah. "I'm not a child. It's a chance in a million, of course. But you know as well as I do you're hoping you've seen him before."

"Your eye's not dim," said Fluff. "If he's the man, I saw him away in Chicago before the War. He was properly screwed one night at a low-down hall. He could have been skinned alive, but nobody liked to touch him because he was using Bethgelert's private box."

"And who's Bethgelert?" said Jonah.

"The high-an'-mightiest fence in the U.S.A."

CHAPTER III

Berry Protests and is Corrupted

Twelve hours had gone by since we had spoken with Fluff, and we were at ease in the valley which lay behind Nay.

There was no doubt at all about it—summer was in: and though our hearts turned to White Ladies and that exquisite tapestry of greenwood which the delicate fingers of June have woven from time immemorial about our home, I must confess that we had no cause for complaint. The sky was cloudless: the fresh air was magically warm: and the blowing meadow in which we were securely disposed was as green and gay and smiling as that of a nursery rhyme.

As a privy council-chamber, the spot was ideal. There were no walls about us to hear what we said: no one could possibly approach us without being seen: the lovely logic of the blackbird and the comfortable sermon of the brook ministered to the mind. As I looked about me, crime and its ways seemed suddenly dim and unreal: the treachery of Casca, the knavish cunning of Fluff took on a fabulous air: as for *The Wet Flag*, the present pastoral gave it the lie direct. And yet it was there—behind that sad court in Rouen, but twenty-five miles away. Thieves' kitchen and eclogue were both of the same round world. I found myself wondering whence Bermuda had come—whether she ever had lain as Adèle lay now, flat on her face by a stream, with a slim arm plunged into the water in an absurd endeavour to find and tickle some trout . . . whether the gentle-eyed prelate had ever gone picking daisies, as Piers was picking them now, because his wife was making a daisy chain. . . .

My sister laid down her novel and stared at the sky.

"I've no doubt he's the man," she said. "The man Fluff saw in Chicago before the War. Of course he may have changed. D'you think he'll know him again?"

"Oh, yes," said Jonah. "These fellows never forget. I must say I hope he is right. It'd give us a definite line."

"You mean," said I, "that if he's in with Bethgelert, he may be proposing to sell Bethgelert the jewels?"

My cousin nodded.

"It doesn't follow, of course. But it's well on the cards."

Adèle spoke over her shoulder.

"How will he do it?" she said.

"There you have me," said Jonah. "Bethgelert won't come and get them, and I can't see Casca lugging them all that way. Even his nerve would give out. Those pearls'll want some smuggling— they take up a lot of room. And the bracelets, too."

"If you ask me," said I, "he'll get them put into the bag—the Embassy bag."

"That's an idea," said Jonah. "I daresay he will. Three or four tins of tobacco would cover the lot."

"They may have gone," said Daphne.

"Don't you believe it," said Jonah. "Casca's not going to part till he gets his cheque."

"But Bethgelert won't buy till he's seen them."

"He might—on a valuation. A valuation made by one of his men. And that's where the letters may help us. You never know."

"It's frightfully exciting," said Jill, looking up from her chain. "Supposing you tear a letter. You know. They do go sometimes, even if you've only just stuck them down. Supposing you tear one badly, so that it shows."

Berry shuddered.

"You don't," said Jonah, calmly. "You simply mustn't do it. Tampering with letters is a devilish serious thing. I don't know the punishment in France, but in England you can get penal servitude for life."

Berry lay back on the turf and covered his eyes.

"How—how frightfully exciting," breathed Jill.

"Yes, isn't it?" said Berry. He laughed hysterically. "And now let's change the subject, shall I? What's the French for 'I reserve my defence'?"

"The point is this," said I. "It's no good blinking the fact——"

"Who's blinking any facts?" said Berry.

"——that if we're to go for the bowling, we've got to go out of our ground. We shan't get our property back by learning some conjuring tricks. We've got to use against Casca the weapons he uses himself."

"And now you're talking," said Berry. "Only say the word, and I'll lace his liquor so tight he won't be able to move his eyes for over a week."

"I'm speaking generally," said I. "Why d'you set thieves to catch thieves? Because they're without the Law. Because they're prepared to do things which the Law forbids. It may be convenient to drug him before we're through. Just now it's more convenient to see what letters he gets."

"All right," said Berry. "Go on. I don't care. D'you draw the line at trunk-murder? Or is that in the trivial round?"

"Don't be silly," said his wife. "All we're going to do is to read a letter or two addressed to somebody else. It isn't usually done, but——"

"I wonder why," said her husband. "Never mind. Do I hold them over the kettle? Or wait at the bend of the stairs to nobble the police?"

"You needn't worry," said Jonah. "Piers and I are going to play this hand. It's easy and safe, but it means sitting in all day. I hope you'll think of us if this weather goes on."

"Brother," said Berry warmly. "I shall be with you in spirit in all you do."

"Oh, you coward," said Jill. "A moment ago you were against it. Now you've not got to do it, you egg them on."

"Sweetheart," said Berry, "if I thought there was any danger, I should demand to be exposed. As an ex-cymbalier of the Salvation Army, I should insist upon——"

"You'll have your chance," said Jonah. "The dirty work will begin when the pearls are out of the safe."

My brother-in-law swallowed.

"Quite," he said thoughtfully. "Quite. Of course that's looking ahead. What—what exactly d'you mean by 'dirty work'?"

"Rough-housing," said Jonah simply.

There was a ripple of mirth.

"Oh, very funny," said Berry. "Quite a scream. D'you think I'm going to rough-house with Bethgelert?"

"Not with Bethgelert," said I. "He never——"

"You shut your head," said Berry fiercely. "The point is this. You can't have a scrap with a common——"

"Oh, can't you?" said Jonah.

43

So soon as he could speak—

"Oh, of course, you *can*," said Berry. "If you want to be kicked in the stomach and spend the rest of your life in an invalid chair, you can arrange it. But I don't believe in knocking the body about. Besides, it's vulgar."

"You'll lose sight of that," said Jonah, "the moment you smell the jewels."

Berry fingered his chin.

"I must confess," he said, "that if I saw Plaza unattended in a street which was not too well lit, I should be very much tempted to accost him. And if he stopped to do up his shoelace . . ."

"Don't be absurd," said Daphne. "You mustn't touch the man. If you saw him, you'd call a policeman and give him in charge."

"Mustn't touch him?" said Berry. "Do you mean it would be un-Christian? And why should I call the police? They'll find his body later. I'm not going to take it away."

"Rot," said his wife. "We can't have any violence. Only a moment ago you said——"

"I said I respected my body, and so I do. You don't get me jostling any bull-necked sons of darkness because Fluff thinks he saw them in ninety-four. But give me good reason to think that if I tripped up a dwarf——"

"Supposing," said Jill, "supposing he was bigger than you. Supposing you knew he had the jewels, but he was bigger than you."

"I must have notice of that question," said Berry. "If I'd had one or two orangeades, I don't know what I mightn't do."

"I honestly think," said Adèle, "we ought to rule out any force. I mean, where force is concerned, we can't begin to compete with a full-dress tough. Besides, what are the jewels compared with anyone's health?"

"Baubles," said Berry. "That's what they are. Baubles. And I entirely agree. Let's claim the insurance money and overlook Casca's lapse. After all, he's very amusing."

My brother-in-law can be more crisply and devastatingly provocative than the most malignant baboon that ever grimaced. In an instant the argument was lost in a welter of indignant controversy to which he unctuously subscribed.

Out of the incoherence—

"*I* said he was attractive?" screamed Daphne. "*I* said——"

44

"For your sake," declared her husband, "I tolerated the man. Never mind. It's too hot to argue. Let's sing the Gugnunc psalm."

By the time that my sister had established that Casca de Palk was not and never had been anything but repulsive to anyone not gifted with the mentality of Rabelais, that her husband seemed deliberately to suppress those instincts of decency which even the lower animals sought to acquire, that lies and perversion were his glory and misrepresentation his crown, the author of discord was only too patently asleep.

As she looked round for some missile—

"Hush," said I. "Here's François. He's not my idea of Nemesis, but we can always hope."

The *maître d'hôtel* was coming down from the terrace by the rude and laborious zig-zag which led to the valley below. When I say "laborious", I am thinking of its ascent. On a hot day this made the head swim.

"There's a card on the salver," said Jill. "Somebody's called."

The cynosure of twelve eyes, the butler completed the zig-zag and took to the turf. A moment later he was stooping by Daphne's side.

"The Abbé Gironde," read Daphne. "It must be the parish priest. Did you let him in, François?"

"Yes, madame. He is seated now in the *salon*."

"Good," said my sister quietly. She put the card back on the salver and rose to her feet. With one consent, the rest of us rose also, Berry, of course, excepted. He was sleeping the sleep of the just. "Monsieur will see him. Wait till we're out of sight, and then wake him and give him the card."

François grinned obediently.

"Very good, madame."

One minute later we had withdrawn to the woods.

I shall always regret that we were out of earshot : all we could do was watch the pantomime.

With difficulty awakened, Berry stared from the card to the butler, as a man who is not fully conscious, yet conscious enough to perceive that he and no other is the object of some most poisonous demand. As the horror of his fate became clearer, he shot one frantic look round. Then he began to argue . . . François however, was relentless. With a wealth of polite gesticulation, he pointed the only path. Berry put his head in his hands. Then he crawled to the stream and laved the lot. Finally he got to his feet and screamed for his wife.

"No, you don't," said Daphne, from behind a magnificent beech.

"Adèle!" howled Berry. "Adèle!"

My wife's reply was to laugh immoderately.

"Jill," yelled my brother-in-law. "Here's a very important wire for the Duchess of PADUA."

"Oh, you liar," piped Jill.

At last, with an inaudible but obviously bitter apostrophe, in the course of which his gestures suggested that he was contrasting the respective destinations of the upright and the unrighteous, the scapegoat turned to the house. With frequent rests, he toiled up the sunlit path. Then he heaved himself on to the terrace and disappeared.

"What could be better?" said Jonah. "All the same, we must stay out of sight. He must be simply bursting to get back on us, and I've not the faintest desire to cope with the combination of Berry and Monsieur Gironde."

Nor had anyone else. We had met such combinations before. And they had shortened our lives. We strolled in the woods securely until it was time for tea. . . .

As we entered the *salon*—

"Yes," said Berry, "a most delightful man. I should think he'd broadcast very well. And a great believer in garlic. By the time we were through with the weather you couldn't see across the room. Then we had a misunderstanding. He said he was enchanted to see us. Maintaining the fiction, I said he wasn't half so enchanted to see us as we were to see him. My construction may have been loose, but he got the foul end of the rod. When at last we straightened it out, he started in breathing goodwill until I was ready to swoon. Then we discussed expiation—whose, I don't know. I was past finding out, and he wouldn't let on. It's not much of a game, really. Whenever it was my turn, I said it was all I lived for, and when I'd said it four times he touched me for a hundred francs. However, we can lay for him on Sunday. Unless he belies his figure, he won't be at his best after lunch."

"You asked him to lunch?" shrieked everyone.

46

Berry Protests and is Corrupted

"That is my impression," said Berry. "I may be wrong. But he won't be any trouble. If I should be kept in Rouen, give him my love."

Jonah and Piers left for Paris the following day. And Carson with them.

It is right to record that their going was sharply opposed. As the hour of their departure approached, their unattractive mission took on an extremely ugly look. Speaking for myself, I became extremely uneasy. Trick the thing up as you please, the two were setting out to commit a definite crime which, though not especially grave, entailed the continual treading of very thin ice. As if this were not enough, they were to work hand in glove with a well-known crook. And this in Paris, where plain-clothes men were patrolling from dawn to dusk. If Berry and I were restless, Daphne, Adèle and Jill were worried to death, and when the car was announced their smouldering apprehension burst into flame.

Jonah heard their entreaties with an eye on the clock.

When they had done—

"Piers is your hostage," he said. "Do you seriously think I would risk a hair of his head?"

And while the rebuke was still warm, he took his leave.

There you have Jonathan Mansel. Quiet, astoundingly efficient, seemingly invariably forearmed, he can be more compelling than any man that I know. Not that his word is law unto us, his relatives. Oh, by no manner of means. And he has many faults. But I will wager that he is more honoured in his own country than any prophet that ever was foaled. And that with justice.

Not until the Rolls had disappeared did Daphne remember that he had left no address.

Since then two days had gone by, and life seemed particularly aimless when François appeared on the terrace and stepped to my side.

"Monsieur Carson is below, sir."

Carson!

For a moment there was dead silence. Then—

"Show him up," said everyone.

The butler bowed and withdrew.

One minute later Carson was standing before us, letter in hand.

This was addressed to me, but before I could rip it open, Daphne, Adèle and Berry were crowding about my shoulders to see what it said.

Dear Boy,
    Fluff was right. Please see the enclosed. The original was posted at Tours. It may be a mare's nest, but reason suggests investigation. Sorry I can't spare the Rolls. I should stay in Tours at the best hotel.
                                                    Yours,
                                                        Jonah.

In some excitement I turned to the second sheet.

                                        14 rue Malleyband, Tours.
Dear Monsieur de Palk,
    I have delayed answering your kind letter until I should be in Europe, and I may say that I shall be very disappointed if we do not renew our acquaintance before my return. I am expecting Maimie to join me any day now, and, as at present arranged, we shall be over for four of five weeks : although I know you are always full of engagements I think that should give us good time to fix something up. Our movements are rather uncertain, but this address will find me until you reply.
                                        Cordially yours,
                                            Paul K. Woking.

    I surrendered the sheets to my wife and turned to the messenger.
    "Right-oh, Carson. Tell Captain Mansel that I'll get busy at once. Are you going back straight away?"
    "Yes, sir."
    "Everything quite all right?"
    "Yes, sir."
    "Very good. Get what you want in the pantry before you go."
    "Thank you, sir. I've a note for the Duchess, sir."
    We shouted for Jill. Carson plainly believed in delivering letters to those whose superscription they bore. All things considered, I do not think he can be blamed.
    When Jill came running, he gave her a little note.
    "Is he all right, Carson?" she cried.
    "Yes, your Grace. Couldn't be better. He gave me this letter himself."

The next moment he was gone.

I crossed to the balustrade and stood looking into the valley asleep in the sun.

"Reason suggests investigation."

"I'm coming with you," said Adèle.

"Oh, that's not fair," cried Jill, looking up from her note. "When I wanted to go with Piers——"

"The penalty of greatness," said I. "The Duchess of Padua is just a shade too well-known."

This was true. If Jill were less startlingly attractive, her resonant title would bear less dazzling fruit. But add to the rank of Duchess all the artless charm of a beautiful child, clap strawberry leaves on the brow of a grave-eyed, laughing playmate of all the world, and you will be sounding a fanfare whose summons no one can miss. To go abroad with Jill was to make a royal progress. She had music wherever she went. It was, indeed, frequently embarrassing —but not to Jill. She was usually sublimely unconscious of the interest which she evoked. When this was too marked to be mistaken, she charged it, naïvely enough, to her lack of dignity.

"That's the worst of my going," said Berry. "I mean, if the Press were to get it——"

"I think we must chance that," said I. "If Adèle likes to come, well and good. She can play about with the car and order our food. But I'm not going to have her smelling out Casca's doom."

"If I am to come," said Berry, "I must have a room adjoining, and she must unpack my things. Daphne will show her how I like my bath, and if I should cry in the night——"

"Any ministrations," said I, "will have to be made by day. If Woking is crooked, our only chance is to make the most of the night. Without our cloaks of darkness, he'd see us before we saw him."

My brother-in-law frowned. Then he took up the letters and read them again.

"Of course," he said, "this is Jonah all over. 'Reason suggests investigation.' Possibly it does. Reason suggests that I should put half a million on the winner of The Stewards' Cup. Then why don't I do it? Because in the first place I haven't got half a million, and in the second I haven't the faintest idea what's going to win. How the devil can you investigate the manners and customs of a man you've never set eyes on without being heard or seen?"

"It's been done before," said I.

"In the *Boy's Own Paper*," said Berry, "it's done about once a week. But this is that tonic called life. If Woking was blind and deaf and wore a bandeau—Oh, and what price Maimie?"

"That," said I, "is what we've got to find out."

Berry expired.

"Assume," he said, "that two snakes are lying asleep—impulsive, poisonous reptiles that have no use for man. Assume that for some good reason you wish to inspect the bellies on which they go." He shrugged his shoulders. "Well, of course, you *can* turn them over with the toe of your shoe."

"I'm not half-baked," said I. "If we can't sight our friends from a distance, that's where we go home."

" 'Sight them'? Did you ever hear of the pigeon that sighted a hawk? He saw him damned well—quite a close-up, just at the end of his life."

"At least," said I, "we can go and have a look at the house. That's the first step, obviously. If he keeps late hours we may see the fellow come in."

Berry sank into a chair and closed his eyes.

"What a dazzling prospect," he said.

"We must begin somewhere," said Adèle. "Besides, you can sleep all day."

"What if it rains?" said Berry. "Pours all night?"

My sister put in her oar.

"You can't stand out in the rain—either of you. I mean, what *is* the good of——"

"We're not going to," said I. "We're not going to do anything to damage our health. He's simply being obstructive because he sees in the distance a job of work."

"Would it be inaccurate," said Berry, "to describe you as a venomous and bile-sodden leper? Or shall I be downright and call a skunk a skunk?"

"I repeat," said I, "that you are work-shy. The difficulty always was to make you take off your coat. We'd better leave here at ten and lunch at Chartres."

"I wish I could come," said Jill wistfully. She came to my side and put a warm arm round my neck. "Don't you think if I sat in the car—I mean, you could have a puncture in front of the house, and while you were changing the wheel——"

"A crowd would collect," said I. "And the following morning a basket of flowers would arrive 'for the beautiful child'." This had actually happened at Florence the year before. "No, my pretty. Stay with Daphne this round and hold the fort. Somebody must be here to pass on our news to Jonah, whatever it is. Besides they'll be back before we are, and Piers would call me out if he found you gone."

"I'll tell you what," said my sister. "Why don't you wire for the Fauns? This place would be perfect for them and they can go on to White Ladies as soon as the painters are out."

The Fauns were Jill's babies—twins: two unbelieveable mysteries of pink and white. We were all quite insane about them. To do them pleasure Berry had inhabited a dog-kennel for thirty-five minutes on end.

"Shall I?" said Jill. "I'd love to. Nanny's splendid at trains and we could meet them in Paris and bring them down."

Berry addressed his wife.

"My dear," he said, "your mind must be coming back. You've made the best suggestion I've heard for the last ten days."

Our journey to Tours was not dull.

It was June, it was Sunday, it was fine: and on such days a French highway is a racing-track. Everyone drives all out all the time. To slow up seems to be a sin. The rule of the road is in abeyance. If there is no room on your right, you go out of your ground—and the devil take the hindmost. The great god Pace is in his heaven: my lord of Misrule is enthroned. Engines that were built to do fifty, scream by at sixty-five: old cars rave on their way, leaping like rams: gigantic char-à-bancs fall down steep hills like lifts: a burst of machine-gun fire argues a racer's approach. The average speed is appalling: the risks which are taken make your blood run cold. What saves your life is that there is plenty of room. All the same we were glad to reach Tours. Throughout the two hundred miles we had never ceased to wonder what the next bend would bring forth. That sort of excitement soon palls. As I brought the car to rest before the steps of the hotel, I had a definite feeling that we had been spared.

"I can't get out," said Berry. "I've lost the use of my legs. That char-à-banc this side of Chartres. . . You know. Big Bertha. The one that looked like a piece out of the dress-circle. Well, when that looked round the corner, something inside me snapped."

"Come on," said Adèle, shuddering. "I still feel all weak myself : but if we lie down till dinner . . ."

"I must have a water-bed," said Berry. "I must——"

"Will you get out?" said Adèle.

Berry groaned.

"She's getting like Daphne," he said.

Then he descended and followed her into the lounge.

The porters off-loaded the luggage, and I drove round to the garage and put up the car.

Then minutes later I entered a decent bedroom which commanded the hub of the city and, with this, a steady uproar to which horns, gears, trams, stone setts and two large cafés fought to subscribe.

Berry's suitcase was open and most of its contents were out : Adèle was sitting, shaking upon the arm of a chair : and my brother-in-law was lying supine and peevish on one of the beds.

"Come in," he said weakly. "Come in and share the jest. Darling Daphne's packed me two tops of pyjamas and left the leg-joy behind."

"That's all right," said I. "You pin the two tops together and put your legs through the sleeves."

"Thank you," said Berry. "And what about the neck? I suppose I stuff that up with the *Daily Mail*." He sat up and clasped his head. "Can anybody tell me why I came? Two hundred miles of death-dodging for the privilege of lying awake in the noisiest room in Europe and insulting my body by following the filthy fashion set by performing baboons. I've never seen one of their garments disengaged, but I should say they could wear them upside down. We'd better suggest it to Worth. He'll carry it out in old rose, coin an appropriate perfume and call it *La Nuit des Singes*. But, of course, this venture was doomed before we set out. It was revealed to me last night in a vision. I dreamed I was a pond at sundown. Lovers passed by me, whimpering—whispering, a dead cat was flung into me, and I was drunk by several cows. Then the drought came, and I dried up. Which reminds me—d'you think that beer is coming? Or will you *jouer* with the telephone?"

"This noise is cruel," said I, putting the windows to. "Haven't they any other rooms?"

"Plenty," said Berry. "But not with bathrooms, my son. You bathe or sleep in this shrine : but you can't do both. Never mind. Think of the good we're doing. Fancy being actually in the same town as a man who wrote to Casca to say he was here. We don't know him. We shan't ever see his face. We daren't go and look at his house until after dark. But we're sharing the same *abattoir* and breathing the same foul air." He laughed idiotically. "You know, I'm so excited my gorge is beginning to rise. Perhaps he's out there now, standing Maimie a syrup under the shade of the trams."

"That'll do," said Adèle. "It's a bow at a venture, of course. But when you've got nothing to shoot at, what can you do?"

"Reserve your fire," said Berry. "Sit tight and reserve your fire."

I got to my feet.

"You go to bed," said I, "and reserve your strength. If we dine at half past eight, that'll give us just nice time to be out and about by ten."

With my words came a knock on the door. Then a waiter came with some tea and cakes for Adèle and a bottle of Evian.

Berry gave one look at the tray. Then he made a noise like a lion demanding its prey.

When I say that I have never heard a more convincing repro-duction of the majestic roar, the devastating effect upon the waiter may be conceived. The unfortunate man jumped almost out of his skin, blenched, gave visibly at the knees, set down his tray anyhow and made for the door.

Another roar of protest overtook him and shook him halfway.

"And the beer?" wailed Adèle. "The beer?"

"The b-beer, madame. D-did madame desire――"

"Two b-bottles of beer—at once."

"Very good, madame."

As the door closed—

"How c-could you?" quavered Adèle, fighting for breath. "How could you? And now he'll be afraid to come b-back."

"Confess it was lifelike," said Berry.

"I'll give you that," I said weakly. "But I wish you'd keep these turns for some desert place."

" 'Turns'?" said my brother-in-law. "That was a giddy urge. Instinct. The monarch of primæval forests speaking his mind. If that ewe-necked son of Belial isn't back in five minutes time . . ."

As though incensed by the reflection, he broke off to roar with a violence that shook the room.

Tearfully we implored him to behave, but he only flung himself down and lashed the bed with the cord of his dressing-gown.

There was, of course, nothing for it. When three minutes had gone empty away, I went for the beer myself.

We entered the rue Malleyband about half past ten.

This was a quiet street, perhaps two hundred yards long. It was fairly well lit and must have been pleasant to live in, for on one side rose its houses and on the other a wall which was bounding some park. It was purely residential, and might have belonged to England instead of to France, for the buildings were not uniform and most of the houses were low. Here and there we saw gables rising against the stars, and though no house was detached, it seemed that each had been built by a different man.

We sauntered along, smoking and marking the numbers as we went.

Number Fourteen was in darkness, except for a lantern hanging above the front door. As luck would have it, a street-lamp was shedding a flood of light three paces away.

As we passed on—

"And that's that," said Berry. "What did I say? You can't lurk under a searchlight. And if we withdraw to the shadows, we shan't be near enough to have a look at our man. Let's ring the bell and ask for the Comte de Wishwash."

"How will that help us?" said I. "We want to see Mr. Woking— not the inside of his hall. And I find this house suspicious. If he's a genuine tourist, why doesn't he use a hotel?"

"Because of the noise," said Berry. "He's probably been here before and knows his Tours. So when Maimie said it was time that she did the Loire——"

"Assume he's a crook," said I. "Assume that he's come from Bethgelert to buy those jewels."

Berry wrinkled his nose.

"Could he have done it?" he said.

"He could," said I. "His letter was posted on the seventh—eight days after America heard of the theft. Very well. You can lay that Bethgelert knew that Casca was after our stuff. One day he opens his paper and sees that the trick has been done. His representative leaves for Europe at once—with instructions to get into touch and buy if he can."

"Assume you're right," said Berry. "What can we do? I imagine Bethgelert's travellers have eyes in the small of their back."

"That won't help him," said I, "if we keep out of his sight."

At the end of the street we turned, crossed the roadway and walked back under the wall. At thirty paces we stopped and stared at the house. All its windows were shuttered, as were the windows of most of its fellow mansions. Indeed the street seemed dead. No man or beast had used it since we arrived.

"Well, I've seen some wash-outs," said Berry, "but I think this rings the bell. Fancy driving two hundred miles to——"

"Not so fast," said I. "There's a board up at Number Fifteen. If Number Fifteen is 'to let' . . ."

"I know," said Berry excitedly. "I know. We take it on a seven years' lease with the linoleum as laid. Once we're in, we tunnel under Number Fourteen, lift a flag out of the cellar, and there we are. You know, you ought to be confined."

"Perhaps you're right," said I. "Any way there are no back doors. That means there's a street at the back. Let's go and have a look at it, shall we?"

"I can think of nothing," said Berry, "that I should dislike more. Of course if you insist . . ."

There was no one in sight, so we strolled across to the pavement and had a look at the board on Number Fifteen. This stated that the house was "for sale". The keys might be had of an agent whose name was Bros. I noted his address carefully. Then we passed on down the street and turned to the right.

As I had expected, the houses of the rue Malleyband were served by a secondary street. This was a noisome alley some four yards wide. In its mouth the pathetic corpse of a mongrel sprawled like some hideous legend against the wall. The row itself was unlighted, very imperfectly paved and ankle-deep in refuse from end to end.

On either hand, houses rose up like cliffs. I began to count them faithfully, feeling my way by the wall. Berry followed behind me, laughing hysterically and arguing with himself.

"Yes, isn't it lovely? You know, I often come here just to be quite alone. . . . Oh, no. I—I like a good stench. And the crisp brush of the garbage about my insteps. It takes me back to the days of my childhood, you know. The dear old sewage farm——" The insolent growl of a cat cut short the memory. "Oh, I beg your pardon. I fear that was your sardine. I do hope I haven't hurt it. There's a nest of putrid tomatoes a yard or two back, if that's any use to you . . . No? Oh, I'm sorry about that. You couldn't come a little closer, could you? No, I thought not, you craven. Never mind. Here's a little present from Uncle Rex." An empty can met the base of the wall with great savagery, and four or five cats took flight. "Yes, isn't it provoking? You know, we caught it in Tours. We just popped over there for the weekend, and two days later they sent the fever-cart. Of course we'd not the slightest idea till one of my hands came off. But then they say leprosy's like that . . ."

"Will you be quiet?" said I. "We're nearly there."

This was a fact. I had counted thirteen doors. But I must confess that for all the good we were doing we might have gone home to bed. The exterior of no jail could have been less encouraging. Every door was fast shut : if there were windows, the rooms behind them were dark : the walls were as smooth as they were sheer.

We stumbled and slipped ten more paces to stand before Number Fourteen. The better to see what we could, we set our backs against the opposite wall, but the house rose up gaunt and lifeless, no different from any other that was flanking that filthy row.

Suddenly, high above us, a window leaped into light. Not a window of Number Fourteen, but of the barrack behind us, on the opposite side of the court.

We stood as still as death. The last thing we wanted was to be asked our business by any man.

The light from the window illumined Number Fourteen.

We saw a shuttered window, eight rusty feet of downpipe and two sagging telephone wires. And that was all.

After perhaps three minutes Berry put his lips to my ear.

"You see that downpipe?"

Berry Protests and is Corrupted

I nodded.

"I expect that relieves his bath. If we could bring a bloodhound down here next Saturday night . . ."

A shadow appeared on the wall of Number Fourteen.

Somebody was standing at the window above our heads. They seemed to be peering . . . listening . . .

Frantically I tried to determine how to reply to the challenge which I was every moment expecting to hear. I supposed furiously that they had heard the clatter of the can which Berry had launched. How they could possibly care who used their bestial alley was more than I could conceive.

They were moving . . . leaning out of the window. . . .

The next instant the contents of a slop-pail pitched directly before us three feet from where we stood.

To say that we were bespattered is half the truth. When about five gallons of fluid are discharged from a height of forty feet on to a cobbled pavement, the fountain induced is bold and generous. A venomous wave of muck thrashed us from head to foot.

There was a dreadful silence. Then the window above us was violently shut.

"Can I go home now?" said Berry. "I mean, I don't want to miss anything, but if that's the end . . ."

With a full heart, I led the way out of the alley and into the light of a lamp.

"But how delicious," said Berry, wiping his face. "What a wonderful stroke of luck. Did you get any fish? I did. Hake, I think—mostly. Never mind. You've got more spaghetti than I have. Oh, and look at my gent's waistcoat." He laughed hysterically. "Why, I do believe that's spinach. . . . Of course, if I had my way I should go and drown myself. I don't feel I'm worth washing. All I ask is to become unconscious. If anyone offered to flay me, I'd put my arms around his neck. The enamel has entered into my soul."

"We can burn our clothes," said I. "Considering what they cost, it seems a pity: but fire's a wonderful purge. And after a bath or two——"

"It won't be the same," said Berry. "I can pick the fish out of my ears, but it won't be the same. I've touched bottom or something. When I think that we actually waited—stood there waiting

57

in silence until that she-goat was ready to pour her stinking libations into the street. . . . No, I won't smoke, thanks. I've too much banana on my hands. I dare say it's quite a good skin-food. And what's the betting we have the lift to ourselves?"

In some dudgeon we repaired to the hotel. I cannot pretend I enjoyed traversing the lounge. Neither, I think, did Berry. But he carried it off with the air of a musketeer. As luck would have it he had the key of his room. . . .

With a flash of slim stockings, my wife started up from a chair.

"Splendid," she cried, glowing. "And now—what luck?"

"Oh, middling," said Berry. "Middling. You might almost call it pot luck. No, I shouldn't kiss him, darling. In fact, if I were you I should stand on the balcony. We—we don't smell very nice."

Adèle looked from Berry to me with parted lips.

"For heaven's sake, Boy. But—"

"To tell you the truth," said Berry, "we met with a little contretemps. Nothing serious. Our minds are slightly affected, but that is natural. You see, we've been filmed. Filmed and impregnated with filth. The ordinary grease-trap isn't in it. We're a little lower than the cesspools. We should have been back before, but the operator wasn't ready and so we had to wait."

"What on earth do you mean?"

Berry removed his hat, smelt it and chucked it into the grate.

"There is," he said, "a statute which requires that every citizen should give audible warning before discharging liquid or other garbage into a thoroughfare. To-night to our knowledge that wise and reasonable law was set at nought. A vessel of incredible dimensions was employed."

He laid his hand upon a match-box. When he raised it again, the match-box adhered to his palm.

Adèle watched the performance with widening eyes.

"There's no deception," he said. "My hands are glutinous."

"Do you mean to say——"

"Covered," said Berry. "Caked. We're a walking mass of corruption. If we entered a fried-fish shop, they'd ask us to leave. You're still too much to windward, but the lift-boy was worried to death. I think he had an idea we'd been raised from the dead. And now be as sweet as you look and turn on the baths. I want to get away from myself. What we really need is a lonely steppe and a torrent and half a gale : but with several relays of water . . ."

"And the basins," said I. "And if you could spare us some bath salts . . ."

Adèle flew to the taps, while we stood inspecting ourselves, perceiving new imperfections and wondering where to begin . . .

My wife reappeared twittering.

"But what about Woking?" she said. "Have you——"

"The answer," said Berry, "is in the unmentionable negative."

CHAPTER IV

Adèle Stoops to Conquer

Sharp at six the next morning three lorries laden with milk-cans flung down the ill-laid pavement, touching the ground in spots. As this burst of frightfulness faded, the iron shutters of some shop were raised with a shattering roar. Then a bell rang smartly, and a hideous convulsion, which suggested that some powerhouse had had a seizure, declared that a municipal tram was starting from rest.

Wondering what Berry was thinking, I turned myself over to steal a glance at my wife. From a welter of sheet and pillow four feet away a gay, brown eye was regarding me steadily.

"I have a feeling," said I, "that the working day has begun."

Adèle pushed back the clothes.

"My dear," she said, "it began half an hour ago. How on earth you've gone on sleeping I can't conceive. That's the third tram that's been in trouble, and they've finished cleaning the café across the road. I must say they did it very well. All the iron tables were moved."

"The Frenchman's ears," said I, "are specially made. They must be. They've some sort of silencer inside before you get to the drum."

"I think he's just deaf," said Adèle. "Take any two peasants in the country walking along a lane. They shout and bawl at each other as though they were miles apart. And now what's this hand I'm to play? I'm simply beside myself to be told its shape."

"It's very simple," said I, "but you'll do it very much better than Berry or me. Besides, I don't want to show up." I propped myself on an arm. "A certain Monsieur Bros is a house-agent here. I want you to take the car and go to his lair. Tell him what lies you like, but make him believe that you want to settle in Tours. You require a decent-sized house in a nice quiet street, not very far from the cathedral, non-basement and facing South. You don't want a house on a lease—you're out to buy. Well, unless he can't understand French, he'll take you to see Number Fifteen rue Malleyband. If he doesn't do it at once, you must let him go on till he does. Now, Number Fifteen is empty—he's got the keys. For you to see the house, the windows and shutters, will have, of course, to be opened right and left. Very good. On the ground floor there are two windows. When you leave the house, one of those windows and its shutter must be left undone. Not open, you know, but unlatched."

Adèle nodded intelligently.

"Consider it done," she said. "Poor Monsieur Bros."

"Your company will more than repay him for any trouble he takes."

"I trust," said Adèle "he will see it from that point of view. And that's that. You are clever, you know. And once you're inside—what then?"

"My hope's in the roof," said I. "It's lower than that of Fourteen. Very much lower in parts. And it may command some window—you never know. Frankly, I haven't much hope, but I don't see what else we can try. To stand in that street all night is the act of a fool. To go there by day is madness—there isn't an inch of cover of any kind. If there were shops, it would be different : a garage would give us a chance : but there's only the row of houses, facing a long high wall. Woking may or may not be a knave, but he's dug himself in."

"Perhaps I shall see him—or Maimie."

"I very much hope you won't."

"Why, please?" said Adèle.

"Because you're very striking. The sight of you makes people think. And I want Paul K. to have a rest-cure. So far as we are concerned, I want his mind to be an absolute blank."

Adèle blew me a kiss. Then she locked her fingers and set them behind her head.

"D'you think he's anything more than his letter pretends?"

"I think he's Bethgelert's man."

"And Maimie?"

I shrugged my shoulders.

"I hope she's not his partner. She may be his wife."

Adèle frowned upon the quilt.

"I don't believe Maimie exists."

I looked at her sharply.

"What makes you think that?" said I.

"I'm probably wrong," said Adèle, "but I believe 'Maimie' 's a password. I think it means 'I'm Bethgelert's agent and ready to do a deal.' Of course this is pure surmise. But I don't believe Woking's a tourist. I think he's been sent hotfoot to buy if he can. To say nothing of Daphne's bracelets, the Padua pearls are a very unusual bag : and I don't mind betting that Bethgelert's not the only receiver that Casca knows."

Here a knock fell upon the door.

Adèle twitched a shawl from a chair, slipped it about her shoulders and cried "Come in."

The door opened to admit my brother-in-law.

His appearance was remarkable. He was wearing the smart black hat which my wife had left in his room and a dressing-gown which only Paris would have dared to create. Its bright canary field was covered with wine-red dogs, each of which was pursuing a royal-blue cat. In the background, apple-green rats were laughing heartily.

"When," said Berry, "do we quit this venerable town? I don't want to seem exacting, but if I'm to subscribe to its customs, I must be born again. The difficulties, however, with which that operation would be fraught are too manifest to be insisted upon : and so I propose to withdraw. I've a great admiration for industry, but a community that beds down at two and is in full blast again at a quarter past five makes demands upon my sense of decency which I am not prepared to honour. Watts puts the whole thing in an eggshell.

> How doth the little busy bee
> Delight to bark and bite :
> Its little hands were never made
> To twinkle all the night.

I learned that fragment face downward on my nurse's knee."

"Don't exaggerate," bubbled Adèle. "*Half* past five."

"Pardon me," said Berry. "Precisely at a quarter past five some person or persons unknown caused a long string of iron-tired tumbrils to negotiate the granite setts outside this hotel. I rose and observed the pageant, following it with my prayers."

Here another tram got going, and the savage clang of a girder clawed at the brain.

"That's right," said Berry. "They're building over the way. One of the rites of construction is to belabour iron. I warn you, that girder's for it."

His prophecy was hideously fulfilled.

When he had closed the windows—

"We can't leave to-day," said I, and told him my plan.

"I see," said my brother-in-law. "Fancy gambolling on a roof at midnight. And what do you take me for?"

"We can take some rope," said I, "and make it fast round a stack."

"Quite so," said Berry. "And who's going to make it fast? That'll be a succulent job. And supposing we fall into the alley. Think of the shock to the cats."

Adèle shuddered.

"You must keep in the gullies," she said. "You know. Where the roofs run down. Then if you slipped, it wouldn't matter. But if you can't see from there, you must give up and come home."

Berry sat down in a chair and laid back his head.

"I wish," he said, "you wouldn't talk like this. I know it's your idea of humour, but it makes my hands all hot. The Matterhorn outlook has never appealed to me. Besides, it's not right. Look at the Tower of Babel."

"I've no intention," said I, "of trying to get to heaven——"

"I've noticed that," said Berry, "for twenty years."

"——but if the roof of Fifteen commands Brother Woking's bedroom, it seems absurd not to have a look at his face."

"Now is it likely?" said Berry.

"I don't say it's likely. I say it's possible. It's more than likely that a man who is perched on that roof——"

"Perched," said Berry. "Oh, give me strength."

"——can look bung into some room of the house next door. Whether that room will be Woking's I've no idea. In fact, I think it's unlikely. But I'm going to go up and see."

"Well, heaven go with you," said Berry. "I've left my ice-axe at home. Provided that a small step-ladder is forthcoming, I may consider entering Number Fifteen. If I'm observed I shall say that I am your keeper and you have escaped. If you keep your mouth shut and look natural that ought to get us away. But if no one sees us go in, I'm ready to sit in the attic and hold the end of the rope. I can conceive more exhilarating pastimes, but then I'm like that. Besides, I don't suppose I shall be lonely. A place like that is sure to be crawling with bugs. And now what about some breakfast? Or d'you think the still-room only opens at eight?"

At ten o'clock that morning we were standing beside the car.

"You quite understand, my lady, you're to take no manner of risk. If you can bring it off . . ."

" 'If'?" said Berry. " 'If'? Look at that hat. Look at that face and those legs." Adèle got into the car and shut the door. "Bros doesn't stand an earthly. If she wanted to rent the cathedral, he'd take her to see it and promise to do what he could."

Here a page appeared with a parcel as big as a sheep. This he seemed anxious to introduce into the car.

"You've made a mistake," said I. "This isn't ours."

"Yes, it is," said Adèle. "Let him put it into the boot. I'm going to call at a cleaner's. Something was spilt on the coat of a man I know."

"Oh, you darling," said Berry. "And here's philanthropy. I wouldn't acknowledwge that raiment for fifty pounds. How will you explain——"

"I shan't," said Adèle. "I shall simply say they want cleaning. If anyone gives it a thought, they'll think you're a careless feeder and leave it at that."

As soon as he could speak—

"I see," said Berry. "I wonder what they'll think of my diet. Never mind. Beneath your ministration it's probably losing its sting. You'd sweeten bilge-water, if you bent over a bucket to powder your nose."

"Oh, Boy," cried Adèle, "I've got off." She set a small foot on the clutch. "Keep him going, will you, until I get back? Oh, and don't forget to teach the bar-tender his job. That Manhattan last night was a libel."

"It shall be done, sweetheart."

"That's right," said Berry. "The moment we get back from Matins . . ."

But brown-eyed Adèle was gone.

Three full hours went by before we saw her again.

Berry strolled off to the station to buy what papers he could, and I went to look at the pictures which the Musée des Beaux Arts displays. After an hour and a half I made my way home, but before I went to my bedroom I asked to see the head waiter and mentioned the question of drink. Our interview was illuminating. He seemed surprised to learn that cocktail, Manhattan and Side-Car were not synonymous terms: and when I explained that a wine-glass of gin and water laced with French Vermouth and tainted with lemon-peel was not only not worth two shillings but tended to irritate those to whom it was served, he seemed aggrieved.

"It is carefully stirred," he insisted.

When I could master my emotions, I ordered some ice and some glasses to be sent to our rooms exactly at one o'clock. Then I went out in search of a wine-merchant's shop. . . .

Pen in hand, Berry regarded my purchases with an approving eye.

"This is quite American," he said. "I suppose the bar-tender's ideas . . ."

"Won't bear repetition," said I. "I can't have Adèle eating out of that sorcerer's hand."

"Quite so," said Berry, rising. "Quite so. Shall I ring for some ice? Only to try the shaker."

"When she comes in," I said firmly.

With an awful look, Berry returned to the letter which he was writing his wife.

I regret to say that your brother is making no attempt to subdue those instincts which have been my abiding sorrow for several years. Even the compilers of the Litany do not seem to have contemplated those failings which he delights to indulge, and he has lately developed a most distressing tendency to procrastination which as you know has never been among my faults. Indeed, my cross is heavy . . .

I finished uncorking my bottles, put them away in the wardrobe, picked up a paper and let myself into a chair. . . .

Near half an hour went by. Then a well-known tap on the door

65

brought us both to our feet, and an instant later I admitted my wife to the room.

"Tired, my darling?"

Adèle sank into a chair.

"I must confess," she said, "that I'm glad to sit down. So, I should think, is Monsieur Bros. But that's his fault. No, he's not a nice man at all. And he wouldn't last long in New York. His misplaced and unfounded self-confidence gives you an actual pain. My hat and my smile went for nothing : he's not that type. So far as he was concerned, I was the female of man : and so, his inferior. And I'm not really."

"Never again," said I, in a shaking voice.

"But that's a detail," said Adèle, laying a hand on my sleeve. "The point is, I've done the trick. It was easy enough, but he took me the long way round. D'you think I could get that man to show me Number Fifteen?" She took off her hat and pitched it on to the bed. "First of all he took me to see a flat. When we got to the place, I protested.

" 'But I told you I wanted a house : and this is a flat.'

"D'you know that man argued with me that it *wasn't* a flat? There was a porter, and in the hall was a lift. And a plate outside, saying 'Numbers One to Six'. And when I refused to go in, he said it was all he had. . . . Well, I had to climb down and be civil and smile *and go in*. It was that or failure, you see. He'd called my bluff.

"At last I got him away, and we went off to look at a villa which was 'to let'. I had made it perfectly clear that I had no use for a lease. But he knew better. Of course it was miles from the cathedral, but when I pointed this out, he said that that didn't matter because I'd a car."

"There are human beings like that," said Berry. "But most of them die young. People go mad and scream and do them in."

"Well, I felt quite weak," said Adèle. "Exhausted with impotent rage. But what could I do but submit? Of course, his game was obvious. He'd Number Fifteen up his sleeve—I saw it down on the paper. But the others would pay him better, and so, if he could, he was going to force my hand." She paused there, and I lighted her cigarette. "We drove to see four more villas—all with basements, none of them near the cathedral and only one 'to be sold'.

Then we went to another flat. I don't know how I avoided a first-class row. My voice was trembling as I said that I wanted a house. Then he played his ace of trumps.

" 'Mademoiselle,' said he, 'I am a man of the world. Permit me to know your mind.' "

"Oh, I can't bear it," cried Berry. "Why didn't you gouge out his eyes?"

"I choked, instead," said Adèle. "And the tears came into my own. Then I wrung out a maddening smile and said I was late for lunch. . . . So we came to the rue Malleyband. I had an eye out for Woking, but no one at all showed up. Well, I got a bit of my own back. Bros was expecting, of course, that I should fall over myself directly I saw the outside. He soon perceived his mistake. From the moment I saw it, I obviously hated the house. And I watched his triumph change to injured amazement and then to despair. The colder I got, the more frenzied he became. Believe me, I twisted his tail. Every virtue he pointed, I found a vice, and I kept on comparing its features with those of the rotten villas he'd shown me first—unfavourably, of course. This, I may say, sent him nearly out of his mind, and before we left he was barking with mortification and rage. In fact, his state was most helpful. As for leaving a window open—well, if I'd pushed the front of the house in, I don't think he'd have noticed that there was anything wrong. I actually had to remind him to shut the front door."

"Well, that's something," said Berry. "I should like to think he'd had a stroke : still, the Frenchman hugs misfortune. He'll scourge himself with your perfidy for months."

"Don't let's discuss it," said I. "It sends the blood to my head. If I'd dreamed——"

Here a waiter arrived with the ice.

As he withdrew, Adèle threw me a questioning glance.

"A present for a good girl," said I, and opened the wardrobe door.

"Oh, Boy, what a brain-wave." She turned to my brother-in-law. "He is nice to me, isn't he?"

Berry raised his eyes to heaven.

"Unselfishness itself," he said brokenly.

"By the way," said I over my shoulder, "did you notice the way to the roof?"

"I saw a ladder which led to a large trap-door. Bros said it gave to the finest box-room in Tours, but I fear he may have exaggerated. He was rather overwrought at the moment. I think he'd have said that it led to a swimming-pool, if he'd thought that that would incline me to take the house."

As we were drinking her health, a page arrived with a parcel containing ten metres of rope.

"What's that?" said Berry, frowning.

"A measure of precaution," said I. "To be taken after dinner— in the finest box-room in Tours."

At half past nine that evening Adèle put her arms round my neck.

"I've not stuck in my toes," she said, "because I don't want to be tiresome and cramp your style : but until you come back I'm afraid I shan't sleep very well. Will you promise to be very careful and think what it means to me before you take any risk?"

"I promise," said I, and kissed her, and Berry and I set out.

I had a torch in my pocket and was wearing rubber-soled shoes. So was Berry. But I was also wearing ten metres of rope. As a garment, this was a complete failure. It restricted my action and caused a discomfort of body which will not go into words. Before we reached the rue Malleyband it had begun to come down.

"The trouble is," said Berry, "you're not wearing it next to the skin. Let's go behind this kiosk and get it right. We can always pretend something's biting you."

"I warn you," said I, "you're going to wear it back."

"Don't be indecent," said Berry, "or I shall tell Adèle. Oh, and here's Love Lane. How quiet and peaceful it looks. But what a shame. Somebody's moved the dead dog."

Now I am not so foolish as to expect favours of Fate, but I must confess that I had not anticipated that an hour and a half would go by before we were able to enter the house we sought. The street was as quiet as ever : hardly a vehicle used it whilst we were there : and all the time it was almost entirely deserted—but never quite. Someone was always approaching Number Fifteen. Times without number we halted beneath the window which we were to use, only to see some figure stroll out of the shadows and into the light of a lamp : again and again I raised a hand to the shutter, only to hear a new footfall coming our way : and once I had it open when a warning touch from Berry told me the chance was stillborn. There were times when I asked myself if the street was bewitched. Not caring to loiter directly before the mansion, we strolled to and fro as though we were taking the air, and though, if the house had but stood at the end of our beat, we could more than once have entered without being seen, always before we could reach it someone or other drew near. Never was luck so dead out. The air was most hot and heavy and promised a thunder-storm : the rope about my body had sunk to the seat of my trousers and seemed annoyed at being arrested there : after an hour of walking I was ready to drop in my tracks. All the time I was pricked by the reflection that before I could reach my crow's nest the man I was hoping to study would have retired. What saved my heart from sinking was that the lantern was burning at the door of Number Fourteen.

As we approached the house for the ninetieth time—

"Nothing doing," said Berry. "Here's somebody else. And if anyone told me this, I'd call them names. It's like rehearsing a scene in a pantomime. There's something to be said for these coves that sling bricks into jewellers' shops. The marvel is they don't murder the passers-by. And I wonder how far we've walked."

We met and passed the new-comer and after a moment or two began to return. As we reached Number Fourteen, someone ahead in the darkness was lighting a cigarette.

"No good," said Berry. "The fellow we passed was smoking. It's somebody coming this way."

So it was. We repeated our simple manœuvre. As we drew near to our goal, a lamp betrayed two lovers approaching with linger-ing steps. . . .

"There was once a King," said Berry, "who had no roof to his mouth. This was a source of sorrow to all who knew him—par-ticularly the palace telephone-operator, who always tried very hard, but never got there. One day, on his way back from the cemetery where he'd been playing golf, a large and venomous toad asked him an alms.

" 'Flngsnift gelvuzwoath,' said the King.

" 'No, I never wear 'em,' said the toad. 'But don't you want to be cured?'

"After a dreadful scene, the King got out his brassy and wrote in the dust that he did.

" 'Ah, I thought you must,' said the toad. 'Well, so long,' and with that, he loped off and disappeared in a wood. By the time the King had recovered the power of motion he was out of ear-shot.

"What the King said on reaching the palace that evening can be better imagined than described. His incoherence was frightful. That something untoward had happened was clear to all, and at last it was gleaned that someone or other had said or done the wrong thing and was meet to be killed.

" 'But where did it happen?' said the Chamberlain.

" 'Glyloleyush,' mouthed the King. 'Othwfrenthfrwzzbgr.'

" 'On the fourteenth green,' said the Chamberlain. 'Take that down, someone.'

" 'Blzzwlmoprstutt,' said the King, and hit him under the jaw.

"The rebuke precipitated matters.

"The Master of the Horse, whose ears were quicker than some, commanded the trembling guards to search for a penniless goat with a basket of worms.

" 'Mmwtt ghffwote,' howled the King. 'Plboaffe.'

" 'Not goat, you fool,' yelled the Comptroller. 'Stoat. Besides, goats don't eat worms.'

"The correction was well meant, but the cataclysm provoked by his words was truly awful.

"When the fit was over, the King sat up and wiped the foam from his lips.

" 'Fetch me pen and paper,' he said in a loud and resonant voice. And now, by heaven, 's our chance. Quick. I'll put you up, and then you can give me a hand."

In a flash I was on the sill . . . over . . . down on my hands and knees in a musty room. Then my arm was out of the window, and Berry's hand was in mine . . . And then he was standing beside me, and the shutters were shut.

We groped our way out of the room, shut the door behind us and ventured to use my torch. One minute later we stood at the foot of the ladder which led to the roof.

When Berry had helped me to slough my offensive coil—

"You stay here," I said, "and hang on to the torch. If I flash it about up there, I may tear everything up."

Here a leisurely scamper above us announced the presence of rats.

Berry shuddered.

"Then you—you don't want me up there?"

"Not yet," said I darkly.

I am prepared to believe that the trap-door had not been opened for several years. Never have I disturbed such a layer of filth, while, as for the rats. I might have exploded a mine. I heard them flying headlong on every side. Almost before I was up I hit my head, dislodging a shower of dirt which fell all over my hair and down my neck—a blunt but definite warning not to proceed any further until I could see. As my eyes grew accustomed to the darkness, Adèle's suspicions of Bros were more than confirmed. There was no floor : furrow after furrow of grime showed that the joists were bare and that if I took a false step my leg would go through the plaster into some room below : above me the naked rafters were hanging so low that only a child could have managed to stand upright. Much of the space was taken by a barrel-shaped tank, and the pipes which ran from this made a rude but effective fence by which no trunk could have passed. Beyond this barrier, a sudden break in the rafters argued that here was a casement which led to the slates.

The casement was but twelve feet away, but by the time I got there I might have passed through a bog. The heat was awful, and I was streaming with sweat : the filth which I was disturbing settled upon me like a cloak and, finding my skin receptive, hung there in drifts. I reflected that whoever wrote *Per ardua ad astra* knew his world.

I found a hinged, iron frame, containing four panes of stout glass. The hasp which had held it was broken, but the frame had been wired to the staple to keep it from moving in a gale. All this I discovered by touching. The wire was thick and had been made fast with pliers, but after ten minutes of hell, I was able to wring it free.

My state was now lamentable. I was indescribably filthy, my joints were stiff and aching from the postures I had had to maintain, my hands were torn and bleeding and I was choked and stifled for want of air : but the way to the roof was open, and after resting a moment to steady my swimming head, I lifted the casement up and laid it back on the slates.

After the horror of the attic, hot as it was, the night seemed Paradise. It was spacious and clean and friendly, and I could breathe and see. I rested my elbows on the roof and gave my face to the breeze. After a moment or two I felt a new man.

When I had got my bearings I found that I had my back to Number Fourteen. Below me was one of those gullies in which Adèle had begged me to stay, and behind me the pitch of the roof was masking all but the chimneys of the house I had come to watch.

After a moment or two, I fought my way back to Berry and made my report.

"I shan't need the rope," I said. "It's a patent safety roof, and an infant couldn't go wrong. When you're out, you crawl up to the ridge-pole and just look over the top. If you slip you slide back into a gully. And now I'm off to observe. If I don't come back for a while——"

"Lead on," said Berry stoutly. He put the torch in his pocket and started to mount the steps. "After all, what is death?"

"You'd better stay here," I warned him. "The roof's all right, but the attic's a poor resort."

"Tripe for two," said Berry. "What's foul for the gander is only fit for the goose." He heaved himself on to the joists and put out an arm. "Where do I hit my head first?"

"Don't talk so loud," I breathed, beginning to move. "Keep low and make for the draught. Bend yourself nearly double, and after six feet or so you'll come to the pipes. Whatever you do, be careful to step on——"

With my words, the unspeakable happened.

With a crackling and rending sound, lath and plaster gave way beneath a burden which they were not meant to bear. Berry had missed his footing, or I had spoken too late.

"Are you hurt?" I cried anxiously.

In a steady unemotional voice Berry described the attic and spoke at some length of Monsieur Bros. When he paused for breath—

"Are you hurt?" I demanded.

"My trunk's all right, but I don't think my legs'll go back. One's been taken, you see, and the other left. Never mind. If I should swoon, think this of Bros—that there's a leper in a foreign town. . . ."

I found his right arm and put it about my neck.

"Heave," I commanded.

"D'you think I'd better?" said Berry. "I mean, I shouldn't like to flout Fate. It may be written that I'm to be eaten of rats. Besides, it's a case for a crane. I don't mean the bird. Those things that lean out and——"

"Now," said I, and began to take the strain.

A grunt of relief informed me that he was out of the pit. Then he straightened his back without thinking and hit his head. In vain I tried not to laugh.

"Oh, very funny," said Berry. "Very funny indeed. And I suppose that's the catch. Quite mediæval, isn't it? Dismembered first and then your brains dashed out. And now let's make for the draught, shall I? I suppose the pipes are another parlour game. Here we go gathering smuts in May, On a fine but frowsty morning. When I fall down and kiss you, that means you're out. And who said it was dusty up here—the optimists? To my mind, it beats Rotten Row. 'Hell gone dry' is an under-estimate. And don't say Woking'll hear, 'cause I hope he does. For twopence I'd scream the house down."

"There are the pipes," I said weakly. "Straight ahead. The best way is to pass between them."

"Indeed," said Berry. "And where shall I find the barbed wire? I wish I'd got Bros here. I'd lead him up the draught."

"Now think what you're doing," said I. "Steady yourself with the rafters and keep your feet on the joists. When you come to the pipes——"

"I know," said Berry. "I mingle with them, and God defend the right. When I come up for the third time——"

A flurry of squeaks and thuds cut short the sentence.

"There now," said Berry. "And I only wanted to stroke them. I didn't want to do that, really. In fact, if I'd known it was their rafter. . . . You know I've never liked rats, in spite of their pretty ways. I know they're useful. They carry bubonic plague and— Oh, these are the pipes, are they? How very convenient. Of

73

course, curvature of the spine would help you here. And what happens if I touch them? Do they give way, or only burst into tears?"

"You'll dirty your hands," said I.

"That were impossible," said Berry. "If I massaged a goat in a coal-mine, I couldn't dirty these hands. Or anything else that is mine. And what are the slates like? Can you find a loose one? I want to wipe my nose."

"Will you be quiet?" I breathed.

A moment later I was out on the roof.

Berry followed gingerly.

"There's the park," I whispered. "And that's Fourteen. From the ridge of the roof we shall see the side of the house."

With that, I began to go up on my hands and knees.

This was easy enough. The pitch was steep, but the slates were dry as a bone. After a moment or two I had my hands on the ridge.

I lay down and drew myself up. . . .

Slightly to my left were two windows of a considerable size. Plainly they lighted a room at the back of the house. They had no outside shutters, but the room beyond them was dark. Whether the curtains were drawn I could not tell.

"One to you," said Berry. "I don't suppose they're Woking's, but that's not a servant's room. Shall we move a bit to the left?"

I crawled along in silence, feeling absurdly depressed. My hopes, which had been fanatic, had fallen flat. We had found what I had expected—and that was all. In the sweat of our brow we had won a commanding position, and there was nothing to see. Paul K. Woking's ways were not for our eyes. The truth of the matter was—I was out of my depth.

"I'm much afraid," I said, "that this is where we get off. For the look of the thing, I'm going to stay here till dawn. As far as that room's concerned, we're in the front row of the stalls, but I can't believe that the curtain is going to go up."

Berry was rubbing his chin.

"What about a close-up?" he said.

"That won't help us," said I. "If the light was on, we should see rather better from here. Of course, there may be curtains."

"Well, I'm going down," said Berry. "After that attic I feel like a beast enlarged." He cocked a leg over the ridge. "And don't get disconsolate. The beacon was still a-burning when we came up, and if this should be his room . . . ."

He swung his other leg over and let himself slide by inches towards his goal. He was, of course, in no danger. The houses were joined together. A gutter of some sort must run at the foot of our roof. Then came the bare, brick wall of Number Fourteen.

Left to myself, I studied the wall of that house. I found it fifteen feet higher than that of Number Fifteen, an I judged that it masked two rooms. One of the two faced South, overlooking the park, and the other would have faced North, but for the filthy alley which bounded that side of the house. Better look on to a roof than on such a row : so the windows I saw had been set in the western wall. They were decent, casement windows, some six feet high. Five feet of wall lay below them, and a man that had wished to do so could have entered with the acme of ease. I began to wonder. . . .

Berry was down now, and had his hands on the sill. I could see his head and shoulders against the pane. And as he was peering, the lights in the room went up.

CHAPTER V

Perfect Ladies

Whether my heart stopped beating I cannot tell, but now I can say that I know how a burglar feels when the darkness in which he is working turns suddenly light as day. The shock of discovery flicks a year from his life.

I ducked instinctively. Then I remembered Berry and cautiously raised my head. But his silhouette was gone, and I guessed he was flat on his face in the gutter below. How the inmate of the room had come to suspect his presence I could not conceive. The windows were loosely curtained and he had made no noise. Of course if they had been standing, watching the roof . . .

I began to wonder how they would raise the alarm. If only Berry could make his way over the ridge, we could beat a retreat, and once we were clear of the attic, we stood a good chance. I strained my eyes to try and make out his form.

A shaft of light streamed out, and I hid my head. I heard the rasp of curtain rings, rudely used. Then someone flung open the window at which Berry had stood.

I lay awaiting their challenge with my heart in my mouth.

But none came. And after a moment the other window was opened and somebody coughed.

Hardly daring to hope that they had but opened the windows to let in the air, I ventured to lift my head.

Sure enough, the casements were empty, and I could see into the room.

This was heavily furnished with old-fashioned stuff. I could see one side of a bed and a deep *chaise longue*. A ponderous chest of drawers stood by the door, and a gleaming basin, fed by two plated taps, argued a degree of comfort which not everybody demands. What set my pulses leaping was that the quilt was drawn and the sheets were folded over, ready for use.

A man strolled into view, with his hand to his chin. He was fairly tall and well-knit, and his jaw was square. His fair hair was turning grey, and his features were not unpleasant, but rather rough : his clean-shaven face was sallow and heavily seamed, as is the face of a man accustomed to use its muscles to point his argument. His hands were smooth, his sober suit was well-cut, and he had the look of an excellent business man. Of his nationality there could be no shadow of doubt. Woking or no, he was American.

His eyes wandered round the room. Then he stepped to the side of the bed and lighted a table-lamp. Almost at once, however, he switched it out. I watched him pass to the basin against the wall. Again he put on a light, only to quench it again as soon as lit. Then he crossed to the door and put his hand to the wall. Once more he looked round. . . . An instant later the room was black as before.

Trembling with excitement, I tried to marshal my thoughts. It was done. We had brought it off. Paul K. Woking was now no longer a name. I had seen him—studied the man. I could describe him to Fluff. Out of a million others I should certainly know him again. His habits might be a secret, except that he kept late hours : but now at least we should not go empty away. Our journey . . .

I brushed my triumph aside and set myself to interpret what I had seen. This was easier said than done. One enters one's bedroom at midnight to go to bed. Or one may come up for a book or for cigarettes. But . . .

Here Berry crawled up from behind me and laid himself down.

"How did you get here?" I whispered. "I thought——"

"Circuitous route," he panted. "What do you know?"

"I've seen him," said I. "At least, it must be Woking. Not a bad-looking chap. Going gray, with a hell of a jaw. American every time."

"I thought I was done," said Berry. "I just lay down in that gutter and damned near died. And he must be deaf or something. You could hear the slam of my heart on the other side of the park. When the light went out, I nearly burst into tears. Reaction, you know. Still, I must say he knows how to hustle. Or did he go to bed in his boots?"

"He's not in bed," said I. "He went out of the room."

Berry stared.

"Then what was he doing?"

"That's what beats me," said I. "He had a look round and tried a couple of lamps. Then he opened the door and went out. The bed was made and turned down. But I saw no paraphernalia —no clothes or shoes or brushes or stuff like that."

"Can't be his room," said Berry.

"Then what was he doing there? Why did he open the windows and try the lamps?"

There was a moment's silence. Then—

"I've got it in one," said Berry. "*It's Maimie's room.* What did that letter say? 'I am expecting Maimie to join me any day now.' Well, there you are. The thing's as clear as a fly in a glass of champagne. Maimie stayed in Paris, but he came through. No reason why she shouldn't, and you know what women are. The rue de la Paix and the rest. And now she's coming to join him. There's her room all ready, and he came up to see it was all O.K. And it wasn't O.K.—there wasn't a breath of air. 'This won't suit Maimie,' says Paul. And so he opens the windows and leaves them wide. Not that he's done much good." He wiped the sweat from his face. "If we don't have a storm before sunrise, I'll take the veil."

This admirable explanation simply compelled belief. I could find no fault in it. An express—the *Côte d'Argent* itself—was due at Tours about midnight. And Maimie was on it, and Woking was waiting for her.

"You're right," said I. "You've got it. I take my hat right off and hang it up on the peg. If we don't hear a taxi below in half an hour I'll wager that's only because she's missed her train."

"It's a gift," said Berry. "Clairvoyance. I don't often talk about it. I've always hidden my light under a quart pot. As one of the pure in heart——"

"Quite so," said I. "And if you were more often encouraged instead of reviled by a lot of rotten wasters who aren't fit to wash your socks——"

"Brother," said Berry, "who told you?"

"It's a gift," said I. "Clairvoyance. And now be quiet for a moment. I want to think."

The point was this. From the ridge of the roof we could see clean into the room, but if any words were spoken we could not hear what was said. From the gutter below we could hear, but we could not see. At least, when I say that we could not, I mean that we dared not look. After a little I decided that Berry, who as yet had seen nothing, had better remain on the ridge, whilst I went down to the gutter and used my ears. That Woking would escort Maimie seemed likely enough and I could hardly believe that before he bade her good night their talk would not have told me whether they were honest or no.

Berry heard me out gravely.

"I see," he said. "And supposing she begins to undress."

"I can't help that," said I. "You're here to keep observation. It might be very useful to know that she wears a wig."

"All right," said Berry. "I don't know what Daphne'll say, but I'll do my best. Who was it watched some goddess and got done in by his dogs? Oh, I know. Actæon. I suppose the cats won't turn on me." He rose and peered over the ridge. "You're quite sure I can't be seen?"

"Certain," said I. "If they should come to the window I think I should lower my head. If they should stand looking out, they might see the line of the ridge-pole against the sky. But that's not likely."

"I see," said Berry. "Supposing—just supposing they got some stupid idea, some utterly irrational notion that they were being watched. Supposing Woking comes to the window and says 'Who's there?' Do I say 'Pass friend' or 'Advance one and mind the counterweight'?"

"You lie perfectly still," said I. "Then he'll think he's mistaken and go away. And now I'm going to leave you. I take it the gutter's of stone."

"That is my belief," said Berry. "Nothing but stone could have been so extremely harsh. At present it's bung full of soot, so I can't be sure. The soot, I may say, yields to pressure, same as a swamp. It's the best place to sprain your ankle I ever saw."

I wiped the face of my wrist-watch and peered at the dial.

As I did so, some clock or other began to beat out the hour. Twelve o'clock.

"Any time now," I said, and went over the ridge.

Arrived at the gully, I set my feet in the gutter and sat on the slates, ready to rise in an instant and go on my knees by the wall. If anyone came to the window, I could then fall flat on my face, a movement which, if I were standing, it would not be easy to make. What Berry had said of the soot was perfectly true. I could have kicked myself for not bringing overalls. Then I raised my eyes to the heaven and wondered whether the rain or the taxi would be the first to appear.

Looking back I find it strange that we should have been so certain that Woking was sitting, awaiting that midnight train. If she can do so, a woman avoids a journey which keeps her abroad so late. For myself, if I had to travel by rail from Paris to Tours, I should do so by day. After all, three hours and a half is nothing at all. Be that as it may, I knew that a taxi was coming as sure as the dawn, and when I heard the drone of an engine abusing a neighbouring street, I rose to my feet without thinking, the better to hear its approach.

The drone grew louder and faded. Then the car must have rounded a corner, for the note swelled into a snarl. This in its turn died down. Then came the crash of gears. An instant later the peace of the rue Malleyband was savagely torn in two. The racket grew louder and louder. For one dreadful moment I thought that the taxi had passed. Then the brakes squealed to glory. . . . The hubbub died, and a loose irregular hiccough took its place. The car had stopped.

After a little while I heard the slam of a door.

As the taxi began to move off, I went down on my knees.

Perhaps two minutes went by—no more than that.

Then the lights in the room went up and I heard a man's voice.

"I give you my word for that, sir. I shouldn't be here if I wasn't sure of the house."

"I 'ave bin a dam fool to come," said Casca de Palk.

If from each end of the gully a brace of machine-guns had suddenly opened fire, I could not have fallen more quickly flat on my face, or, being there, have lain more unearthly still. As it proved, however, I might have stayed where I was, for Casca's first overt act was to rush to the window beside me and slam it to with a violence which showed that his temper was up. And here our luck came in with a Harlequin leap, for such was the force which he used that he shivered a pane.

A large piece of glass fell on to the window-sill, to split itself into fragments, some of which lodged in my hair. Had they gone down my neck, I could not well have complained. Never had accident dealt me so handsome a hand.

I heard Casca let out an oath. Then he tore at the curtains until the window was dark. As he did so, the other window was shut, and an instant later I heard the rasp of the rings.

In a flash I was up on my feet and had clapped my ear to the hole.

"I guess it's my fault," said Woking. "But when I looked in a while back, this room was as hot as hell."

"But you 'ave expose me," cried Casca. "I was not wish to be seen in a 'ouse like this. When I 'ear from you, I say 'No'. It is mos' important my 'abits shall not be change. And I 'ave not bin to Tours for thirty-five year. But I 'ave no like to write letters which mus' not be read. And so I am going to Biarritz to visit my aunt. An' then because why I was sick, I get out at Tours. And when twenty-four hours are go by, I shall catch the same train I 'ave to lose an' go to my aunt. It is all arrange an' thought for. An' then you mus' go an' expose me to all the public of Tours."

"See here, Monsieur Palk," said Woking. "I guess I know too much to be showing you off. These windows give to the slates of an empty house. They couldn't be better masked if they gave to a well. Keep them to, if you please—it's nothing to me. But I fancy you've nothing to fear from the birds of the air."

"I do not care," said Casca. "I will not come 'ere again. I 'ave plenty of friends I shall visit, and you shall come to their 'ouse. By and by you mus' go to Dinard, and I shall stay with my frien' the Countess de Nux. And I shall find you in the street and bring you 'ome. She is very 'ospitable, and because you 'ave bin my frien' she shall 'ave you to stay."

"I'm in your hands, sir," said Woking. "I'm here to value the stuff and make you a bid. Where and how I do it is up to you. If you don't fancy this setting, I'll meet you outside Paris where-ever you choose. As to where I take over from you, if we come to terms—well, I guess, if we get that far, you'll honour my point of view. And here's a note from Bethgelert. He doesn't often write."

Casca de Palk grunted. Then I heard paper torn. After a little Casca grunted again.

"I do not care," he announced, "who buys the goods. But 'e mus' buy everything. There are five pairs of cuff-links."

"That's understood," said Woking. "The small stuff follows the big."

"*Eh bien*," said Casca. "An' now I shall go to bed. I 'ave not wish to be call, but when I shall ring who is it will bring me my chocolate?"

"The man of the house," said Woking. "And you needn't dream about him. I've got him where he belongs. He's wanted for murder in Dayton. The warrant's five years old, but it's still on the file."

"*Mon Dieu*," said Casca faintly. "I 'ave not bin meant for these things. An' I do not want any chocolate. I shall not ring. Perhaps you will come and fin' me about midday."

"Oh, he's meek as mild," said the other. "If I hadn't told you——"

"I will not 'ave him," screamed Casca. "He 'as not bin meek in Dayton an' I do not like 'is sound."

"That's for you to say, Monsieur Palk. If you change your mind, just ring, and he'll be right there. But I'll be with you at noon in any event. Are you sure you won't have a night-cap after your run?"

"I am obliged," said Casca, "I will not drink. An' when you shall come to-morrow, you will blease to knock three times. So I shall know it is you. I was not wish to open to all the world."

"Quite so," said Woking, "quite so. Three times, then, about midday. And now I'll bid you 'Good night', sir. You must be tired."

I heard the door open and close.

For a moment there was dead silence. Then came a choking sound which I recognized as the prelude to greater things. I was not mistaken. After what sounded like an epileptic fit Casca got down to it. He cursed Bethgelert and Woking, and he cursed the city of Tours: he cursed the train that brought him and the bed-room in which he stood: and he cursed his folly in coming with a sibilant blasphemous vigour that warmed my heart.

What had touched off this explosion was not immediately clear, but I presently gathered that the absence of a bolt to his door had confirmed his worst suspicions of his environment. A moment's reflection should have shown him that he had little to fear, but I think that the slip which his host had made at Dayton had served to ram home the truth that he had gone out of his ground. That he had brought the jewels with him I could not believe. No one in his position would have done such a childish thing: he had come to see Woking's credentials, and, if these were good, to arrange another meeting by word of mouth. The break in his journey to Biarritz was cleverly planned. He was stealing twenty-four hours. While he lay in the rue Malleyband he was out of his world. Paris would believe him to be at Biarritz, and Biarritz would believe him to be at Paris. Casca was above suspicion and there he proposed to stay. But now he was rattled. Dr. Jekyll had broken his golden rule—which was always to be Dr. Jekyll and never to be Mr. Hyde.

The maledictions died down, to be succeeded by a perfect fanfare of grunts suggesting physical effort of a rare and unpleasant kind. Then the scroop of wood upon wood declared that the chest of drawers was being pressed into service to bar the door.

Here I decided to retire.

I could, of course, see nothing and while Casca's disquietude of soul delighted my ear, it was hardly likely that he would divulge any secrets in his soliloquies.

One minute later I was lying by Berry's side.

"Talk about luck," said the latter. "And of course it's as clear as paint. *Maimie's Bethgelert's name for Casca de Palk*. 'I am expecting Maimie any day now.' There's the summons direct. Oh, very hot. 'Any day'. If you remember, the lantern was burning last night. And fancy his smashing that pane. I suppose you heard every word."

"Every word," said I. "He's put the rope round his neck. Whether we can get hold of the end remains to be seen."

With that, I told him the truth.

When I had done—

"He's got something with him," said Berry. "I'll lay to that. That's why he's scared stiff of the wallah that's under a cloud."

"You may be right," said I. "Any way it doesn't help us. He can't have more than a sample—he's not such a fool. Bit by bit, he's going to submit to Woking the whole of the stuff: but he'll never come out with the lot till the deal is done."

"At Dinard?"

"I don't believe it. He's going to take his time. But we must be there somehow. They're not going to write any more. Our only chance is to overhear what they say."

"And if he parts with it piecemeal?"

"I don't think that's likely," said I. "Woking's not buying the cuff-links without the pearls : and Casca won't sell him the big stuff unless he takes the small. And I don't suppose either trusts the other an inch—no doubt with reason. And so at some given moment the whole of the stuff will pass."

"I hope you're right," said Berry. "And I hope we're just as near as we've been to-night. But we shan't be. This luck comes once in a lifetime, but never twice."

With his words the glow behind the curtains went suddenly out.

"Curtain," said Berry. "Maimie's going to sleepy-weeps. I suppose it'd be utter madness to make a noise like a Stilton robbed of its whelps."

"I confess I'm against it," said I. "My impulse is to enter and break his neck. But I'm going to tread it under. And now lets pray for rain. Thanks to the soot in that gutter those slates must be thick with footprints which we have made : and unless it rains before daylight I must evolve some method of wiping them out."

"And then?" said Berry.

"We go," said I. "We use the back door and emerge into Rotten Row. We leave it unlatched—we can't do anything else. And this evening, as soon as it's dark——"

"Hell's blunted bells," said Berry. "Haven't we done enough? D'you mean to say we've got to return to this messuage? Pass through that filthy mantrap and lie out here in the rain? And all on the chance of hearing that white-livered blackguard clean his teeth?"

"Why argue?" said I. "You know as well as I do——"

"All right," said Berry, "all right. If I can stagger, I'll come. It's not a tempting outlook, but I'm getting used to that. We shall remember Tours, shan't we? And here's the rain. Shall I go and shut the skylight? We don't want the rats to get wet."

As he spoke the sky was split by a blinding flash, the roof of Number Fifteen seemed suddenly bathed in fire, and I received a powerful electric shock. The simultaneous clap of thunder resembled the noise of torn silk, incredibly magnified.

Half-stunned and deafened, we scrambled towards the casement which a veritable curtain of rain served to obscure. Long before I had shut the window, I was drenched to the skin.

"God bless our home," said Berry. "And how many million volts d'you think that was?"

"I've no conception," said I. "I know I thought I was dead."

"I'm not certain I'm not," said Berry. "I've half an idea my body's out on the roof. No, it isn't. I can feel it hurting itself against the pipes. And isn't that Fortune all over? One minute she glues her lips to yours, and the next she bites you in the neck."

"If you ask me," said I, "I think we owe her our lives. That was a damned close call. And if you look at it that way, it's been a pretty good night. Woking, Casca and an escape from death."

"That's my point," said Berry perversely. "And the wise one knows when to stop. If we come again this evening, she'll let us down. Oh, and hark at the rain coming through."

"That's the main water," said I. "I've opened the cock. We may as well use the bathroom before we go."

"But what a brain," said Berry. "Why didn't you bring any soap?"

"In my left-hand pocket," said I. "And you go on, will you? I must stop and turn this off. If there's air in the pipes, just put your head in the basin and suck the tap."

I heard a hysterical laugh.

"You know," said Berry weakly, "you think of everything."

Forty minutes later we were within our hotel.

The polite way of describing the events of the following night is to say that we drew blank. Neither Berry nor I put it like that at the time. When for two solid hours you have lain or crouched on a roof in continuous rain, when you have seen and heard nothing except the snarl of the taxi which comes to remove your prey, when you emerge from a house which all the world believes empty *into the arms of a stranger with a malignant eye*, your account of the matter is likely to be unpolished, not to say blunt. After four hours' sleep, however, our sense of proportion returned, and a wire from Jonah, which came while we were at breakfast, fairly completed our cure

If quite convenient will one of you meet me at Chartres at three p.m.

There is nothing more agreeable than reporting progress—provided you have progress to report. We were all agog to declare our valuable news : and, what was still more to the point, we had already determined to leave Tours that very day. Casca was gone: we had accomplished our purpose : and we had no mind to be connected with Number Fifteen.

"In fact," said Berry, "it couldn't be more convenient. We can have a snack at Chartres and dinner at Nay. And I must confess I'll be glad to get out of this town. I've several things against it, and after last night . . . He'd a nasty look, that wallah." Here he took the remaining roll and bit a piece off. "Does any one want this crescent?"

"The light was behind us," said I. "He couldn't have seen us well. I admit it shook me up, but he wasn't the sort of fellow to go to the police. Probably up to no good, and we surprised him."

"He'd a watery eye," said Berry. "And when I'm committing crime, I don't like being observed by wallahs with watery eyes. Why shouldn't we leave at noon and lunch at Vendôme?"

"Why not?" said Adèle. "We might even leave at eleven and lunch at noon."

"I'll leave at eleven," said Berry, "with heart-felt joy. But I will not eat before one. Never rush the digestion. Never muck about with the maw. Never monkey with——"

"Spare us the superlative," said Adèle, "and you shall lunch when you please. But not at Châteaudun. If you remember we corrected a gendarme there a year or two back. We were well within our rights, but I don't want to meet him again."

"So we did," said Berry. "This side of the world seems unhealthy." He got to his feet. "How long will it take you to pack?"

"Half an hour," said Adèle. "But I can't make bricks without straw. As soon as you've finished dressing . . ."

By eleven o'clock we had left the city behind.

The rain was over and gone, and the sun was blazing out of a clearing sky. Majestic bergs of cloud sailed in the brilliant heaven before the breeze : the countryside was cloth of green and silver : and the black road coursed to a horizon as clean and sharp as the edge of the moon may be on a frosty night. The coolness and sweetness of the radiant air beggared description.

After a little we decided to lunch by the way.

At Vendôme, therefore, we purchased some food and drink, and ten miles short of Cloyes I took a convenient turning and brought the Lowland to rest in the shade of an oak.

As I got out of the car—

"Gideon's rug," said Berry. "We forgot to buy any knives."

My wife started. Then she sat back in her seat and closed her eyes.

"No glasses," she said. "No knives. Not so much as a paper plate. I thought of them twice and then forgot them again."

I put my head on one side.

"I can hear a brook," I said. "If I wash a couple of screw-drivers——"

"And a pair of pliers," said Berry. "We must have something to spread the butter with. And if that's your idea of being helpful, I should go and jack yourself up and change your head. And what do we drink out of? The hub-caps?"

"Adèle and I," said I, "are going to share the shaker. You can pour your beer in the tool-box and lap it up."

After a little while we decided to proceed to some village and purchase some implements.

We had gone about and were just on the point of leaving the lane for the highway whence we had come, when I heard a car approaching at a tremendous speed. I set my foot on the brake and waited for it to go by. An instant later a low, black car went by like a shot from a gun, heading for Chartres. And on the front seat sat a gendarme, staring ahead.

There was a dreadful silence.

Then—

"Hue and cry," said Berry. "What did I say?"

"Oh, Boy," breathed Adèle. "D'you think . . ."

"No," said I. "I refuse to. The thing's absurd."

"Utterly ridiculous," said Berry. "They're probably after some crooks. Some woman who's fooled a house-agent : or a couple of strangers who keep peculiar hours and break and enter houses and come home bruised and bleeding and covered with dirt." He laughed hysterically. "I—I wonder where they'll take them."

'Don't be a fool," said I shortly.

"All right," said Berry. "Drive on to Châteaudun. But don't blame me if the road's up. He's done it on us, that wallah. I said he would."

"Rot," said Adèle. "Besides, I want my lunch."

"Neither do I," said Berry. "Never mind. Let's look on the seamy side. They're probably going racing. After all, police will be police."

"The point is this," said I. "I don't believe for one instant that those fellows are after us. I don't believe they're aware of our existence. But because of Adèle we simply can't take any risks."

"Very beautifully put," said Berry. "We'd better proceed in reverse. Then when they see us coming, they'll think we're going away."

"We can take to the by-roads," said I. "We did it before about here with some success. But we'll have to come in at Rouen because of the Seine."

"But we've got to meet Jonah," cried Adèle. "And Jonah's coming to Chartres."

"Better and better," said Berry. "They've seen the wire, of course. They'll let us keep the appointment, *but they're going to keep it, too.* Fluff'll go well, won't he?"

"Which is absurd," said Adèle. She turned to me. "Put her along, Boy. If you like to miss Châteaudun, I won't complain. As far as I'm concerned, there's no luck about that town."

"Give me the map," said I.

After a little, I found the way that I sought.

By this we could leave the main road before coming to Cloyes, and, after fetching a compass, join it again a mile or so south of Chartres. There, though I did not say so, I proposed to set down Adèle, and while Berry stayed with her, I would drive on to meet Jonah—and anyone else who was waiting for me to arrive. If after half an hour neither Jonah nor I should appear to pick them up, they must beg a lift to some station, other than Chartres.

"And where do we lunch?" said Berry. "Not that I feel like food, but we may as well have a square meal before we crash. Those trays they send in are no earthly. The warders pouch the beer, and the food gets cold."

88

"I refuse to argue," said Adèle. "Supposing they were to stop us—our hands are clean."

"But not our trousers," said Berry. "The moment they open a suitcase . . ."

I swung us on the tarmac and put down my foot.

Two hours and a half had gone by.

I had led my wife to the water and now in the mouth of a by-road, a mile or two south of Chartres, Berry and I were using our best endeavours to make her drink.

But she would not. Chin in air, eyebrows provocatively raised, the shadow of a smile playing about her red mouth, Adèle gazed dreamily over the edge of the windscreen, resembling some beautiful image that has no ears to hear.

" ' 'Tis time,' " said Berry. " 'Descend : be stone no more.' "

The shadow of a smile deepened, but that was all.

"My sweet," said I, "I'm already half an hour late. Be a good girl and get out, and Uncle Berry'll tell you a fairy-tale."

"I won't," said Adèle. "If it comes to a pinch, my French is better than yours."

"There was once a giant," said Berry, "who went in for bumble-bees. One day——"

"Nothing doing," said Adèle. She nodded her head towards Chartres. "That is the way the ladies ride," and, with that, she sat back in her seat and crossed her legs.

"My darling," said I, "be reasonable. Berry and I have committed a technical breach of the law. We are both of us guilty of trespass : and if we should be summoned, we might have to pay five francs. So long as you don't appear, it can go no further than that. But once they connect our trespass with the visit you paid on Monday with Master Bros——"

"Of putrid memory," said Berry.

"—— the business takes on a very much blacker look. Conspiracy, misrepresentation——"

"Fraud," said Berry, "false pretences, causing a house-agent to bark. . . . You know, I believe she wants us to be transported."

"Listen," said Adèle. "If we hadn't seen that car, the idea that we were wanted would never have entered our heads. When it did enter, we dismissed it, as being entirely absurd. But it left its

mark. Ideas do. And so we went out of our way—just in case
there was something in it. And now you ask me to sit here while
you drive into the Narrows, to see if it's rough or smooth."

"Entirely wrong," said Berry. "He's got a date with a girl at
The Grand Monarque. She's got green eyes and a mouth like a
melting-pot. I didn't mean to tell you, really, but——"

"Go on," said Adèle. "This is much more exciting than the
giant and the bumble-bees."

"Oh, the jade," said Berry. "Oh, the ungrateful——"

The sound of a horse's hoofs cut short the diatribe.

Then two mounted police rode easily round the corner and into
the lane. They seemed much amused about something, and
though, as soon as they saw us, they tried to pull a straight face,
they could not altogether recapture the stern and unbending dignity they had put off.

The lane was none too wide, and they passed us in single file,
looking us over carelessly as they went. I smiled and gave them
good day and they nodded and touched their hats. An instant
later they were riding abreast again, talking and shaking with
laughter, as though we did not exist.

We watched them pass round a bend. Then Berry got into the
car and shut the door.

"Personally inspected and recommended," he said. "That
doesn't look as if any warrant was out. And now if you feel any
calmer, d'you think that we might go on? Of course I always said
it was fantastic."

"But then, you see," said Adèle, "you've got such a wonderful
nerve."

"Rude child," said Berry. "Now I shan't let you take off my
boots to-night."

As I started the engine—

"I think," said I, "that we might keep this to ourselves. If
Jonah heard of our detour he'd pull our legs for a month."

"I quite agree," said Adèle.

"Your secret," said Berry, "is perfectly safe with me."

Then we rounded a corner, to see the Rolls at rest by the side
of the road.

Carson was standing beside her, talking to Piers: and my
cousin was on the back seat, reading *The Sportsman* and smoking

and generally taking his ease.

"Well, I'm damned," said Jonah. "And there's a capful of luck. It's the merest chance we stopped here. We started to come and meet you. And what's the main road done?"

"Lost our way," said Berry.

"Lost your what?" said Jonah.

"Way," said Berry. "Road. Route. Death-trap. You see we'd forgotten the knives, and when we saw a fork in the road—well, before we knew where we were, we'd no idea. Not an inkling. And the further we went, you know, the worse it got. Talk about *The Wandering Jew*. Why, he's never been out of the garden compared with us. I may say that I charge the blunder to want of sleep. Never mind. How's Casca?"

"Out of town," said Jonah. "How's Woking?"

"Lonely," said Berry. "Maimie left him last night."

Jonah opened the Lowland's door.

"Come to the Rolls," he said, "and tell me the truth."

Without a word we descended and crossed the road. And when the others were settled, I took my stand beside them and told our tale.

When it was done, my cousin took off his hat.

"A splendid show," he said. "And this'll shorten our price."

"We'd the devil's own luck," said I.

"You went out and got it," said Jonah generously. "And now I've a bit of news. The Plazas have split on Casca."

I could hardly believe my ears.

"The Plazas have split?" I repeated. "Then——"

"But not to the police," cried Piers.

There was an electric silence.

Then—

"Rough-housing," said Berry faintly. "I can smell it coming. Stand back and give me air."

"Do you remember," said Jonah, "the night that we picked up Fluff? Do you remember his saying that someone was very sick about losing the pearls?"

"Auntie Emma," said Berry. "I remember thinking 'What an attractive name!'"

"That's right," said Jonah. "Well, the Plazas have split to Auntie Emma. I suppose they're cross with Casca. If they wanted to do him down, I don't think they could have gone to a better man."

"Thanks very much," said Berry. "And where do we come in?"

"First, I hope," said Jonah. "But I give you my word—it's going to be some race."

CHAPTER VI

Plot and Counterplot

" 'Gain," said the Marquis Lecco.

"Have a heart," said Berry. "I've done it three times, and I'm tired."

" 'Gain," said the Marquis, inexorably.

With an awful look, Berry remounted the table, strolled about for a moment and then, as though by mistake, stepped into mid-air. As he crashed to the floor, the Marquis and Lady Elaine were convulsed with laughter. So, indeed, were we all. Everyone, high and low, rejoiced when the Fauns rejoiced. It was inevitable.

From her chair between the two beds my sister lifted her voice.

"Do be careful, old fellow," she said. "You'll hurt yourself."

" 'Gain," said the Marquis swiftly. "And hurt 'self."

There was a roar of laughter.

"Oh, you Nero," said Berry. "This comes of living in Rome. Any more for the shambles?" He turned to me. "And why don't you do something to shorten your life?"

I shook my head.

"They wouldn't have me," said I. "The best is good enough for them."

The Marquis was growing clamorous.

Adèle leaned down from her seat on the foot of his bed.

"Darling," she said, "poor Berry's tired now. Let him sit down and tell you a fairy-tale."

The Fauns appeared to consult. The way in which, before deciding such questions, they caught one another's eye, was most attractive. Then Lady Elaine gave judgment.

"Belly tell fairy-tale," she said.

A chair was produced, and Berry sat down in the gangway, facing his wife.

"Once upon a time," he said, "there was a chocolate house."

"All tocklate?" said Lady Elaine.

"Nothing but," said Berry. "Even down to the stranger within the chocolate gates. They had running hot and cold chocolate in every room."

"Tocklate beds?" said the Marquis.

"Of course."

"Tocklate windows?" said Lady Elaine.

"Yes," said Berry. "And choco-electric bells."

"Tocklate stairs?" said the Marquis.

"Look here," said Berry. "We can't take the inventory now. I tell you, it was *all* chocolate. ALL. Well, of course, such a residence has its points. If you were hungry you just went and bit a piece off the nearest mantelpiece : but if it was a hot summer—well, you had to watch your step. If you didn't, before you knew where you were you'd taken half the hall into the dining-room. Well, in this delicious mansion there loved a lively—I mean, lived a lovely Princess."

"She tocklate?" said Lady Elaine.

"Certainly not," said Berry. "How dare you? She was the real thing. Both her eyes looked the same way, her hair was a glorious mud-colour, and during the winter you could have eaten off her hands. The only trouble was that she had big feet."

"Biggern yours?" said the Marquis.

I saw Jill cover her mouth.

"Yes," said Berry gravely. "Even bigger than mine. When she sat in the train, they went under the opposite seat. And boys in the street called after her, and——"

"Rude boys," said the Marquis.

"Oh, most unmannerly," said Berry. "Dead to all sense of shame."

The Fauns nodded sagely.

"Big whip," said Lady Elaine ominously.

"Every time," said Berry. "With lumps on it."

"Whips have no lumps," said the Marquis.

"This one did," said Berry.

"Which one?" said Lady Elaine.

"Well, the one we're speaking of," said Berry. "The one to whip the rude boys that called after the Princess with flat feet with."

Again the Fauns consulted. Then they hid their faces and laughed immoderately.

Meakin, gentlest of nurses, was speaking to Jill.

"I think, perhaps, your Grace . . . They've had a long day."

"Quite right," said Daphne, rising.

The Marquis was up in a flash.

"Belly go on," he commanded.

"To-morrow," said Berry. "I couldn't tell you to-night, because there's a bear coming and—well, he hasn't arrived yet. He's not a bear, really, you know. He looks like a bear, and walks like a bear, and he smells like a bear. I mean, if you saw him in the garden, you'd go and get the carrots at once. Which reminds me, when I was in the Prshewalski Mountains . . ."

Under cover of the outburst of joy provoked by his pronunciation of the name, we made our escape from the room. As I turned to the stairs, my brother-in-law touched my arm.

"Come," he said. "I've someone I want you to meet."

I followed him to his bedroom.

Propped against the side of the bed, was standing the biggest sham-bear I have ever seen. On being measured, it proved to be five feet high.

"Marvellous," said I. "But how did you get it down here?"

"Carson," said Berry. "He'd time to burn in Paris. So I gave him a cheque and told him to do what he could. If it's fine to-morrow, we'll put it out in the meadow before they come down."

"You're a man of your word," said I.

"That remains to be seen," said Berry. "I shouldn't have said that it smelt."

"They don't know what bears smell like."

"Not now. But they will one day. One day they'll go to the Zoo and find me out. Never mind. D'you think you could make me a Stinger? This Auntie Emma business has lowered my tone."

A Stinger is two thirds brandy and one third white Crême de Menthe.

"Too drastic," said I. "If we've got the stuff in the house I'll make you a Rosy Glow."

"Never heard of it," said Berry. "What I want is something to make the bloodstream think."

"Leave it to me," said I. "After my medicine you'll want to go back to Tours."

"In that case," said Berry, "I'd rather have a Manhattan. I don't believe in playing about with the brain."

The tempestuous *Habanera* came to its magnificent end : the sunlit street of Seville faded again into our comfortable *salon* : and Adèle looked round from the piano and picked up a cigarette.

"And now to business," she said.

In vain we pleaded for more.

"To-morrow," said Adèle. "I promise. I'll practise to-morrow morning and you'll see a world of difference to-morrow night. My voice is rusty."

This statement was false. More. If anyone else had made it, they would have been assaulted : but Adèle had taught us to suffer her own abuse of her gift.

With a sigh, my cousin got to his feet, crossed to the great fireplace and carefully knocked out his pipe.

Then he turned to face us.

"If you remember," said Jonah, "I told you that Fluff was no fool. He's been spending his evenings in Montmartre. I believe there's a café there. It's not patronized by receivers, but you sometimes see go-betweens. . . .

"Three nights ago—on Sunday—Auntie Emma called him across and made him sit down.

" 'I'm told,' he said, 'that Mansel's been looking you up.'

" 'That's right,' said Fluff. 'The poor fish. He wanted the Plazas' address. Seemed surprised they weren't in the telephone-book.'

" 'Ah,' says Auntie Emma. 'I guessed as much. The dog returns to his vomit.'

" 'And, with that, he fairly lets fly, as though he would never forgive me for losing Jill's pearls.'

"Fluff subscribed to his censure for half an hour. Then he came straight to my lodging and asked for the letters he'd brought me a few hours before.

" 'They're going back now,' he said. 'That block of flats isn't safe.'

"He's got an instinct—that man. Auntie Emma had a tout there the very next day. And when I saw Fluff again, he'd borrowed or stolen the truth. How or who from I've not the faintest idea. He'd drunk someone under the table to make them talk, and though he's a head like an anvil, he couldn't stand up. But, as I say, he was wise. The Plazas have split on Casca, and Auntie

Emma is out to skin him alive."

"Ah," said I. "And that wallah we startled last night was one of the gang."

"If he was," said Jonah, "he was pretty late in the field."

"He'd been to Biarritz," said Berry. "That's why he was late."

"Well done," said Jonah. "That's right. He'd been on to Biarritz, of course. And when Casca didn't get out, he began to throw back. They're pretty hot, these coves. Fancy losing a trail like that and picking it up again within twenty-four hours. Any way, he was late in the field, and you've wiped his eye."

"Will he shadow Woking?" said I.

"I doubt if he knows of his existence. If he saw Casca go, he'll probably follow him up."

"And what about us?" said Berry. "He didn't see us too well, but I don't suppose he thought we were leaving a Bible Class."

"No," said Jonah, "I don't suppose he did. And please don't bank on his not knowing you again. Never mind. In a show like this you can't expect roses all the way."

"No, I'd gathered that," said Berry. " 'Roses'. Of course, either you're being indecent, or else you've no idea of the *flora* of Tours. 'Roses'," he repeated brokenly. "D'you think we shall find some at Dinard?"

"I don't know," said Jonah. "I'll tell Fluff to go and find out."

"But," said Adèle, "they may meet somewhere else first."

"That doesn't matter," said I. "We don't have to tread every step."

"I'd much rather we didn't," said Jonah. "What we want is Casca's list of engagements, and then we can pick and choose. Daphne must write to-morrow and ask him to come and stay. I don't think he will—too busy. But when he makes his excuses, he'll probably say where he's promised to go instead."

"One moment," said Daphne. "Supposing the man accepts. D'you mean to say we must have him? Have him here, in this house?" I saw her take a deep breath. "I don't believe I can bear it."

"My dear," said Jonah, "you must. What would Auntie Emma give for a chance like that? If he comes we press him to stay. We make much of him. We urge him to come to White Ladies. We show him that our common misfortune has drawn him closer to us. Intimacy and confidence must kiss each other." My sister shuddered. "I know. Never mind. Don't worry. I don't think he'll come."

"Supposing he does," said Berry. "Supposing he gives us a list of the houses he means to visit during the next six weeks. I can conceive no reason why he should, but supposing he does. What do you propose we should do?"

"Visit them, too," said my cousin. "Not every one, you know."

"Unseen and unheard?" said Berry.

"Of course."

"I see," said Berry. "Does it matter if we're smelt? I mean, I only want to know where I am."

"It shouldn't be hard," said Jonah. "The trouble is you're not accustomed——"

"And there you're right," said Berry. "Sorcery's not in my line and never was. If I knew how to turn myself into a dog's bark or a footprint or a smell of cooking, I'd gate-crash all over France: but never having mastered the faculty of transformation, you must forgive me if I doubt my ability to dignify a French house-party, to which I have not been invited, without my presence being observed. What does Wordsworth say? 'All the guests can't be blind all the time.'"

Jill looked up from the hearth.

"But why," she said, "why don't we go to the police? They wouldn't laugh at us now."

"The answer," said Jonah, "is short, but painfully true. If we were to go to the police, we should lose our match. Casca is above suspicion—do please remember that. He's a well-known, highly respected man about town. If the police touch him—and they're wrong, there's going to be a hell of a row. They wouldn't lift a finger without most positive proof. And even if we could convince them, what would they do? Arrest him? Not on your life. They'd *approach* him—apologetically . . . request an interview at his convenience . . . and so tear the whole thing up. Casca would smile, set his house in order, give them their interview and never go near his safe-deposit for the next three years. Woking and Auntie Emma would both go empty away, and so should we. I tell you, these 'A.S.' cases have an almighty bulge. Direct action is futile—bound to fail. Their position is impregnable. Their good name compels consideration, and they use that consideration to make their escape."

"Jonah is right," said I. "It's a question of moral courage. If a man like Fluff is suspected, he is arrested and charged. But if Casca was seen picking pockets, they'd refuse to believe their eyes."

"Well, I think it's a beastly shame," said Jill, hotly. "Just because——"

"It's human nature," said I. "And there you are."

"I don't care. It's a beastly shame. We know he's taken our things, but, just because he's not poor, we've got to sit still and let him keep them, unless we're clever enough to be there when he's actually giving them to Woking to take away."

"That, I'm afraid," said Jonah, "is an accurate statement of fact. We have got to *know*—not believe, *know* that he has the stuff on his person, before we strike. If we strike without knowing that, and he hasn't the stuff upon him, we've lost the game."

"And Auntie Emma?" said Berry.

"I think it goes without saying that Auntie Emma is out to do exactly the same. A burglar never goes for an empty house."

"Collision," said Berry. "What fun we shall have. Fancy mixing it with Auntie Emma on somebody else's roof?"

"I can't have that," said Daphne.

Berry shrugged his shoulders.

"Better write to him, too," he said.

"I don't think," said I, "we need fear any horseplay. The last thing anyone wants is that Casca should get ideas, and violence in his vicinity would give the whole show away."

Adèle looked at me very hard. "Are you just saying that," she demanded, "to keep us quiet?"

"No, my darling, I'm not. If we manage to regain our property, then we must look out for squalls: but until that desirable moment I think Auntie Emma will leave us strictly alone. He may try and bluff us, you know."

"I entirely agree," said Jonah. "And now what about some Bridge?"

"Not for me," said Berry. "Curiously enough, I'm tired. Picked too many roses, or something. And what's the programme to-morrow? I suppose I leave for Biarritz on foot at eight o'clock."

"I hope," said my cousin, "you'll come for a country walk. Not very far. Just down to the end of the valley, soon after lunch. I believe Fluff's going for a picnic : and I think we might see him if we went down that way."

"How do?" said Fluff, nodding. "Lemme present my young lady—Miss Susie Dones."

As we uncovered—

"Pleased to meet you," said Susie cheerfully.

The sight of our new ally would have done anyone good. To say she was fat would be misleading : her style was rather cherubic, and her bright flowered-linen dress was a shade too tight and too short for her sturdy form. The day being hot, she had removed her hat, to leave it perched, like a chef's, on the top of her golden curls, but, though she must have known this looked ridiculous she neither forbade nor demanded that we should smile. Her amiable, baby face was distinguished by keen, gray eyes, and the gaze with which she calmly appraised us, one by one, was unabashed, but not forward, yet not so guileless as it looked. I came to the immediate conclusion that to get the best of Susie, one would have, so to speak, to arise the night before.

"Miss Dones," explained Jonah, "is going to be a great help."

"You needn't tell me that," said Berry. "My deeps are calling." He turned to Miss Dones. "It's fellow-feeling, you know. I'm a great help myself."

"The point is this," said Jonah. "Miss Dones can dance in where not one of us can tread. You see, she's not known by sight."

"Show me the way," said Susie. "I'm all for a husband with twenty thousand quid."

"And the city of Tours," said Fluff, looking at me. "Did you get Woking's number?"

"They've done the sum," said Jonah. "Bethgelert's sent Woking over to value and buy. De Palk rolled up on Monday and showed his hand. And they were behind the curtain and listened in."

"Go on," said Fluff incredulously.

"Hard fact," said Jonah, and told our tale.

When he had done—

"And here's fruit," said Fluff. "I'd better be off to Dinard and take a look at the house." He pushed back his hat. "What was it

Woking said about receiving the stuff?"

I shut my eyes.

"He said that he'd meet Palk wherever he liked—to value the jewels. But not in Paris. 'As to where I take over,' he said, 'I guess you'll honour my point of view.' "

"He's afraid," said Fluff. "He's known. What was he like?"

I described Woking faithfully.

"I can't place him," said Fluff, "but he knows that somebody can. He won't touch Paris, and he's dainty about where he receives. Why shouldn't he do it at Dinard? Or some other private house? Because he's afraid—that's why. He don't want to travel the stuff."

"He's got to," said Jonah. "He can't expect de Palk to carry it out of France."

"He'll try and make him," said Fluff. "Woking's afraid."

"Well, de Palk won't do it," said Jonah. "I'll lay to that. He might send it out, but he'd have to be paid in advance."

Fluff shook his head.

"C.O.D.," he said, "but never before. And why shouldn't Palky oblige?"

"Never," said Jonah, shortly. "I know I'm right. Never mind. We're not there yet. Could Miss Dones pick up Woking? Pick him right up and put him under her arm?"

"It might be done," said Susie, guardedly.

"Well, it's like this," said my cousin. "Tours is the man's headquarters. He's going to pay some visits—so much we know. Now if he's afraid, as you say, in between those visits he's likely to go back to Tours: and in any event it's well on the cards that he'll touch there before he leaves for good."

"That's right," said Fluff, nodding. "An' if he had a girl-frien' there, to make it a 'ome from 'ome . . ." He turned to Susie. "Once you know 'im, you should 'ave it all your own way. His visits'll give him a pain—standin' about in sallongs and bowin' to the Countess of Nooks. 'As pants the 'art'. He'll fairly streak back to you, to get new strength."

"I'll make him well," said Susie. "Churchy le fum. Once I can pick him up . . ."

There was an admiring silence.

Then—

"May I speak?" said Berry, demurely.

His saintly expression was ominous. Susie and Fluff exchanged an eloquent glance.

"Among my failings," said Berry, "is a weakness for hard-baked facts. I simply dote on them. But just at the moment I'm starved. You're all among the prophets, and the diet of a prophet is notoriously light. But I'm not a visionary, and though I've drunk in your wisdom, I'm still as dry as a bushel of bran. You're founding your plans on what Casca and Woking will do : but all we *know* is that those two are going to meet—we don't know where—and that, if they can strike a bargain, Woking will buy the stuff."

"Quite," said Fluff, nodding his head. "And 'ow do we know that?"

Berry shrugged his shoulders.

"Modesty," he said, "forbids me to——"

"Maybe," said Fluff. "I'm not sayin' you didn't get it." He jerked a thumb towards me. "You and he won it together, and won it well. I tell you, I give you best. There's no one I know would 'ave gone to all that trouble on such a chance. But tell me this. *What facts 'ad you to go on?* Never a one. You worked on a prophecy—and a —— thin prophecy, too."

Berry swallowed before replying.

"That's true," he said. "But what did you say just now? You said that no one you knew would have gone to all that trouble on such a chance. And that's what gets me." He laid a hand on my arm. "But for my cousin here, we shouldn't have taken that trouble. I was dead against it : I thought it wasn't worth while. And that's why I'm sitting up, begging for hard-baked facts. I don't care how few we've got—let's found some plan on them. And then I'll take off my coat. If you showed me a five-acre field and told me the jewels were buried within its fence, I'd dig the swine up if it took me the rest of my life."

"Sorry," said Fluff. "Ninety-five per cent guesswork an' only five per cent fact. That's the shape of a job like this. An' always will be." He sighed. "With only ten per cent fact, I'd be a million-aire. You read about the shows that come off, but 'ow many fail? Some 'itch, some prophecy out, some chance what you 'ad to take goes letting you down. I know—you want to make sure. Well, you

—— well can't in this game. There's no such word."

Berry shook off his hat and wiped his brow. Then he turned to Susie.

"Knows how to clear the air, doesn't he? I feel all swept and garnished after he's done."

Susie nodded sympathetically.

"I know," she said. "Empty like. But when he talks that way, you can take what he says. That's what I like about him."

"Ah," said Berry gravely. "I wondered what it was. Now I was married for my influence for good. It's most marked, you know. Almost skewbald. Why, when I was in the Eighteenth Eiderdowns —well, I leavened that lump all right. Before I'd been there six weeks, the chaplain got the bowler because he was late for lunch. 'The good old Duckrugs' they used to call us. Ah, that was something like a regiment. Our motto was *When it was dark*, and our crest, *A string-bag reversed*. We gave no quarter—not half : and when our blood was up, why, we used to outrun the mascot. And he could shift some."

"Oh, stop 'im, someone," said Susie weakly. "The moment I see his face, I knew his style."

"It's my eyes," said Berry. "They're really more soul-traps than eyes. Love inhabits them. I used to be called Silvia at Borstal."

"Reminiscence," said I, "is no earthly. It's worse than prophecy."

"Quite so," said Piers. "Let the past steam in peace."

" 'Steam'?" said Berry, frowning. "Is that an engineering metaphor?"

"No," said Piers. "Agricultural."

"Down with the Dukes," said Berry excitedly. "Down with the Dukes. Why, when I was in the Seventh Underwear——"

Out of the roar of protest, a general conversation emerged. Jonah strolled off with Fluff, and Piers and Berry and I devoted ourselves to Susie for a quarter of an hour.

At the end of that time Jonah sat down on a log and fondled his pipe.

"Our aim," he said, "is to find out when and where Woking going to receive the jewels. Nothing else matters at all. When we have that information, we can prepare fresh plans. In the hope of gaining that news, Miss Dones is going to nurse Woking, and we've got to do our best to watch over de Palk. That's going to be very hard. But for Auntie Emma, Fluff could have played that hand. But now he's washed out. If Auntie Emma finds us where Casca is, he'll be very rude : but if he were to find Fluff there, he'd do him in. So Fluff must stay in the background. He won't be wasted, you know. Now that Auntie Emma's come in, there's a hell of a lot of background for Fluff to work."

There was a little silence. Then—

"I—hate rudeness," said Berry. "Supposing——"

"I decline to suppose," said Jonah. "You taught me that. I'm as sick as you are of guess-work, and I think we've been guessing too much. Fluff will go to Dinard to-morrow, to spy out the land : and to-morrow morning Miss Dones will leave for Tours : and we shall sit still until Casca replies to our note. And now please tell Miss Dones where the rue Malleyband is and give her your best description of Woking's style."

"I never saw him," said Berry. "At least, he was only in my sight for one ninety-fifth of a second—that's the time it took me to hide. I don't think he's got a spade-shaped beard. But I'm very hot on the rue Malleyband. I could talk about it and its environs for several hours. Now the way to get there is this. Assume you're in the place des Epars. It's not——"

"That's Chartres," said I.

"So it is," said Berry. "Never mind. From there you proceed to Tours. When——"

A shriek of laughter from Susie cut the direction short, and I took up the running as well as I could.

When I had done—

"Good enough," said Miss Dones. "If Woking's for sale. I'll buy him. Where do I write?"

"Here, if you please," said Jonah. "But take your time."

"You bet," said Susie. "But these things go, or they don't. The moment I see him I'll know if it's fine or wet."

Five minutes later we bade the two good-bye and started back to the house.

"That girl inspires me," said Berry.

"What with?" said Piers.

"The will to win," said Berry. "What is she?"

"She's out of the chorus," said Jonah, "of some revue. She's toured all over France and she knows her world. And I quite agree with you. Susie Dones is one of the bull-dog breed. If she had a motto, it'd be *Gimme the daggers.*"

"That's right," said Berry. "Crest—*A vulgar gesture of contempt.* Do I hear music? Or is it somebody's boots?"

Piers spoke over his shoulder, quickening his steps.

"*L'Après-Midi des Faunes*," he said. And then, "Good God!"

That his words should make us start forward was, I think, natural enough : and an instant later we were in view of the meadow which was our garden and lay like a jolly apron beside the stream.

In the midst of the sward a portable gramophone was discoursing a lively tune. To this Adèle and the bear were dancing furiously, while Jill, with a Faun on each side, was keeping such step with the music as her tiny partners allowed. A little apart, regarding the light-hearted masque, my sister Daphne was sitting beneath a chestnut-tree, her bare arms stretched behind her, propping her up, and her delicate fingers planted upon the turf. Her pose was most easy and careless : her shapely ankles were crossed as though to point her content. This to her infinite credit, for, *standing beside her, smiling, was Casca de Palk.*

My heart gave one leap, and then stood perfectly still. Mercifully, however, my legs continued to move. No doubt this was due to what is called presence of mind : but I must frankly confess that my wits were all over the place.

In the midst of our plotting against him the wolf had strolled into the fold. The man we had believed to be at Biarritz was actually here—in the flesh. The thief who had robbed us was sharing our holy of holies and watching our most intimate rites. The crook I had spied on at Tours was waving his cane in greeting and wagging his graceless head.

As I strove to collect my thoughts, query on query leaped and spun in my brain. Why? How? What—what did it mean?

As I hastened my steps, the answers began to appear.

Casca de Palk had left Biarritz the same day that he had arrived. He had spent a short twelve hours there, but that was all. On his return he had come straight to see us—*to see what we were doing down at Dieppe.* He had purposely given no warning : he wished us to be unprepared. And Daphne could not send for us, for Carson was gone to Rouen and no other servant must be allowed to see Fluff. . . .

My sister was calling.

"Where have you all been?" she cried. "I do wish you wouldn't go off without saying a word. François———"

"Beloved," said Berry, "we've been to look at a horse. Carson reported a Shetland pony at Vigues and we had a sort of idea it might go with the bear. But I fear it's a wash-out. The owner has large ideas. He wants one hundred pounds and it's worth about twelve. Never mind." He pointed to Casca. "Where did you get that from?"

"It just arrived," said Daphne.

"How very convenient," said Berry. "Has he had his *foie gras* yet?"

"Hush," said I. "He'll hear you."

"I think he's grown," said Jonah. "Laterally."

Then we crowded about the blackguard, shaking his treacherous hand and slapping his back.

"You shall have the haunted room," said Berry. "The ghost is a large blood-stain. Your starting eyes watch it spread over the ceiling and down the walls. As it reaches your bed———"

"I am desolate," panted Casca. "I cannot stay. You know———"

We shouted down his protest and haled him up to the house. . . .

On the hour and a half that followed I will not dwell. To suffer Casca de Palk was unpleasant enough : to make much of the sweep was revolting : but the fear of affording foundation for the doubts which had brought him to Nay like some high explosive upon our souls—a high explosive which one idle word would touch off. What was almost worst, the fear of betraying this fear sat like some spectre beside us in all we did. We sought to be natural, found ourselves being fulsome, and became cavalier. We discussed the crime and the Plazas with our hearts in our mouths. By no means sure of himself, each was frightened to death of what the other would say—a frequently groundless fear which threw us into confusion again and again. We perceived crises approaching, advanced *en masse* to meet them, got in each other's way, found they weren't crises at all, laughed forced and apologetic laughs and then went out on the terrace and said "My God".

With the greatest care we led our guest to suppose that since we had come, we had never been further than Rouen—only to remember with a shock that the presence of the Fauns insisted that someone had travelled to Paris to bring them in. When he spoke of his visit to Biarritz, a sudden inability to comment smote us like some disorder which cannot be overcome, and the deadly silence which followed turned his statement into a sentence of death. In a word, it was a nightmare business, for Casca was a *cordon bleu*, while we were seven cooks to a kettle of delicate broth.

At last he got to his feet and asked for his car.

We protested naturally, but Casca was mercifully firm. He had an engagement that night which he could not break.

"But when are you coming," said Daphne, "coming to stay?"

The villain spread out his hands.

"My dear lady, I cannot. All my 'opes——"

"But you promised," cried Jill. "At luncheon in Paris, before we——"

"My pretty grace, I 'ave say so because I desire to come. But all the time I was bound to Madame de Nux. She 'as a château at Dinard, and I 'ave got out of it twice. But now since two days she 'as written that all is ready for me to come to her 'ouse, and, *mon Dieu*, what can I do?"

"But after that?" said Adèle.

"That was the devil," said Casca. "That I shall not go to Dinard was all my chance. When I return I mus' go to the Bluchers at Loumy. That is a long engagement. And you—you will not be here. 'Ow long do you rest at this château?"

"Only," said Jonah, swiftly, "only until White Ladies is ready to take us in."

"Ah, yes. The painters," said Casca. "Another two weeks?"

"Ten days at the most," said Jonah. "But don't let that stop you, my friend. Come over and stay with us there."

"That's right," said Adèle. "Come to us from the Bluchers, whoever they are. And we'll all go over together and——"

"Why not?" cried everyone.

"No, no," said Casca. "You are most kind and charming and once I shall 'ave the good pleasure to rest at your 'ome : but then I mus' be in Paris and after that I 'ave other engagements to fill.

I must go to Vichy, by example, to make my cure."

"Have the water sent over," said Berry, "and make it with us. I'll—I'll massage you."

"*Mon Dieu,*" cried Casca, blenching. Then he took Berry's arm and looked round " 'E 'as want to kill me with kindness. But I think I know 'is massage—he pulls the leg. And then, in the last, my leg will come off in 'is 'and."

Here the car was announced and we bore him into the hall.

With the end in sight, we fairly let ourselves go. I fancy his departure resembled the finale of a revue. And then at last it was over, the curling drive was empty, and our arch-enemy was gone.

Slowly we returned to the terrace, without a word.

My sister sank into a chair and closed her eyes.

"I'm through," she said faintly. "All in. I can't ever see him again. The mental and physical strain is insupportable. Do—do you think he suspects?"

"Well, we didn't accuse him to his face," said her husband, "but I think we did everything else. We fawned upon him : we told him manifest lies : we contradicted one another : at the mention of Biarritz we burst into gleaming sweats."

"Rot," said Adèle. "I think we were wonderful. When you remember——"

"You all overdid it," said Berry. "If you had left it to me——"

"You damned near bent it," said I. "The word 'Tours' was on your lips when I dropped my glass."

"Whose fault was that?" said Berry. "Who went and said that ever since we'd been here we'd never been out of the grounds? How could I assimilate that statement? You might as well try to digest a pint of slack lime. As for Casca . . ."

"I agree with Adèle," said Piers. "All things considered, I think we did awfully well. We'd no time to consult : we'd no time even to think."

"The first I knew," said my sister, "was the horrified look on Jill's face. And when I turned to the terrace, there was François descending, with Casca behind. We three had one minute's notice —not even that, for we had to go and meet him. I tell you, my brain was just reeling, and I felt all weak at the knees. I've no idea what I said except that I know I told François to find you and say he was here."

"She was cooler than Casca," said Jill. "She gave him the finest smile you ever saw, and Casca went red and grovelled and dropped his hat."

"As well he might," said Jonah. "And that's a slice of good news. Hot and bothered, was he? Hoist with his own petard? Comes to see what we can give him, and gives himself away. If Jill's right and Daphne shook him, you can bet your life that he spent his afternoon cursing and wondering whether she'd noticed anything wrong. And that'll mean that he didn't hear half we said."

"If you ask me," said Berry.

"We don't," said everyone.

Berry expired.

"Vulgarity," he announced, "is the soul of guilt. When in the wrong, be rude. That's the maxim by which the lot of you live."

"But we're not in the wrong," shrieked Jill. "I don't believe for an instant——"

"Neither do I," said Berry. "Not for one muddy moment."

"What don't you believe?"

"Everything," said Berry. "I'm the complete agnostic. I don't believe that you believe that he believes that we believe——"

In the storm of disapproval the ultimate tenet was lost.

"Two things stand out," said I. "The first is we made one mistake."

"Oh, don't exaggerate," said Berry.

"We shouldn't have hidden the fact that we'd been *en voyage*. If his chauffeur talked to the servants . . ."

"Quite true," said Jonah. "But I think it very unlikely that Casca would trust a hired chauffeur with such a charge. That's not the way of the people I call 'A.S.' "

"Once," said Berry, "I had a little book. There were six names in it and I used to call it 'B.F.' I never got any of them."

Adèle began to shake with laughter.

I addressed myself to Jonah.

"I expect you're right. Well, the second thing is that you've pledged us to leave this place in ten days' time."

"I was coming to that," said Berry. "Talk about rushing in."

"I know," said Jonah. "I had to. To stay here, with White

Ladies waiting, would be an eccentric act. And as we're not eccentric——"

"But only insane," said Berry.

"——Casca's suspicions would instantly crystallize. While Casca is watching we *must* do the natural thing."

"Yes, I see that," said Adèle. "But we can't operate from White Ladies."

"I don't propose to," said Jonah. "We must leave here for England not later than Sunday week. If Casca returns—as he may—Jean and his wife will tell him we've gone to White Ladies, by way of Dieppe. But that will be misleading, for we shall be 'somewhere in France'."

There was an electric silence.

Then Berry yelped with dismay.

"I knew it," he howled. "I saw it coming. Disguise, secrecy, concealment. All the hellish discomfort of lying low. Some cave in the woods near Loumy. No baths, no bedding, no beer. Rubbing two sticks together to make a third—I mean, a fire. Dinner —tomato soup and a box of dates. You know, it isn't decent."

"Wrong again," said Jonah. "People can lie very low in a first-class suite."

"If you'll guarantee me a bathroom——"

"I'll do my best," said Jonah. "I value my creature comforts as high as you. And one thing I will guarantee—and that's good food. The rougher you lie, the finer your fare must be. If we ever came down to a cave, one of our bits of baggage would be a case of champagne."

Berry fingered his chin.

"Of course," he said, "there are worse places than caves."

CHAPTER VII

We Get Together

I pulled up behind the Rolls, and Berry got out.

"I decline," he said, "to drive any more in this car. It's not that I mind being alone with you, for I'm a broad-minded man, but the function of the lungs is to aerate the blood—not to garner and secrete as many ounces of dust as they can accommodate. Damn it, my tubes are choked."

"So are mine," said I. "I propose to stop and clear them at the very next café we pass. It's quite a simple operation and costs exactly two francs."

"I see," said my brother-in-law. "Well, you must be specially built. I'll gargle with beer all day, but it never appealed to me as a nasal douche. Besides, it stunts your adenoids."

Here he sneezed four times with great violence and turned to the Rolls. As he came alongside, Adèle, who was sitting with Piers, looked suddenly over her shoulder and saw his plight.

"For heaven's sake!" she cried, starting. "Don't say that's dust."

"No," said Berry shortly. "It's dandruff. I've been brushing my teeth."

"But why," bubbled Jill, "why didn't you——"

"Look here," said Berry. "If you were to guide us, we had to stay in your wake. Well, the moment you left the main road, your wake became a pillar of cloud about four miles long. . . . Oh, yes. We shut the windows. But there is a degree of temperature at which life becomes extinct. Possibly a resurrected fiend . . ."

Adèle was out of the Rolls and had opened the Lowland's door.

"My darling," she cried. "But how dreadful! You look like a ghost."

I fancy I did. When the car which is playing pilot maintains an average speed of forty-five miles an hour, when the weather is hot and dry and the roads have never been tarred—after twenty minutes or so one goes *poudré*.

"Unpleasant," said I, "but inevitable." I slid from my seat to the ground. "Now you know why I made you go in the Rolls. But it looks much worse than it is. Why did you stop?"

"To view the promised land." She took my arm and led me to a gap in the hedge. "You see that village? And, slightly below and beyond it, that scrap of a house? Well, that's our lair."

"It's lovely to look at," said I. And so it was.

Three miles away, across a valley, the white-walled inn lay safe in a little dell on the slope of a hill. This then rose, fresh and green, about three of its sides, while the fourth stood back from a road and, beyond this, a placid stream, spanning which I could see two bridges of old, gray stone. The valley was plainly rich—square upon square of wheat and maize and pasture, and sleepy barns and miniature yokes of oxen and bottles of hay tied up in squares of sackcloth which tiny figures were bearing upon their backs. Straggling schools of toy cows argued the course of lanes which we could not see, and orderly ranks of poplars were painting neighbouring meadows with regular stripes of shadow, clear-cut and soft and vivid as the grass they clothed. For the sun was going down on this Canaan, and, since it ran east and west, all the valley was flooded with golden light. This gave it a fabulous air, remembering famous pictures and pastorals singing of husbandry and content, and though I later saw it at every hour of the day and never failed to find it grateful, I think it was fairest at sundown when the breeze of the day had fallen and the shadows were long.

"Isn't Jonah clever," said Jill, "to have found such a perfect place?"

"I'll tell you when I've had a close-up," said Berry. "I suspect these dinky gobbets of the good old days. The Middle Ages are superb in retrospect : but I'd rather have constant hot water than any priest's hole."

"And Loumy?" said I.

"Ten miles off," said Jonah. "The other side of that hill. What decided me was its approach—the inn's, I mean. We needn't touch the village—we shan't to-night. We go and come by the West. And the host is of the old school. While we're there, he'll be in our service, and how we live and move will be our affair."

"I see," said Berry. "No bathroom?"

"Yes, said my cousin, "a beauty. All it lacks is a bath. But we can remedy that."

As soon as he could speak—

"Oh, easily," said Berry, shakily. "All you want's a couple of bowls. Kneel in one while you wash your neck in the other. You've only got to find your length. After that you move up— sit in the other and put your feet in the one. That's the really luxurious moment. Besides, it gives you a chance to pick the splinters out of your soles."

"As you please," said Jonah, setting a match to his pipe. "As a matter of fact, I've ordered a large *lessiveuse*. You know. What they wash clothes in. It's just as good as a tub : only you bathe vertically."

"Why not a cabin-trunk?" said Berry. "When you've done, you shut it. Then you've got something to step on when you get out."

"I don't care," said Jill. "I think it's a wonderful find. And I want to get in and have dinner. Can't we go on?"

I let them get well ahead before I restarted the Lowland to follow behind.

With our occupation of the inn, the disposition of our forces would be as good as complete. Daphne and the Fauns were in Hampshire, and there it had been decided that she must stay. Casca was likely to write there—to reassure himself that we were indeed at White Ladies—and somebody must be there to send a reply. Susie Dones was at Tours, and Fluff was now at Loumy, getting the lie of the land. Carson had crossed with Daphne, but was now on his way to join us at *The Fisherman's Arms*.

Since we had talked with Casca, we had made no progress at all. Neither, we hoped, had Auntie Emma, although he was gone to Dinard with two of his men. Susie had recognized Woking, but so far Bethgelert's agent had not walked into her net. In fact, when last she had wrote, he had disappeared. We assumed he had gone to Dinard, according to plan. Still, we were banking on Loumy. There we proposed to launch a mighty effort to repeat our success of Tours : in a word, we meant, if we could, to attend one or more of the enemy's councils of war.

Now that I had seen its environs, to find my way to the inn was easy enough, and twenty minutes later I stopped in front of its door. As I applied the handbrake, my cousin emerged with a glass and a bottle of beer.

"Drink," he said, "and listen." I took the glass. "In the first place, Woking is back at Tours. Susie wired yesterday morning to say that she'd seen him again."

"Here's luck," said I, and drank deep.

"In the second place," said Jonah, "here is a letter from Fluff. It was posted yesterday evening and got here this afternoon."

I took the letter and gave him my glass to refill.

This is some place. House like an Oxford Colege with a yard like a barruck square. Stands in a park. No dogs. Easy enough to walk right up to the walls. Shutters to the windows —no bars. But God help you once inside. You'd want a map like an atlas to find your way. Stables galaw and three cars. And here's where we come in and go up to the top. *Chauffer's English*. Name of Walker. Had one with him last night. He says the Count and his lady are very decent folk. True blue, if French, and does him a treat. And that's why he stays, for what he sees is enough to break a man's hart. If you ask him, the place is Robbery Hall. Servants no better than a dirty pack of thieves. Fighting and biting over their illgoten gains. And not a bill questioned. And the guests the same. Sponging and grumbling and swanking from morning to night. And the rest. Well, I took his length very careful and to-day I see him again. Funny he comes from Putney where this was born. Used to be took as a kid to play on the Eath. Same here. Presently he starts on the houseparty *opening Thursday next*. Raft of greedy bounders he says you wait and see. And worse says I. What about making the old ancestral home a den o' thieves? Go on says he we aint sunk to that—not yet. That's all you know I tells him and asks why he thinks I'm here. You bet I opened his eyes. I guess you should see him Wednesday before I go. I put him wise about A.E. for he'll be on to him like a cat on a fileted soal.

"And very nice, too," said I. "Fluff's pulling his weight all right."

"I thought he would," said Jonah, returning the glass. "How

far Walker can help remains to be seen, but so far as Auntie Emma's concerned, this is a deuce of a scoop."

"Here's more luck," said I. . . .

Jonah pointed over his shoulder.

"Courtyard on your left," he said. "Leave her there, and they'll wash her as soon as they've done the Rolls. We've got the place to ourselves."

"And a bath?" said I. "I must get some of this off."

"First floor back," said my cousin. "I believe the room to be occupied, but I think I should walk right in."

When I had berthed the Lowland, I made my way upstairs and took his advice.

Crouched in a large iron vessel, which was shaped like a bucket and was standing some three feet high, my brother-in-law regarded me with a suspicious stare. At length——

"You're late," he said grimly. "This is the second act."

"Be good enough to get a move on," said I. "I, too, have a toilet to make."

"No one," said Berry, "can hasten in a utensil like this. One false move and it ejects you. The most trivial gesture has to be most carefully weighed. At the present moment, for instance, I've dropped the soap. It may be hours before I get it again."

I looked at my watch.

"One minute more," said I. "And at the end of that time I shall hand you this excellent towel. The inference will be obvious."

"Look here," said Berry. "I prepared this rotten bath in the sweat of my trunk. I carried up most of the water : I mixed it to a convenient temperature : I sought and procured those accessories without which no lavation can be decently observed. In these most poisonous circumstances I'm damned if I'm going to be rushed," and, with that, he folded him arms, closed his eyes and lay back against the side of the *lessiveuse*.

It was a most natural movement, and rather dignified : but it was fatally infectious.

As did its occupant, so did the *lessiveuse*. The two leaned back together, and before the former could attempt to correct his pose, the latter had lost its balance and fallen incontinently on to its galvanised side.

The catastrophe was truly overwhelming. Let alone the appalling uproar, a ravening wave of water broke upon the wall, to fall back shattered and swirling and streaming across the boards, lapping against the skirting and flowing under the door.

That Berry did not fracture his skull was due to his frantic endeavours to save the game. Ere he made them, the game was lost, but when the crash came he was clutching the rim of the "bath", and, still in that trying position, he dealt at length with my presence, with Jonah's choice of a lodging and finally with *lessiveuses*.

Weak with laughter, I helped him out of the welter and on to his feet. As I did so—

"What ever has happened?" cried Adèle from the passage without. "The water's simply streaming into the dining-room."

"Is it, indeed?" said Berry. "Well, you go and turn down my bed. I've had a great shock. And in view of your statement I'd just as soon dine upstairs. But I shall have to go very carefully. Have they got any sweetbreads?"

As soon as she could speak—

"But it's simply pouring——"

"That's water all over," said Berry. "Why, I've seen——"

"You must mop it up," screamed Adèle. "Look out, Piers. there's a pool . . ."

I seized Berry's sponge and started to swab the floor.

Piers was beating on the door.

"I say," he cried, "the dining-room ceiling——"

"I know," said Berry. "It's leaking. I'm having my dinner in bed."

There was a furious silence. Then—

"Berry, dear," said Adèle, "do have a heart. I tell you——"

"Sweeting," said Berry, "be of good cheer. An expensive sponge has been ruined, but the percolating water has been stopped. I regret the incident, but as usual the fault was not mine. But five minutes since, whilst I was in the throes of ablution, a vulgar and beastly apparition entered this room. Startled by this invasion of my modesty, I recoiled, as might some naiad shrink from the gross gaze of Silenus. The brush of a Boucher, perhaps, might have captured the scene. Alas, the preposterous vessel—the lavatory to which I had committed my perfection, betrayed its sacred trust.

We Get Together

In an instant all was over, the tragedy of Shelley was re-enacted, and I was b-belched like some Hyacinth on to the b-boards. The *lessiveuse* had given up its dead. Conceive the desolation of my awakening from the swoon. No Ariadne in Oxo—Naxos was more distraught. On one side, the wanton——"

"The translation is this," said I. "He upset himself. Sheer, damned negligence. I saw it done."

"Oh, Boy, I never dreamed you were there. Has he really mopped——"

"Not a drop," said I. "But I have. But why did you trust him here? He ought to have had it in the coach-house."

"That's just what I said," said Piers.

"I know," said Berry. "I heard you. I shan't forget. Baying the old lion. Get my pyjamas, someone. When do we dine?"

"Dine?" howled Piers. "The dining-room is a swamp."

"That," said Berry, "is the worst of these old houses. Damp as hell. Never mind. I should dine in the coach-house if I were you." I stepped to the door. "Where are you going?"

"To get your pyjamas," I said.

This was untrue. Before I did anything else, I locked the door of his bedroom and took the key. Then I sent Piers to find Jonah and ask him to straighten things out with the host of the inn.

"But, my dear," said Adèle, "what will you do for a bath?"

I put her small hand to my lips.

"Come with me, Amaryllis," said I, "and turn my Georgic into an Eclogue."

Two minutes later I had a change of clothing and we were out of the house. We made our way up stream, and half a mile on we found an excellent pool. Here was a little foot-bridge, leading I know not where, but, when I had stripped, it made me a landing-stage. The flow of the stream was gentle, and the water was clear and warm : as I let myself sink to the gravel, I knew that comfortable refreshment which steals between the lines of Solomon's song. Ophelia died kindly. The Malmsey which Clarence preferred never made so indulgent a bed. And whilst I dived and floundered, my wife leaned against the oak handrail, bare-headed and slim and smiling, and looking as though she belonged to some nursery rhyme which has not come down through the ages, but, because the gods loved it, died young.

Night stole in as we sauntered the way we had come and hung a moon in the heaven to light our steps : a nightingale was singing in a thicket, and far in the distance I heard the drone of some car that was climbing some hill : ahead of us the inn was glowing like the jolly mansion of some gnome, and the cool, soft air about us was charged with the simple perfume of new-mown hay.

Adèle, her slight arm in mine, inhaled luxuriously.

"Mown with a scythe," she said. "No machine-cut hay ever smelled so sweet. The Middle Ages had secrets which we're doing our best to lose."

"I'd back you against any Queen of Beauty," said I.

"You're very sweet," said Adèle, "but I didn't mean that."

"What then?" said I. "Stained glass? Chivalry? Mulled wine? The liripipe? I should love to see you with a liripipe down your back."

"Manners and customs," said Adèle. "We've turned away from Nature—and that's a shame. Will you get up early to-morrow and watch for me while I bathe?"

"Of course," said I. "But there'll be an edge to the breeze."

"I know. I don't care. The bathroom was bound to be a failure. It was putting new wine into old bottles : and when you do that, they burst."

"I'm against you, my lady," said I. "The bathroom failed because it entailed putting Berry into a *lessiveuse*. When you do that, you ask for trouble with a couple of b's. As for Nature, you're one of her darlings, and so, whenever she smiles, you dart to her side. To-morrow at five in the morning Eve will be bathing in Eden, and that's a fact."

"I must kiss you for that," said Adèle, and slid an arm round my neck.

"But when the fine weather breaks—well, *Mademoiselle Lessiveuse* will come into her own, and Eve, the Bather, will bless good cousin Jonah, the Abbot of Aberbrothok."

Berry's voice came booming out of the inn.

"Here is an S.O.S. Missing from her home, *The Fisherman's Worms,* at Mose, an American darling—unforgettable brown eyes, mouth like a red flower, legs must be seen to be believed, last seen in the company of a treacherous drawlatch—prominent blear eyes, flat feet, bullet head. . . . Will the two, who are believed to be philandering in the shadows, return home at once, as their soup is getting dangerously cold?"

We hastened our steps.

A moment later we entered a pleasant parlour, to find the others at table, discussing the vanguard of a most promising meal. That we were received in silence argued a healthy hunger which would not wait, but the wireless set in the corner was rendering *The Nutcracker Suite* as though those making the music were sitting outside the window, under the stars.

Two things struck me at once.

The first was that the garments which Berry was wearing had been drawn from the slender wardrobe which I had hoped would last me until the big baggage arrived. The second was a telegram, lying by the side of my plate.

"What, again?" said I, picking it up.

The wire was from Susie Dones, and its message was commendably short. It was, in fact, one word long.

Clicked.

Three days had gone by, and Berry and I were seated by the side of the road some ten miles from Mose. Below us, the domain of Loumy lay like a billowing quilt, all gay green shot with silver, for the sun was in all his state and, since it had rained like fury the night before, the landscape was quick with magic and summer seemed to be wearing the tabard of spring. The house stood not in the midst, but at the head of the property and was a handsome château of a considerable size. It resembled no college of Oxford that I have seen, but it was broad and spacious and all its walls were of stone. Its dormer-windows and turrets were picturesque, and, though it was not stately and did not belong to the landscape as castles may, Time and Weather had naturalized the stranger and a cordial riot of creeper had taken him in her arms. As Fluff had said, the house made with the stables three sides of a vast courtyard : this to the North, for the south of the château was open and gave to the park.

Casca was there—somewhere. Walker had brought him from the station some twenty-two hours ago : and a wire from Susie suggested that Woking was arriving to-night. The station lay twelve miles off and Walker was under orders to meet the evening train. On the way he was going to meet Jonah and tell him where in the château Casca was lodged.

From the left a laboured jingle came floating up to our ears. The old church clock of Loumy was telling the hour. Half past twelve.

"Nothing doing till two," murmured Berry. "We're wasting our time."

"Perhaps," said I. "But I'd just as soon waste it here as anywhere else."

Berry frowned.

"There is," he said, "a great art in wasting time. If you waste it as it should be wasted, you're not wasting it. Assume you've two hours to spare. The first thing to do is to relax. Well, you can't relax here and now without a mackintosh-sheet. I am sitting, not without the gravest misgivings——"

A sudden, high-pitched laugh brought us round in a flash.

Three feet away was standing the silliest-looking man I have ever seen. An idiot grin was distorting his vacant face and his air was as awkward and futile as the senseless burst of laughter with which he had greeted our ears. So far from seeming nervous or ill at ease, he plainly believed in himself, and such was his self-esteem that, if he had any manners, he clearly regarded their use as beneath his dignity.

"A match," he shrilled, waving a cigarette. "My kingdom for a match."

With the coldest of stares, Berry produced some matches and gave him the box.

Without a word of thanks, the other inspected the gift.

"Not sulphur, are they?" he said.

The French sulphur match is very cheap and highly offensive. To offer a smoker one is a hostile act.

"Unfortunately, no," said Berry, and turned away.

The fellow was clearly English and had, of course, perceived that we were his countrymen. For an instant I wondered if he was the enemy's man, but before the natural suspicion had taken shape, it had faded away. Knaves are not fools. And this man was the complete and absolute ass. His looks, his air, his conduct were those of a poisonous fool. Æsop has drawn him over and over again, but only once before had I seen his like. Probably he was a tourist—for there were many about—and, if Berry's patience survived, would presently leave us in peace. But, whatsoever his business, he was not in Auntie Emma's employ. Of that I was certain, and, as it turned out, I was right.

"I'm doing châteaux," said the stranger, and lighted his cigarette. He put the box into a pocket and set a foot on the bank between Berry and me. "That should be Loumy down there, if my map's not wrong."

For a second time I wondered if he was playing a game—if this was indeed a member of Auntie Emma's gang. Then I knew that the man was not acting, for no man on earth could have played such a part so well.

"What about those matches?" said Berry icily.

The other laughed idiotically.

"There now," he cried, and clapped a hand to his coat. "You know, I'm always doing that."

"I believe you," said Berry.

"I'll tell you what," said the other, producing an empty box. "I'll take half. I can't be without a match."

With that, he produced Berry's box, flicked it open and upset all its matches into the dust.

"Oh, keep the lot," said Berry, averting his eyes.

"But I thought you wanted them back."

"My desire has failed," said Berry.

"Good," said the other, shovelling the matches up. "I said 'That should be Loumy'."

"I know. I heard you," said Berry. "I daresay it should."

"Well, is it?" said the other.

"I've no idea," said Berry. "We're strangers here."

"So'm I," said the other, beaming. "Where's your pitch?"

"We haven't got one," said I. "We're moving about as we please."

The other produced a map.

"That's Loumy, all right," he said, pointing. "Where did you sleep last night?"

Glancing over his shoulder, I saw a town named Larogne.

"At a place called Larogne," said I.

"I know," said the other. "At the *Hôtel du Parc*?"

It seemed best to nod my head. Better to suffer the impudent cross-examination, than to arouse suspicion in any man's mind.

"Loumy," said the other, and took out the *Guide Michelin*. He turned its pages and read. Then he slid the book into a pocket and pushed back his soft brown hat. "Funny our meeting like this, isn't it?"

"Most droll," said Berry.

"You're brethren, aren't you?"

"No," said Berry. "We're not."

"Cousins, then?" said the other. "You're very alike."

"Make it uncle and aunt," said Berry. "I don't care."

The falsetto rang out like a bugle call. For a moment its author abandoned himself to his mirth. Then—

"I like getting together," he crowed. As though to illustrate this statement, he again set his foot upon the bank three inches from Berry's knee. Then he leaned on the stay he had provided and grinned into Berry's face. "Where's your bus?"

I could have done the man violence. The Lowland was carefully hidden in a thicket a furlong away.

"With the chauffeur," said Berry, rising.

I got to my feet.

"What's it look like?" said the other, turning.

"Pneumatic tyres," said Berry, "and a couple of steps."

The other shrieked with delight.

"I meant 'What make?'," he panted, "you silly fool."

I began to shake with laughter. I think I may be forgiven. The look on my brother-in-law's face was charged with an indignation which seemed to pass even his comprehension, while more than once he regarded the blue vault of heaven as though expecting some sympathetic bolt to expunge what he clearly regarded as a blot upon the moral system.

At length, with a manifest effort, he mastered his voice.

"Look here," he said. "You go and do your châteaux—lest a worse thing befall," and, with that, he turned on his heel and began to walk down the road.

Before I could overtake him, the other was by his side.

Berry stood still.

"Did you hear what I said?"

"That's all right," said the other. "I've plenty of time."

"So it appears," said Berry. "Unfortunately we haven't. We have some affairs to discuss."

"Well, don't mind me," said the other.

"Private affairs," said Berry.

"Let them wait," cried the other, grinning. " 'Begone, dull care'." With that, he gave a horse laugh and slapped Berry upon the back.

For a moment the world stood still. Then, to my infinite relief, Berry put his hands in his pockets and raked his poisonous assailant from head to foot.

"I have no wish," he said, "to appear unfriendly, but I have a definite feeling that we are better apart."

"Don't you believe it," said the stranger. "I'm all things to all men."

"Well, I'm not," said Berry shortly. "What's more I detest——"

"Now, don't you worry," said the other, taking his arm. "You come with me to Loumy, and——"

Berry disengaged himself.

"I am not at your disposal," he said. "I have been at some pains to point out that my cousin and I desire to be left alone. This, unhappily, in vain. I must therefore desire you to allow us to go our way and to trespass no longer upon a forbearance which is almost extinct."

No man born of woman could have mistaken the meaning with which Berry spoke these words. The last rags and tatters of his patience had gone to the making of this speech. One more idle rejoinder—and the balloon would go up.

With my eyes on the man I waited. . . .

All of a sudden the stranger began to laugh—to yell and howl with laughter, as though possessed.

I decided that the man was insane.

As I made my decision, he found his voice.

"I've been pulling your leg," he gasped. "Louis Blucher is one of my oldest friends. What's more, he loves the English. He'd never forgive me if I didn't bring you to lunch."

There was a dreadful silence.

This idiot was going to Loumy . . . *to sit down with Casca de Palk . . . to give our presence away with both of his clumsy hands.*

Of course he would report his encounter, and the instant he mentioned two Englishmen, Casca would prick up his ears. One leading question, and all the rest would come out—how he had found us seated, regarding the Loumy estate, what we were like, that Berry had said we were cousins . . . I wondered what we had done to deserve misfortune like this.

With a hand to his head, Berry was regarding our tormentor dazedly. I remember thinking that, when his ass protested, Balaam must have gazed upon the animal in very much the same way.

I pulled myself together. Something had to be done.

"W-well, why d-didn't you say so?" I stammered. "I mean —Never mind. I'm sure you meant well. I'm afraid we can't possibly come."

"Out of the question," said Berry, wiping his brow.

"Oh, but you must," cried the other. "I absolutely insist. When Louis hears——"

"Don't let him hear," said I. "To tell you the truth, we'd rather he didn't know. We—we met him once, and we ought to have gone and called. But we haven't had time."

The stranger stared.

"But you've only just got here," he said.

"Exactly," said Berry. "That's why we haven't had time. And now this business has cropped up. And that's the trouble. We meant to go and see him. I've got a note down in my book, 'See Bloumy', I mean Lucher—I mean, Blucher of Loumy. And now it's impossible. So we particularly don't want him to know——"

"Oh, he's not like that," said the other. "Louis—"

"I know," said Berry. "I know. Dear old Louis. And it's just because he isn't like that——"

"Like what?" said the other.

"Well, you said it first," said Berry. "I mean—The point is this. Loumy Blucher's feelings must not be hurt. Anything but that. And so you must not mention having met us. By the way, my name's Mace—Herbert Mace. What's yours?"

"Rose."

Berry appeared to start.

"Rose?" he said sharply. "Rose? Where do you live?"

"In London," said the other, staring. "But——"

"One moment," said Berry excitedly. "What are your Christian names?"

"John Alexander," said the other. "And now let's——"

"You must go home at once," cried Berry, seizing his arm. "You were asked for last night on the gramophone—I mean, the wireless. You know. An SOS. 'Will John Alexander Rose, of London, believed to be touring in France, return home at once, as his, er, his'—someone or other : I can't remember who it was —'is dangerously ill.'"

Somewhat dazed by the brilliance of my brother-in-law's mother wit, I supported his shining statement as well as I could.

"That's right," I said. "I heard it. Have you got a car?"

The stranger looked from Berry to me. Then his features spread into a grin.

"It can't be me," he said. "I've no one——"

"It must be you," cried Berry. "They—they described you. 'Clean-shaven, fair, gray eyes and a scar on his chin.'"

"But my eyes are green," said Rose.

"They may have said 'green'," said Berry. "Of course it's you."

"I can't see why it should be," said Rose.

"'Can't see'—Oh, give me strength," said Berry. He swallowed violently. "You correspond exactly to the individual whose instant return to London is of such vital importance. You bear his three names : you are doing what he is doing : you look as he looks. If——"

"I don't care," said Rose. "I'm not going. Why should I? I've only just come."

Berry shrugged his shoulders.

"It's up to you," he said. "I've done my bit. I heard the SOS, and I've passed it on. If you like to ignore it, of course that's your affair. I think you're unwise. There are such things as 'deathbed Wills'. You may be losing a fortune, by staying away."

"I know," said Rose. "I've got it. I'll send a wire. I'll send a wire from Loumy to ask what's what."

Berry took off his hat and wiped his face.

The action was eloquent. He could not have declared more plainly that he had shot his bolt.

I took a deep breath.

"Look here," I said desperately. "Why don't you lunch with

us and give Loumy a miss? Louis Blucher's all right, but he has some terrible guests. Of course, if you like a French crowd . . ."

Of all the hopes that ever I harboured, this was the most forlorn. But after ten minutes' hard labour the trick was done. When I say "hard labour", I mean it. We had to make bricks without straw, and with those bricks, when made, to construct a specious fabric to lure away a reluctant and contrary child. But in the end we did it. After a vacillation which shortened our lives, Rose decided to prefer a dinner of herbs in our company to the stalled ox waiting at Loumy a mile and a half away. Only a fool would have considered our invitation : only a fool could have failed to perceive our *volte face* : only a fool would have swallowed the sickly drivel with which we filled him up. And so we come to the price which we had to pay. . . .

Someone has said that there is nothing more terrible than victory, except defeat. As I went for the Lowland, I felt inclined to agree. The prospect of entertaining Rose for the next few hours was simply devastating.

The food we had with us was happily ample for three, and all we had to do was to drive a few miles and then picnic in some sequestered lane. As for the absence of a chauffeur, I decided that Rose must be told that we had made the man up. Here I should say that his car was three miles off. He had left it, it seemed, at some garage, because he had broken a spring. It was to be ready again at five o'clock. Our programme was therefore obvious. Now we had got him, we must keep him until it was time for him to get under way. If not, he would burst off to Loumy to see his friend.

As I came up with the Lowland, I saw that something was wrong. Berry looked ripe for murder, and a sulky look had settled on Rose's face.

"He says," said Berry, thickly, "he says he doesn't want a cold lunch."

"That's right," said Rose. "We want to get together, don't we?"

"Oh, rather," said Berry, in the tone of one who is subscribing to a suggestion that he shall be burnt alive.

"Well, you can't get together over a slice of cold ham."

"Can't you?" said Berry. "I mean, I expect you're right. What

—what can you get together over?"

"Rose is right," I said quickly. "That's the idea."

Berry put his hand to his head.

"What's what idea?" he said weakly. "And for God's sake don't you start, or I shall go stark staring mad."

The other's face cleared with his words.

"I agree," he said warmly. "People say it's good for hiccoughs, but that's muck."

"Hiccoughs?" screamed Berry. "Hiccoughs? What the devil do you mean? We were discussing grass-seed."

"No, we weren't," yelped Rose. "You said——"

"What does it matter what I siad?" said Berry. "We're out of the realm of coherence. Ham, hiccoughs or havoc—what's the odds? And now let's find some brambles and have a bathe."

Rose abandoned himself to a paroxysm of mirth.

Addressing Berry, I sought to steady my voice.

"He misunderstood you," I said. "He means that if you've got hiccoughs and somebody makes you start, they go away."

"That's just what I don't," said Rose.

"There you are," said Berry. "It's just what he doesn't. And I'm inclined to agree. How many thousand times has it been what I can't?"

"You're all wrong," howled Rose. "The only way to stop hiccoughs——"

"Think of a number," said Berry. "Add a pound and a half of suet and divide by a box of bricks."

"Not at all," said Rose. "You take hold of your tongue and pull it out of your mouth as far as you can."

"I know," said Berry, excitedly. "Then you stand on it with one foot and put the other in your breast-pocket."

If we were playing with insanity, at least our guest's good humour came pelting back, and when I suggested that we should lunch at a town some forty miles off, he clambered into the Lowland without a word.

The hours that followed rammed home the truth of the adage, "Familiarity breeds contempt". Finding his company courted, the idiot became exacting—as idiots will. Rose began to despise us and treat us like dirt. With the spectre of Loumy in the background, we grunted and sweated and summoned up crooked smiles. I ordered a roaring lunch at the best hotel. Rose chose the wine—champagne, tasted it, said it was muck and drank two bottles himself without turning a hair. I paid the bill, which was more than nine hundred francs, and felt like death for the rest of the afternoon. But compared with our mental distress, this bodily inconvenience was nothing at all. To consort with the man was odious: to converse with him brought you to the verge of frenzy itself. The man was "as sounding brass, or a tinkling cymbal". His talk was offensively futile: he argued and interrupted until you felt ready to scream, and he raked us with a fire of questions, the answers to which entailed a network of lies. Worst of all, he began to get fractious: and we had to humour the sweep —with death in our hearts.

When it was four o'clock I got to my feet.

"We ought to be moving," I said. "Our friend has got to get on."

"That's right," said Berry. "We'll run you back to your car, and——"

"I've changed my mind," said Rose. "I'm not going on. I'll sleep the night at Loumy. And you can come in to dinner. There's nothing the matter with Louis Blucher's champagne."

Before this crushing blow I felt rather faint. Berry shut his eyes and covered his face.

As I strove to rally my wits—

"But the SOS," gibbered Berry. "You simply can't ignore a summons like that."

"Must," said the other, yawning. "Drunk too much of that fizz. You run me back to Loumy, and if I feel like it to-morrow, I'll take the London road. I guess it's my partner's died—the silly damned fool. Have you got another cigar?"

As a man in a dream, Berry produced his case.

Rose took the last cigar and bit off the end.

"All tobacco should be common," he said. "Everybody's tobacco should belong to everyone else. You know. Like air and water. I'm sure I'm right."

But I had no ears for his sapience. I could only see the danger —now ten times as hot as before—of letting him loose at Loumy, with Casca de Palk. After a frightful struggle, after wrestling with more emotions than I ever knew I possessed, I glanced at Berry to find Berry glancing at me. As once before that day, I decided to take the plunge. After all, it was Rose that had driven us on to the plank and down to its bitter end.

"We're sleeping at a village," I said, "not far away. Not far from Loumy, I mean. Some—some friends of ours are there and —and I'm sure they'd be very happy to take you in."

"Loumy's more in my line," said Rose.

"Oh, be a sw-sport," said Berry, with bulging eyes. "They're a cheery crowd and you won't have to try and talk French."

"That's all very well : but where do I come in?"

At once offensive and inconsequent, the remark was typical of the man's contributions to the sultry communion which we had done our best to sustain.

"With us, of course," I said with a sickly smile. " 'The more we are together', you know."

"That's right," said Berry somehow. "Don't—don't let us down."

After another struggle we had our way. But not without swallowing insults that sent us half out of our mind. The man was insufferable. He stipulated, he condescended, he patronized, he was incredibly rude. There was no grace in him.

A thousand times I have wondered what else we could have done : but, short of murder, I think that we had no choice. Rose was a very firebrand. Let him come within range of Casca, and all our hopes would be ashes in ten minutes' time. He *had* to be kept out of Loumy at any cost. Had he been other than he was, we might have charged him to make no mention of us. But no one on earth could have trusted so poisonous a fool, while we should have been at the mercy of as brazen a curiosity as ever I had to endure.

Sick at heart, I went off to get the car, cursing our bitter fortune and wondering what Jill and Adèle would say to our monstrous guest. As for Jonah . . . I remembered suddenly how Jonah was to have met us three hours ago. If only that pelting idiot had been content with our lunch, long before now we should have been joined by my cousin, and his quick brain might have found a way out of the pass. We must have missed him by minutes : Jonah was to have joined us at one o'clock.

As I came up to the car, somebody brushed against me and

thrust a piece of paper into my hand. Before I could speak, he was gone—*and I was watching Carson walk out of the yard.* Carson! Then Jonah . . .

Swiftly I entered the Lowland and shut the door. Then I stooped as low as I could and opened the note.

> By the mercy of heaven I saw you without being seen. I cannot believe that you know the identity of your friend. He is known as Auntie Emma. If you can, I should deport him —drive him away from Loumy and leave him in some desolate place. You'll have to be wary : he certainly carries arms.
>
> J.

I have never been able to determine to what extent the fellow had been playing a game. So far from being an idiot, he was unearthly shrewd. That goes without saying. Yet I will swear that his manner was not assumed : and, as I have said, I never have seen a sillier-looking man. I am inclined to think that he was an extreme example of that curious type of genius whom no one who has not seen him in his element would credit with any sort of competence. When next I had speech with Fluff, he confirmed this point of view.

"Of course we're used to Auntie, but he always gives the idea of a full-marks fool. Never heard such wash as he talks—when he's not on the job. You wouldn't think he could reason : but he's as cunning as hell. And tough. That 'igh-pitched laugh of his. I've seen him plug his man in the stomach an' laugh like that when the deader tried to get up."

But if his behaviour was natural, there can be no doubt that he knew how to turn his folly to good account. When he was dealing with strangers, his face and his ways were his fortune— and that he knew. They had been his fortune this sweltering day of July. Neither Berry nor I are naturally credulous men. More. We had reason to be on our guard. Yet Auntie Emma had wiped the floor with us both.

The moment he saw us he suspected that we were the two confederates of Jonathan Mansel who had accompanied the latter to *The Wet Flag*. He, therefore, tested us, to see if we told him the truth and had led me into a lie as soon as I opened my mouth. I had said we had stayed at the *Hôtel du Parc,* Larogne. He had instantly checked this statement, to find that Larogne can boast no hotel of that name. Very good. We were his men. The next thing he wanted to know was the look of our car. Before ten minutes were gone he had his desire and had put us in such a stew as must have done his heart good. So he took us away from Loumy, to leave the coast clear for his men. Finally he had induced us to show him our lair. . . .

With a shock I found myself praying that Berry had not yet mentioned the village of Mose by name.

I think it was this apprehension that stung me out of the stupor in which I sat, and at once I started the engine and set my foot on the clutch. And there I stopped. Before I took any action, Berry had to be told.

I racked my brain for some means to bring this about. It occurred to me suddenly that since we had met Auntie Emma, not for one instant had he left us together alone.

Desperately I looked about me. Then I saw Berry's hat. This he had left in the Lowland, instead of taking it with him into the hotel. In a flash I was out of the car and unlocking the boot. This was empty except for the luncheon-basket we had not used. I set Berry's hat on the basket, with Jonah's note stuck, open, between the ribbon and felt. Then I relocked the boot and re-entered the car. An instant later I was before the hotel.

As our guest took his seat by my side—

"Where's my hat?" said Berry. "I left it here."

"To be pinched," said I. "I took the trouble to lock it up in the boot."

With that, I gave him the key.

"It wasn't worth stealing," said John Alexander Rose.

Looking ready to burst, my brother-in-law withdrew to the rear of the car. With a hammering heart I heard him inserting the key.

Auntie Emma was speaking—

"What's the name of this village?" he said.

"It's a hamlet," said I, "called St. Roch. Our best way will be to strike north and then——"

"The thing is to get there," said the other, launching a frightening yawn. "What's this car worth?"

"About a thousand," said I.

"Francs or pounds?"—this with a giggle of laughter that scorched my ears.

"Roubles," said Berry and clambered into the car.

I let in the clutch. . . .

Almost before we had picked our way out of the town, our dangerous companion was fast asleep.

I shall never forget that drive.

I never once glanced at Berry, and when I found his face in the windscreen, his expression was fixed and dull, and his eyes were staring ahead. The engine was quiet and supple, the roads were free. I might have had no gear-box, made little use of my horn, drove like the wind. And always eastward : but Loumy and Mose lay west.

I knew that ahead lay forest, if you can call it such. A wide stretch of rolling plain, much of it covered with poor, uncared-for trees and all of it wild, rough country, the soil of which was too poor to cultivate. The place was desolate. Roads ran through it, and here and there a peasant's crazy cottage lifted its mournful head, but if a man was afoot there when dusk came in, he might have to walk five miles before he had the good fortune to see a light.

To the best of my recollection this unkind region lay seventy miles away. Consult the map I dared not, but once, some years before, I had made my way across it and driven from there to the town at which we had lunched. I had therefore a very good hope of striking its confines within an hour and a half, provided our guest still slept and so remained oblivious of our preposterous speed. Be sure I was well aware how considerable was this protasis.

Mile after mile we covered without a word : we made no sort of movement, no sort of sound : we had no eyes for the country, no thought for the perfection of the day : we courted speed and silence, and cared about nothing else. Each bend in the road alarmed us, because of what it might hide : the roar of a passing lorry sent our hearts into our mouths : we quailed before the hubbub of echoing village streets : and if ever a waggon checked us, I could have murdered the boor that delighted to hold us up.

But luck was with us.

Heavy with wine and drugged with the soft warm air, the knave between us slept and stirred in his slumber—and slept again.

It was long past six, and we were well into the forest for which I had made.

By now we were going slowly, for the main roads were far behind us and I had been driving at random down by-road and lane. From a swelling which we had just breasted no sign of habitation had met the eye, and as we slid into a hollow, I felt that the time had come.

We were off the map.

As I turned to Berry, Auntie Emma opened his eyes.

"Had a good sleep?" said the former.

"A one," said the man. "Where are we?"

"That," said I, "is the question. I've missed some turning or other. We ran through Loumy a quarter of an hour ago."

As the fellow looked over his shoulder, I whipped the key from the switch. Instantly the engine fainted, and I brought the Lowland to rest by the side of the road.

"That's done it," I said, with an oath. "We ought to have taken in petrol, but I thought we could just get home."

"D'you mean to say——"

"Dry as a bone," said I. "It's a rotten life."

"Well I call it damned careless," said Berry, as though his temper were gone. "You knew the gauge wasn't working. Why didn't you——"

"I tell you, I thought we could do it."

"Why think?" said Berry, offensively. "Why not make sure?"

Auntie Emma put in his oar.

"If you were my chauffeur," he said, "I'd shake you up."

"It might be worse," said I. "We passed a pump half a mile back."

"And what about me? I'm thirsty."

"Walk back with me," said I, alighting. "The pump belonged to a pub."

"So it did," said Berry, and left the car.

"Why should I?" said Auntie Emma. "I don't believe in walking. How long will you be?"

"Twenty minutes," said I. "Perhaps twenty-five."

"I guess if you like you can do it quicker than that."

"I don't believe in hurrying," said I, and wrung out a grin.

"You make me sore," said the other and lighted a cigarette. . . .

As we passed out of earshot—

"Good for you," said Berry. "What do we do?"

"We take the first bend," said I. "Then we go back through the bushes until we can see the car. The swine can't touch her, because I've got the key of the switch and the bonnet is locked. How long he'll keep us waiting I've no idea. I should think about forty minutes. But sooner or later he'll go and see if we're coming, and that's our chance."

And so it fell out.

At the corner we left the lane and made our way back through the bushes which hereabouts grew pretty thick. Using the greatest caution we moved back the way we had come, and ten minutes later we lay in a little depression commanding the car.

Auntie Emma was out in the road. From the way he was nursing his hand I think he had tried to unscrew the cap of the petrol-tank. But this required a spanner, and the tool-box was locked. After a little he took his seat on the step. There he sat smoking and smiling, and once he laughed.

It may have been because we now knew him for what he was, but against the silence of sundown the foolish whinney of mirth sounded most sinister, and I know I shuddered to hear it and hoped he would laugh no more.

At last he got to his feet and frowned at his watch. Then he flung out an oath and stood staring the way we had come. We watched him breathlessly. After perhaps two minutes he started to stroll up the hill.

At once we began to move forward . . .

By the time he had breasted the rise we were behind some brambles not ten feet away from the car.

"Now," breathed Berry. "He may turn round and come back."

"Not he," said I. "He'll go as far as the bend."

And so he did—with never a backward look.

As he passed downhill out of sight, we left our cover and stepped across to the car.

I doubt if he heard us start, for the swell of the hill was between us and would have stifled the sound, but he heard us sail out of the hollow on the opposite side.

"He's stopped," said Berry. "He's staring. He's starting to run. What a fool instinct can make of a man! He's stopped now. I don't know what he's doing." We swept round a bend in the road. "But I'll bet he isn't laughing," he added. "How far are we from Loumy?"

"Roughly," said I, "a hundred and twenty miles."

"Glory be," said Berry. "I give you best. I'd like to be there when he asks some peasant his way. And his map'll take some reading." He laughed luxuriously. "Live and learn. He won't snooze in a car again for the rest of his life. After all, it's an ill wine that does nobody good."

"To my mind, the cream is this. He doesn't know what to think. He doesn't know whether we know he's Auntie Emma or whether we still believe that he's J. A. Rose. In either guise he was a nuisance and in one or the other he has been abated : but he doesn't know which. What's more he never will know how long we've been playing a game. Of course we've won the rubber, but when he remembers the tricks he thought he'd taken, he'll wonder whether they don't belong to us."

Berry glanced at the haggard prairie stretching on either hand.

"Well, he's going to have a nice, quiet time to work it out, isn't he?"

This became increasingly obvious. We were not clear of the forest for half an hour.

As we slid into a village—

"Query," said Berry. "If three can't get together over a slice of cold ham, how far will one get on his own over a blasted heath? And the answer's a hiccough. Which reminds me, this little *coup* has made me completely well. An hour ago I felt that I should have been buried two days ago : now, I could man-handle a lorry into the middle of next week."

With his words, I suddenly found that I felt exactly the same. My distemper was gone, and I was perfectly well.

More than four hours had gone by, and the others had waited upon us until we could eat no more.

As Berry emptied his glass—

"More beer?" said Jill tenderly.

Hebe herself could not have been more enchantingly solicitous. I am perfectly certain she never so filled the eye. Fresh, melting and liquid, my cousin personified the nectar she poured.

"Well, just a heel-tap," said Berry, "in memory of an imperfect day. If you want to be put off champagne drink it at lunch. Of course b-beer's different." With a sparkling eye he regarded the rising tide. "Now there's an honest liquor. Goes down smiling, and never presumes. Never. Beer knows its place. Not so champagne—that's for remembrance. It rounds on you. Invites you to consume it and then disputes your rights. Rebutter and surrebutter."

"You really are disgusting," said Adèle.

"Not at all," said Berry. "Two well-known legal terms. Onomatopœic, perhaps: but that's not my fault. Never mind. I'll put it another way. Take any ordinary paunch—capital P."

There was a shriek of protest.

"I shall write and tell Daphne," said Jill.

"Well, do spell it right," said Berry. "Two L's. All the same, you've been so sweet that I take it back. The truth is I'm suffering from reaction, and the wonder is I've not offended before. The self-control which I have been called upon to exercise to-day passes all comprehension. My output of restraint has been fantastic. These gazelle-like orbs bulged with emotion. Apoplexy was in the air. The vials of exasperation were poured out. Did I tell you he called me a fool—a silly fool? And then committed an assault upon my body? Laughed like a half-baked baboon and slapped me upon the back?"

He broke off to mop his face.

"Well, you got your own back," said Jonah. "And more beside. I know that waste. If he was there at night-fall, he'll be there till break of day. Then he's got to get his bearings. And when the brain-storm is over, he's got to get back to Loumy as best he can. If he takes the field before Monday, I'll be surprised . . . Merest chance I saw you. I'd left the Rolls with Carson, and was walking up to find you by the side of the way. When I saw him talking to Berry, you could have knocked me down. I couldn't think what to do. You see, if I'd appeared there'd have been a hell of a row. Then you came up with the Lowland, and after a little discussion you all got in. You bet I ran for the Rolls. . . . But I devilish nearly lost you more than once."

"You've made him mad," said Adèle, finger to lip. "Mad as a hornet, Boy. And I don't like that."

"On the contrary," said my cousin, "they've won the black-guard's respect. He'll go devilish gingerly now in his dealings with us. His men are with Walker now at the village inn. But I don't think they'll learn very much. But I'm glad to report that Woking and Walker are now the best of friends. Woking rode back from the station by Walker's side. Glad to find an Anglo-Saxon, you know. And Walker has suggested to Woking that Woking should take some drives. Pretty country, you know. I hope and believe the idea will appeal to Woking—and Casca, too. You know. A car to themselves, and a nice fine day. Stop by the side of the road and go for a stroll. That's the way to do private business."

"I should like Auntie Emma's ruling on that," said Berry dreamily.

CHAPTER VIII

Alarms and Excursions

I could fill up a book with our efforts of the next five days, but, since they came to nothing, I will record them only as bearing upon those of the sixth.

While the Count and his guests sat at dinner, Jonah entered the château and actually made his way into Casca's room : but the furniture offered no shelter, and only a bird could have perched outside the windows and heard what was spoken within.

Each night at dusk the ground floor was shut and barred, and, since there were fourteen guests, the *salons* were never empty, except at meals. To this I can swear, for I spent more hours upon the terrace than in my bed. The smoking-room was our Mecca : but all our patience was fruitless, and though we might well have entered when everyone had retired—and that, of course, was useless—until the lights were put out an incredibly perverse fortune kept us at bay.

Of these trespasses, committed and projected, we all of us felt ashamed : we should not have liked such treatment : and more than once we considered the wild idea of approaching the Count : but in the end we laid the blame upon Casca, who after all had led us into these evil ways.

The château proving impregnable, we were reduced to hoping that Casca and Woking would do as my cousin had said—go driving together and make their plans by the way.

If only they did, we were ready.

The map had been studied with Walker, and three routes had been arranged. Each was a different drive of a different length : and every morning the buckets outside the garage were used by Walker to tell us which route, if any, the car would take. No bucket meant no drive : one bucket, Route Number One : and so on. Meanwhile in the first hours of daylight we worked these roads—to and fro, up and down, in and out, until we knew every coppice and the angle of every bend.

Three times we had the signal, and three times at half past

two a car rolled out of the courtyard with only the chauffeur and Woking as occupants.

Auntie Emma and his men were no doubt about their business : but they did not trouble Walker and for all that we saw of them they might have been out of France.

At midnight on Wednesday, Walker met Jonah and me at the edge of the park.

"He's going on Friday, sir—the American gent. The early train on Friday. But I think he'll drive to-morrow—same way as to-day. He didn't half like that drive. Called it a peach of a run. And he did let fall as his friend did ought to see it . . . I thought I'd take the Roquefort—that's an interior drive. So that if they did want to talk business, they'd 'ave to get out."

"Well done," said Jonah quietly. "We shan't forget."

In silence we returned to the car.

There was no doubt about it. Casca de Palk was making our path very hard.

As we slid into the darkness—

"If we fail to-morrow," said Jonah, "we shall have to go back to Tours. And from there we must follow Woking wherever he goes. I think the end is coming. I don't believe they'll stay together again."

"Follow Woking". My heart sank down to my boots. How could we shadow such a man with the slightest hope of success?

After three hours' sleep we took to the Rolls again and spent five solid hours going over Route Two. This was an eighty-mile run. By the end of that time we knew every inch of the way. Sharp at a quarter to nine we came to rest in a dingle, a furlong or so from where we could look upon Loumy and into the great court-yard. I took a binocular with me and walked to the spot.

To the right of the garage door two buckets were standing to-gether against the wall. I let out a sigh of relief. This was by no means unselfish. Had they stood to the left of the door, they would have been declaring that Woking would drive in the morning instead of the afternoon. As it was, we could rest for four hours.

Twenty minutes later we were back at *The Fisherman's Arms*.

Adèle and Jill came flying out of the inn.

"Will you bathe first?" said the former. "Or have your break-fast at once?"

"I'll breakfast," said Berry. "The layers-out can bathe me. I've had six hours' sleep in three nights and I shan't last long."

"Confess," said Jonah, "that you've never felt so fit in your life."

"Oh, blasphemy," said Berry, and shambled into the house.

The simple, abundant fare did much to lift up our hearts: before the fragrant attentions of Jill and Adèle, our impulse to prophesy no good, but evil, began to die down: and when we sat smoking about the remains of our feast, we were able to focus more clearly the possibility of success.

"I'm better," said Berry. "Death has fallen back discomfited. The funeral which had been arranged will not take place. I don't say it isn't partly the omelet. Honour where honour is due. But" —he picked up Jill's hand and kissed it—"I give you my word I could look at your throat all day."

"Adèle's is better," said Jill.

"Nothing in it," said Berry. "The two of you cram the eye. If Daphne were here——"

"There is no goddess but Daphne," said Adèle.

"I agree. She's incomparable. But she couldn't diminish you two. And when I think that that filthy slab of offal, that verminous skunk from which when dead the vultures would turn away, not only drugged you, but touched your lively beauty while you were asleep . . . lifted those hands to strip them . . . raised your heads to unfasten——"

"Oh, don't," said Piers. "I can't bear it. When you talk like that, I want to go straight to Loumy and break his neck."

"A little patience," said I. "I'd much rather have my neck broken than go to hard labour in France."

Adèle shuddered.

"You must let him go," she said simply. "Get back our things, if you can. But——"

" 'Let him go'?" said Berry. "Why it's only the thought of Casca at work in a quarry that keeps me from losing my mind. And think of the good it'll do him. He won't have to go to Vichy when he comes out."

"No," said Jill. "We've decided. We don't want him to go to prison because of us. You can tell him what he's fit for, and then——"

"But we don't know what he's fit for," said Berry. "I can think

140

of no sphere of service which that bladder of slime would not foul. I've always understood that the dogs of Constantinople are by no means particular about their food, but I am prepared to believe that even if his body were distributed about the meaner streets of that city the animals would prefer to go hungry rather than insult a digestion which I have been led to believe is practically invulnerable."

"I decline to believe," said Jonah, "that when the moment comes you will be unable to indicate the office which our gentleman friend should fill. In the meantime, I think I can tell you why Casca is keeping house."

"Why?" said everyone.

"Because he has the pearls with him. He daren't go out and leave them, and while they're on his person he doesn't fancy leaving the shelter which Loumy affords."

"That's right," said Piers. "The small stuff was valued at Tours, the bracelets at Dinard, and Woking was asked to Loumy to see the pearls."

"Well, if you're right," said Berry, "we may as well stay where we are. If the swab's afraid to leave Loumy——"

"It's a groundless fear," said Jonah. "Comparatively, I mean. And I hope very much he'll see that this afternoon. He's got to get back to Paris, and that's a lot more risky than taking the pearls for a drive."

Adèle looked up from her embroidery.

"If he does turn out with Woking, why don't you hold them up? Once you find the pearls upon him, you've got him cold."

Jonah laid down his pipe.

"And if the pearls aren't on him?"

There was an eloquent silence.

"I must confess," said Berry, "I see your point. If we strike when the iron's not hot, we do everything in."

"Exactly," said Jonah. "And mind—if we fail to-day, we needn't burst into tears. Woking won't be easy to shadow, but the four of us, with Susie, ought to be able somehow to bring that off. And Woking has got to take over before he clears out."

"And Auntie Emma?" said Piers.

"I wish I knew," said Jonah. "I wish he'd show up. I begin to get uneasy when the enemy's out of my ken."

"I should worry," said Berry. "You don't know when you're well off. And now let's pray for success. Let's swear to erect a petrol-pump on the spot where we overhear Woking explaining to Casca how to get to the rendezvous. I mean, we must do something. The thought of returning to Tours sends the blood to my head."

Jonah sighed.

"The only way I know of propitiating Fortune is, so far as you possibly can, to leave nothing to chance. That's why I've made our lives hell for the last three days."

"Nothing to chance," said Berry and covered his face.

" 'Ninety-five per cent guesswork'," said Piers.

"Call it ninety-nine," said Berry, "and you'll be nearer the mark. Never mind. If we weren't insane, we shouldn't be here. And, once you're insane, nothing matters—there aren't any odds. I found that out at Tours. The entirely incredible happened—it does in dreams. The preposterous came to pass. And having seen that with my eyes, I know it may happen again. It doesn't seem very likely, but Casca *may* break his rule and go for a drive. And after a while he *may* get out of the car. And he *may* stroll into a thicket and wait for us to come up. And then he *may* raise his voice and broadcast the time and place at which he proposes to part with the stolen goods. I tell you, I'm taking no risks—I've got a pencil all ready to take it down. You know. Like the result of the Grand National."

"Quite right," said Jonah, quietly. "I've got one, too."

As the applause died down—

"I give you best," said Berry. "On with the dance."

By one o'clock that day we were all at our posts.

Jonah and I were lying at ease in a meadow which flanked the road which Walker was going to use. Behind us, between where we lay and the road, an empty barn, which stood on the edge of the field, was concealing the Rolls. Since the barn had a door to the road, we could not have been better placed, for, once the car had gone by, we had but to open the door and start in pursuit.

The word "pursuit" is misleading. It was most important, of course, that we should not lose touch : but it was just as important that, though we followed behind, we should not appear. If Casca in fact drove forth, he would be the soul of suspicion, and one glimpse of a car behind him *which did not catch up* would fan his apprehension into a flame. We must, therefore, be there in the background, but nowhere else. Here our study of the route was to serve us : and this and my cousin's judgment would probably see us through. Besides, we had chosen six viewpoints—places at which we could stop, from which, by mounting the bank by the side of the way, we could observe the road before us for fully two miles.

But the barn had another use. Its stone walls ran up for six feet and then stopped dead : planted upon them, a sturdy, wooden paling made up the rest of the height : but the boards did not meet the wall by more than an inch, and anyone standing within could not only see a car coming, but could look right into the vehicle as it passed by.

Carson lay silent beside us, with field-glasses up to his eyes. He was steadfastly watching Berry, who was standing high above us, some two miles off. Close to Berry was Piers, lying no doubt in the bracken, with his eyes on Loumy's courtyard.

If Berry raised his hat once, that would mean that the car had come up to the door : if he raised it twice, that someone had entered the car, but he could not say who : if he raised it three times, that the car had turned out of the gates and was taking Route Two.

We had arranged other signals, but these will serve.

Once the hunt was up, Berry and Piers would take their seats in the Lowland, make their way to Route Two and follow the Rolls, so that in case of a puncture or any mishap with which the latter might meet, the coupé would be on the spot to take up the chase. I do not think I have said that the Rolls was an open car.

For over an hour we waited, while the honesty of our surroundings ministered to our minds and the dulcet drone of insects and the liquid fluting of birds made us an overture so peaceful as to give the drama which was coming the lie direct.

Then Carson lifted his voice.

"Stand by, sir," he said. And then. "The Major's moving. He's speaking to his Grace."

We waited breathlessly.

"I think there's a hitch," said Carson. "Yes, sir, he's sending

'Look out'."

I smothered an oath, and Jonah got to his feet.

"Car up to the door, sir," said Carson.

There was a little silence. The signals seemed contradictory. If the car had come up to the door, then all was well.

"Something has happened," said Jonah, "for which we haven't allowed. It may be nothing. As long as he doesn't send 'Danger'—"

"Stand by, sir," said Carson. We waited. "Unable to see the occupants of the car."

I groaned in spirit. We had had this message before.

"Natural enough," murmured Jonah. "The car's between him and the door."

"Route Number Two, sir," said Carson, and got to his feet.

I took the glasses, and Carson went into the barn to watch the road. About five minutes must pass before the car would come by.

With my eyes on my brother-in-law—

" 'Look out'," I said. "He's sending 'Look out' again. . . . Now Piers has come up and they're talking. . . . 'Message ends' . . . They're going off to the car." I lowered the glasses and turned to my cousin who was standing with a hand to his mouth. "What the deuce can he mean?" I said.

"I've no idea," he said slowly and turned to the barn.

He took his seat in the Rolls and I stepped to the chink in the wall. . . .

After perhaps one minute I heard the sound of a car.

We waited in absolute silence, Carson and I on either side of the door, and Jonah behind and between us, with his hands on the wheel.

The car was very near now and was travelling fast. In a moment —two seconds now—we should know the truth.

I found my teeth chattering with excitement.

Then the Roquefort swept into sight, and my heart gave one great bound and then stood still.

Casca was there, with Woking. But in the chauffeur's seat sat Someone other than Walker—some man I had never seen.

Then the car was gone, and the slim, black road was empty and Jonah was frowning at Carson, first with the news.

"It can't be helped," he said shortly. "Open the door."

This was in two great leaves and was made to admit a waggon

laden with hay.

Carson's leaf was half open and I had put my shoulder to mine, when I heard approaching the sound of a second car. And as I heard it, the truth leaped into my brain.

Auntie Emma had done it on us. Walker had been 'removed'— put out of the way : and the man who had taken his place had been bought by Auntie Emma, to do as he said. *And here, in this car that was coming, was Auntie Emma himself.*

There was no time for speech.

As Jonah started the engine, I flung myself upon Carson, knocked him out of the way and dragged the leaf back into place. Then I leaped for the loophole—to see a closed car go by and the crook that we had deported framed in the nearside window, as he gave some order or other to the man who was driving the car.

As I turned to the Rolls—

"Are you right?" said Jonah quietly.

My cousin has a quick brain.

I nodded.

"It's Auntie Emma himself."

"Then, heaven help us," said Jonah. "He's going to tear every-thing up. He's after the pearls."

I never remember feeling so much dismayed.

After all our scheming and toil to take one more step towards victory, we stood in most imminent peril of utter and enduring defeat. Our plans were dust and ashes : and we had neither time nor material to make any more. Now that Walker was gone, we had no idea which roads the Roquefort would take : we had no idea how or where Auntie Emma was proposing to strike. All we could do was to make a desperate effort to get between him and his quarry and hold him up. And that, without his quarry's suspecting his presence or ours.

I have often wondered whether so strange a procession ever took order before.

First, Casca and Woking, more or less secure and unsuspecting, all oblivious of what was behind them and certainly finding the country a pleasant place. Then the crook and his two confederates, out to spoil the spoilers of the very cream of the booty the final disposal of which they were about to discuss. Then Jonah and Carson and I, in an agony of apprehension, frantic to balk Auntie

Emma and so preserve Casca and Woking for a far heavier blow. Finally Berry and Piers, who knew that our plans must be back in the melting-pot, yet could do nothing but stick to those we had made.

"Can you see them, Carson?"

On his feet by the windscreen, Carson shaded his eyes.

"Not yet, sir."

My cousin put down his foot.

We flashed between pine-woods, snarled at a high-walled corner and dropped down a sudden hill with a rush of a lift. For a mile now the road was open and straight as a carpenter's rule. For forty-five seconds we seemed to be actually flying—skimming the earth : and then we were at the next corner, and Carson, who had been crouching, was standing upright.

As we swung round—

"There they are, sir," he cried. "About five furlongs ahead."

"Can you see the Roquefort?"

"No, sir. They're slowing up for the village. They're checked. There's a lorry ahead."

The village lay low, at the foot of a serpentine hill. This rose abruptly to a flying column of beechwoods, clothing a great hog's back, its ranks so tall and serried that the road that ran between them might have been the bed of a gorge. It occurred to me suddenly that for robbery under arms this was a likely place.

"Somehow or other," said Jonah, "we've got to pass on that hill. If they get to the top before us, they may overtake in the greenwood and do the job."

"There's the Roquefort, sir," said Carson. "Clear of the village and climbing up to the woods."

"As I thought," said Jonah. "They're closing up."

We floated into the village and swung to the left, slipped between two waggons and round to the right—to meet as nasty a punch as surely ever was landed by a malignant Fate.

The Roquefort was out of sight now—had rounded the first of the bends of the serpentine hill : and the closed car was clear of the village and making a rush at the slope. So much for the middle distance. In the foreground, no more than fifty paces from where we were, a lorry was standing still, on the very fringe of the village and full in the midst of the way. And that, for the best of reasons.

146

The level-crossing was closed. One iron trellis had already been lugged into place, and a sour-faced woman was shutting the farther gate.

That the stars in their courses were fighting against us seemed painfully clear. Fifteen seconds more, and we should have been by. As it was, we were stuck, good and proper, until the train should have passed. But for the lorry, we could have defied law and order and gone our way : we should, of course, have done so : Carson and I would have each flung open a gate and the Rolls would have crossed the metals before the surly keeper had time to protest. But the nose of the lorry was not three feet from the gate, and because of its bulk there was left no room to go by.

Jonah let out a groan. Then he brought the Rolls up to the lorry and threw out the clutch.

As he did so, I left the car, rushed to the wicket and darted on to the line.

No train was in sight.

Without thinking, I crossed the metals and began to run up the road towards the serpentine hill.

By now, of course, the closed car had disappeared : but I had, I suppose, some wretched, hopeless idea of attempting to keep in touch. Had I stopped to think, I should have spared my legs, for the hill must have been a mile and a quarter long, and the closed car would be at the summit before I was more than halfway to the first of the bends. For all that, I pelted along : and I think it was better to be running than sitting still in the Rolls awaiting the train.

At last I came to the bend, and when I glanced back, before turning, the lorry and the gates of the crossing were as they had been when I left them and Carson was out on the metals, with a hand to his head.

I stumbled round the corner, to see the road empty before me for a quarter of a mile. Far above me the range of beechwoods stood up, a screen of elegant verdure against the blue of the sky. I began to wonder when Jonah would catch me up. I remembered fearfully that you may wait half an hour at a level-crossing in France.

The heat was awful, and I'm not good on my feet. I was simply streaming with sweat, and the second bend was farther than I thought. And after that there was another, and then the deuce of a pull before you came to the crest.

As I dashed the sweat from my eyes, a figure stepped out of a by-road, perhaps forty paces away.

It was Piers.

I saw him glance up the hill. Then he glanced down and saw me and started to run.

"What's happened?" he cried.

"The Lowland," I gasped. "Where's the Lowland?"

"She's down in the lane. To save time, we came across country. We came so quick that I thought——"

"Bring her up," I panted. "For God's sake——"

But Piers was in the mouth of the by-road, waving his arms.

I staggered up to a sign-post, leaned against it and wiped the sweat from my face.

"You get back to the village," I said. "Auntie Emma's between us and Casca, and the Rolls is held up. Tell Jonah I'm going to do what I can."

As he sped down the hill, the Lowland shot up to the corner and came to rest.

"Don't talk," said Berry, opening the driver's door. "I know that hunted look. There's the devil to pay, of course." He slid aside, and I took my seat at the wheel. "I suppose Auntie Emma's getting jealous. The moment Piers told me that Walker was not on parade——"

"He's done it on us," said I, and put the car at the hill for all I was worth.

"There you are," said Berry. "I never liked the man."

"Not Walker," I screamed. "Auntie Emma."

"Well, I never liked him, either," said Berry. "Is he out of matches again?"

"He's after Casca," said I. "They're just about three miles ahead. We're stuck at the level-crossing."

"Hence the exercise," said Berry. "I understand. Auntie Emma is preying on Casca. Dog is about to eat dog. Are we hoping to be in at the death?"

"We're out to stop it," said I. "We've got to get between them. Hold Auntie Emma up, and——"

"There now," said Berry, "and I left the bombs at home. You

know, you must be deranged. 'Hold up Auntie Emma'? D'you want a puncture in your abdominal wall?"

Here we rose to the crest of the hill, to see the lovely corridor stretching as bare as my hand.

I heaved a sigh of relief. At least the end was not yet.

As the Lowland slid into her stride—

"They may have turned off," I said. "Look down the left-hand by-roads as we go by."

"I see. In case they've stopped to pick flowers. Shall I wave if I see them?" Here we passed a by-road at seventy-two. "Well, the first five yards of that one were empty. Bare as your hand. After that there was a white lawn-mower. Or it may have been a sheep rolling. If my eye could be cut in half, covered with lamp-black and then photographed, you'd probably get the truth."

"We're coming to a view-point," said I. "Stand by with those glasses, will you? If they haven't turned off . . ."

We spurted out of the beechwoods, swooped at a hollow and tore up the rise beyond. As we made the crest, I set a foot on the brake. . . .

Twenty seconds later I was up the bank which rose to the right of the way.

Trembling, I searched the road, which now dropped down by reaches and then swept away to the right to disappear in a hamlet some three miles off. I found a waggon and then a couple of vans. And then I saw the green of the Roquefort, three furlongs this side of the village, plugging along. The close car I could not see, but I dared not wait.

As I flung myself into the Lowland—

"We'll do it," I said. "I can't see Auntie Emma, but Casca's three miles ahead. And he's running into that hamlet where you turn to the left by a forge and go over a bridge. They'll have to slow up through there, and we ought to catch up on the switch-back the other side."

This was a few miles of highway that rippled across a heath. Because it resembled a switch-back we gave it that name.

"Before the switch-back," said Berry. "There's quite two miles of country before that begins. You know. You go down to the saw-mill and swing to the left."

"Quite right," said I. "I'd forgotten. We'll pass them before the switch-back with any luck."

"I advise it," said Berry. "I—you do see that lorry, don't you? The one we're going to crash on. All full of marble blocks."

There was not much room, but we did it—and saved thirty seconds of time.

As we flung round a bend—

"You were saying?" said I.

"Are we?" said Berry. "I mean, was I? Of course I've never liked marble. It's so—so suggestive. I don't think I've ever been so close to so much before. Never mind. I was about to—Must you pass those vans *as they're passing*. I mean, I always believe in—Damn it, we can't do it. Only a slice of forked lightning could —*Ugh!*"

The on-coming van helped us—to help itself. We proceeded amid scandalized yells.

"Sorry," said I. "As soon as he saw I meant business, I knew he'd give way. And now do announce your conclusions. Beyond catching Auntie Emma, I've no ideas."

"Conclusions be damned," said Berry. "What about my large intestine? It's slipped down behind the seat."

"Let it lie," said I. "Auntie Emma'll never look for it there."

"Don't be indecent," said Berry. He swallowed. "I fear the switch-back. For Auntie Emma's purpose it's almost a perfect place. He chooses a dip in the middle, and posts a man fore and aft. You get me? Auntie Emma's down in the dale, and his men are up on the hillocks on either side. And he holds up the car in the hollow, while they keep a good look-out. If they see a car coming they go at once to meet it: and they stop it on some pretext or other *before it has topped the rise which commands the hollow where Casca is being robbed*. In that way all help is cut off, until the job's done."

"Very ingenious," said I. "I think you're most likely right. And I'll tell you what. We must ditch them. Crowd them as we go by and force them into the ditch. If we can do that, they're finished— out of the race. If we just go by, there'll be a dog-fight. What's more, we'll be throwing away a very good card—the element of surprise. That blackguard knows this car. And the moment we pass——"

"Yes, it will be a pregnant moment, won't it?" said Berry. "To tell you the truth, I've been trying not to anticipate it. And if it could be avoided . . . I mean you might just as well accost a she-bear who has good reason to desire your early decease and explain that it is your immediate intention to deprive her for ever of her whelps, mightn't you? Just as well."

Although I did not say so, I could not help feeling that the comparison was just.

We were now nearing the hamlet which I had seen the Roque-fort approaching a short three minutes ago. And since the latter had not apeared to me to be travelling fast, I judged that the closed car must now be a mile ahead. Roughly, a mile. A start of a mile in two miles—for, from where we were, "the switch-back" lay two miles off.

As we slid out of the village, I let the Lowland go. . . .

We shot up the hill, whipped through a grove of chestnuts and tore down a long, straight stretch at eighty-five. As I steadied her up for the corner, the busy song of the saw-mill came to my ears. One mile was gone. We flung round the bend and another, brushed some hay from a waggon and slashed a thicket in two. For a furlong we swam between meadows. Then we switched to the right and leapt at a ridge.

"Now for it," said I. "We can see the road from the top. It runs dead straight to the switch-back. And if we don't catch them here——"

The sentence was never finished.

As we shot over the summit, I saw the Roquefort before us, at rest, to the right of the way. Two of its doors were open, one upon either side, and the chauffeur was stooping to set a jack under a spring. Of the closed car there was no sign.

Two things were immediately clear.

Auntie Emma had passed the Roquefort—no doubt according to plan : if Berry was right he was even now at "the switch-back", awaiting his prey. But Fate had put a spoke in his wheel. The Roquefort had picked up a puncture just short of the trap.

For an instant my brain zig-zagged.

The puncture was a clear godsend. We had been given a respite —a chance of plucking our fortune out of the draught. *The question was how to use it*. Our plight was no longer desperate. A little reflection would almost certainly point us some obvious path. *But we had no time for reflection.* We had to act now—*at once.* Every fleeting moment was of value. We had not an instant to lose.

I saw a lane on my right twenty paces away. I clapped on my brakes and swung the Lowland round. For a second I thought we were over. . . . And then we were in the by-road and out of sight.

As I brought the car to rest—

"Did he see or hear us?" I said.

"I don't think he did," said Berry. "He never looked round."

"They're out of the car," said I. "They've gone for a stroll."

"I agree," said Berry. "The open doors."

"You must follow them up," said I. "I imagine they're in that wood to the right of the road. If they've gone to the left, you'll see them, it's open moor."

"How can I——"

"You can't, of course. You can't get near on the moor. But if they're in the greenwood . . . But first we've got to stop Jonah from blundering in. He'll be moving faster than we were, and he mayn't have the luck we had. We must back the Lowland over the crest of the hill. The moment he sees her, he'll stop and come on on foot."

"And you?"

"I must pinch the Roquefort," said I. "It's the only way. Knock out that wallah and take the Roquefort on. When I don't stop for Auntie Emma, I guess he'll follow me up, and I'll give him a run for his money and——"

"Let me come with you," said Berry. "That isn't a one-man show."

"Not much," said I. "Two tricks are better than one. And now you get on to Casca. I'll put the Lowland back."

As Berry slid out of the car, I whipped the lever forward and let in the clutch. Happily the gears were not noisy. She swung back into the main road quietly enough. Then I lifted her over the brow and out of the sight of the chauffeur at work on his wheel. As before, the man never looked round.

As I took the key from the switch, I felt we had gained one point. We had set the signals at danger. Jonah would be going all out, but the Lowland would be in his view for a quarter of a mile. But as I slipped out of the car, I must confess that I shot one desperate glance the way we had come. With Jonah and Piers and Carson, the attempt which I was to make would have lost its sting. Indeed, as like as not, my cousin would have perceived a far less crude and far less perilous method of routing Auntie Emma and spoiling his game. The flaws in my plan were glaring. If Casca and Woking returned before I was ready, our cake was dough. If I could not mislead Auntie Emma—supposing he saw that Casca was not in the car?—he would come pelting back to find the sheep at his mercy, awaiting his shears. Would Casca and Woking believe that this daring theft of their car had nothing to do with some attempt, which had miscarried, to snaffle the Padua pearls? Supposing passing traffic prevented my rough design . . .

As though to point this danger, the distant hum of an engine came to my ears. As I stepped over the rise, I saw a blue limousine giving way to a one-ton truck which was laden with calves. Behind them a gray two-seater was discharging its obvious impatience in the shape of intense backfire. The road was getting positively crowded.

As they passed me, I averted my face, as a criminal should. Then I shot a glance at the Roquefort, two hundred paces away. The chauffeur was in the act of lifting the spare wheel down.

A swift reconnaissance showed me the moor was clear. Casca and Woking had clearly chosen the wood. I, therefore, went over the bank which lay between the moor and the road, and ran as fast as I could, until I was abreast of the Roquefort whose top I could see. Then I lay down on my stomach and crawled up the bank.

The car was empty, and the chauffeur was screwing the wheel-cap back into place. His back was towards me : it was the near hind wheel.

I glanced up and down the road and I searched the fringe of the wood. There was no one in sight.

For an instant I hesitated.

The man must not see me and he must make no noise. I must, therefore, strike from behind and knock him clean out. Regarding my victim, I felt a dreadful reluctance to use him so. If we were right, he deserved no consideration. All the same . . .

The pounding drone of a lorry came to my ears—a lorry approaching from "the switch-back". As I glanced up the road, I saw it swell into vision—a thing the size of a truck on a railway line.

If I was relieved, I was shocked.

I could, of course, do no violence until the newcomer had passed : and, since it was moving slowly, the chauffeur would have finished his labour before it was by. Then, again, a great deal may happen in, say, two minutes of time. Other vehicles might well appear on the scene. Casca and Woking might wander out of the wood. Auntie Emma might come back to see why the bird had not flown into the net he had spread. . . .

The chauffeur tightened the wheel-cap, laid down the spanner and stepped to screw down the jack. With a sinking heart, I glanced from him to his protector, and back again. Never did man work so swiftly : never did waggon lumber so slowly along. My precious chance was shrinking before my eyes.

By the time he had put up his tools, the lorry was still about a hundred yards off. Now only the wheel he had removed was waiting to be clamped into place.

As he straightened his back, I saw the man glance at the lorry and slam the near-side door. Then he pushed back his cap and took out a cigarette. As he felt for the match, the lorry came rumbling up. The next moment he was shouting to its driver, but because of the noise it was making I could not hear what he said.

I shall always believe that he asked the man for a light. Be that as it may, the lorry did not come to rest until two thirds of its body had cleared the car, and, when it did the chauffeur was not to be seen.

I leaped to my feet and had crossed the road in a flash.

As I went, I saw the chauffeur—six feet behind the Roquefort, addressing the man in the cab.

An instant later I was within the Roquefort, and the Roquefort was under way.

I fancy the chauffeur must have watched it, as a man in a dream. I had, of course, entered the car from the opposite side and, thanks to the presence of the lorry which was shaking all over and making a frightful din, he neither saw me nor heard the engine start : and I cannot imagine what explanation he offered of the translation of his charge.

But, though I had been very lucky, the worst was to come. I had counted on taking the chauffeur's dustcoat and cap, and so deceiving the ruffians whom I was to lead astray. But now I had no disguise. And Auntie Emma knew me—would never forget my face.

Suddenly I thought of my sun-glasses. These were still in my pocket: for all the glare, I had had too much to think of to put them on. *And Woking was wearing glasses.* Each day he drove out hatless and wearing his big-rimmed glasses, exactly like mine. . . .

I whipped on the glasses and chucked my hat on to the floor. Then I slammed the door behind me and put down my foot.

Berry's prevision was uncanny. At least, I assume that it was, for half way along "the switch-back" I saw a man up on a rise. And after he had watched me a moment, I saw him turn his head.

At once I began to slow down, and when I was fifty yards off I stopped in my tracks. Then, without more ado, I began to turn the Roquefort, with the obvious intention of returning the way I had come.

For a moment the man looked uncertain: then he turned and began to run into the hollow I could not see.

I continued to go about leisurely, keeping a vigilant eye on the tell-tale rise.

I was round and had gone fifty yards, when the closed car came storming like fury out of the dip.

I let the Roquefort go, and twenty seconds later I turned to the left.

When I saw the closed car follow, I could have thrown up my hat.

Such jubilation would have been premature.

The Roquefort was quite a good car, but she had neither the pace nor the manners of the Lowland, and though I could just hold the closed car, it was all I could do.

For such a state of affairs I was not prepared.

I had proposed, in my haste, to lead Auntie Emma a sprightly cross-country dance and then to leave him standing and run right away. And so I could have done—with the Lowland. As it was, it seemed unpleasantly likely that my victim was going to give me the run of my life.

I remember setting my teeth.

Somehow or other I must contrive to evade him for twenty or thirty miles. Otherwise, when he found that he had been fooled, he might return in the hope of retrieving his prey. And he might in fact retrieve it. Casca and Woking might very well be walking until they saw somebody coming whom they cared to ask for a lift. Or perhaps they would sit by the wayside and send the chauffeur off in search of a car. And, in any event, I had no desire to be caught. When he saw me again and perceived that I had beguiled him, Auntie Emma would be very cross. As Berry had said, it would be a pregnant moment. I certainly carried a pistol, but so did he : and I fancy he knew how to use one much better than I. Besides, he had two men with him, but I was alone.

I thickened the spark a little, swooped at a sudden hollow and coaxed the speedometer needle to sixty-nine. . . .

It is not my purpose to set out the chase in detail, though I shall remember each minute as long as I live.

The cars were evenly matched. Sometimes I drew away : at other times the closed car was not twenty paces behind : and once, when a waggon had balked me, Auntie Emma was actually alighting when, with two wheels up on the bank, I was able to pass the obstruction and make my escape.

I tried to read the legends the sign-posts bore, but because of our pace and the poor way in which they were painted, I could not make them out. It follows that after five minutes I had but the faintest idea of my direction and none at all of the country which I was to cross. Of shut level-crossings I went in most deadly fear, but here the gods were kindly, for I never met one : a flock of sheep, however, bade fair to shorten my life and lost me the longest lead which I held that hot afternoon. By hook and crook I had gained three hundred yards, but when I was clear of the sheep the closed car was ten yards behind, and if an upgradient had followed, I must have been caught.

I should say that I had expected that whilst we were in view of other wayfarers, I should not be pressed : but here I was completely mistaken : and though to this day I cannot tell what line my pursuers would have taken if they had boarded the Roquefort when we had not the scene to ourselves, they were plainly prepared for that contingency, for no matter what traffic we encountered, they gave me no rest.

Again and again I doubled to right or left, but the roads were undressed, and even if, when I turned, I was just out of sight, the dust which I raised declared which way I had gone. Still, if I had no good fortune, I had no bad. I might have met some fatal obstruction before I had covered a league. As it was—often enough, I confess, by the skin of my teeth—for more than twenty-five minutes I led that closed car across country I did not know.

Then I saw a townlet coming and gave myself up for lost.

The place was plainly ancient and promised most narrow streets, and, as if that were not enough, such as would enter must cross some stream by a bridge at the head of which stood a gateway not ten feet wide.

Vainly I sought for some turning which I could take.

The closed car was hard on my heels—not sixty yards off. The bridge was clear, but I could not see through the gateway : and, once I was on the bridge, unless the gateway was clear, I was caught like a rat in a trap.

Still, there was nothing for it : not even a cart-track ran out of that strip of road.

I confess I flashed on to the bridge with my heart in my mouth.

As I came to the gateway, the closed car passed on to the bridge. . . .

I was through—in the nick of time.

As I left the portal, another car met and passed me and took my place in the jaws.

I heard the squealing of brakes. . . .

Truly, out of the eater had come forth meat.

Blessing my unwitting friend, I darted between two gigs and flung up the coarse-paved street. This bent at once to the left and I followed it round. Some fifty paces ahead I could see that it curled again, but I swerved up a cobbled alley and round the flank of a church. Behind this, a twisting lane argued a way to the country which only the peasants used and twenty seconds later I was dropping through sweet-smelling lime-trees and down to a wooden-floored bridge. As I swung to the right at cross roads, I glanced behind : but, the way I had come was empty, except for a yoke of oxen—a tiny speck in the distance, swaying out of the sunshine into the shade of the limes.

There can be no doubt that in that pretty, old townlet the fox was lost. Thanks to the stranger who blocked the jaws of the gate-way and thanks to the well-worn cobbles that kept no dust, I there made good my escape : but though I might well have rested, for the last half hour I had sailed so close to the wind that I covered another ten miles before I drew rein and I scoured the landscape behind me a dozen times before I slowed up at a sign-post, to learn where I was.

I was quite prepared to find that I was off the map. When you drive, as I had, at random as hard as you can, in forty-five minutes you can be properly lost.

But my run of luck was not ended.

I was seven miles from the town at which Berry and I had given the enemy lunch.

CHAPTER IX

Pray Silence for Berry

"Go on," said Jill greedily.

I sat back in my chair and looked round.

"I will," said I. "But I'm not at all certain that what I did after that was not the act of a fool."

"Sure to have been," said Berry. "Never mind. Lay the facts before me, and I'll put you out of my pain."

"Be quiet," said everyone.

"Well, I drove to the town, and left the car at the first decent garage I saw. I told the people to wash her and mend the punctured tube. Then I sent a wire to Count Blucher—whose name was, of course, on the dash—saying I had found her deserted some ten miles off and that, as my car was *en panne*, I had left my chauffeur behind and ventured to use the Roquefort to carry me in. I added the address of the garage and signed the telegram 'Rose'. Then I put off my glasses, walked to another garage and chartered a car. And, as you know, I was back here at half past six."

"Sheer insanity," said Berry. "What you should have done was to set her on fire. Then you could have crawled to the coast and stowed away in some tramp that was bound for Japan."

"It's quite all right," said Jonah. "What he's done will stifle inquiry. When once they've got the car back, who's going to take any trouble to find the thief? And now, if you please, let Berry take up the tale. We'll pay the compliments later, but I am most terribly anxious to know where we stand."

Berry pushed back his plate, and I, who had eaten nothing, began my meal.

"You may remember," said my brother-in-law, "that I was to undertake the simple and fascinating duty, first of locating Casca and Woking, and then of drawing nigh unto the swine, unseen, unheard, undreamt of and generally unbeknownst. Well, you've heard that the heath was a wash-out, and so, with the gravest misgivings, I turned to the wood.

"I should like to be able to say that I moved through that wood like a snake. But that would be misleading. I went in fear and trembling, and, in spite of all my precautions, I made so much noise that if I wanted to listen I had to stand perfectly still. Even then my heart and my lungs embarrassed the ear. The only wonder is that Casca and Woking didn't come to meet me, to see what it was. The climax came when I caught my foot in a trailer and utterly ruined, by crushing, a beautiful bramble-bush. I think it's bound to die. You see, it left most of its thorns in me. It was while I was fobbing off Insanity—by which I mean, resisting a very natural desire to withdraw, screaming, re-enter the Lowland and burst—that I perceived a small path, some four inches wide. No sooner seen, than trodden. I minced along it, like Agag, as fast as I dared.

"Here I should like to say that I was not alone. I was attended by an escort of about five hundred flies. My clothes didn't interest them : what they liked was the nude. And, as I'd left my hat in the Lowland, they'd plenty of room. I will say they stuck to the rules. They had to be on me one second before they bit. If I got them off in that time, they had to begin again. Of course I won sometimes. . . .

"All at once I heard some movement directly ahead. Hardly daring to breathe, I stole forward. . . . Then the wood came to an end, and I saw the tarmac before me and the black and green of the Roquefort six paces away.

"Well, of course, I turned round and went back—accompanied by the flies. At least, I now knew where I was, and it seemed extremely likely that I was treading the path which Casca and Woking had taken on leaving the car. I therefore redoubled my precautions, by which I mean that I protruded my tongue and listened to the rumble of a lorry which effectually swamped all sound for the radius of a quarter of a mile.

"Now how far I went, I don't know : but after two or three minutes I saw a little clearing ahead. And there were Casca and Woking, *the latter with a map in his hand.*

"I can't say I got hot all over, for my pores had been working full blast from the moment I entered the wood : but I can honestly say I forgot the flies. You see, the incredible was happening— just as it happened at Tours. There were the two conspiring—

exchanging the information which we were mad to secure. But here there was no gutter, and I was twenty yards off. When the flies didn't buzz too loud, I could hear the murmur of their voices —but that was all.

"Well, I fell back a pace or two and cast a frenzied glance round. *And then I saw my gutter*—like you do in the fairy-tales. Why my brain didn't seize with excitement, I'm damned if I know. There it was—a sort of groove in the ground, about two feet deep : a drain or a gully or something, perhaps the bed of a rill. And it ran towards the clearing by the side of the path.

"A moment later the flies and I were out of sight in this ditch. It *was* the bed of a rill which was nearly dry. The water was only just moving—under the slime. This was in perfect condition, rich, glutinous and fragrant, and the flies got so excited that they forgot the rules and bit me as fast as they could. I have reason to believe that they were now reinforced by large numbers of gnats and other less elementary insects with whose quiet enjoyment of the slime, which no doubt was affording them board and lodging, I was interfering. However, I couldn't help that. I dragged myself down that drain at three miles an hour. I don't think I made much noise—half the time I slid on the slime—and I knew that I couldn't be seen, for the drain was overhung with brambles and, after a little, with bracken as thick as you please. When the bracken began I knew I was out of the wood, so I lay dead still and listened : but, though I could hear them plainly, I couldn't make out their words.

"I went on as fast as I dared, when all of a sudden I heard Woking's voice so close that I give you my word I thought he was speaking to me. They must have moved or something, but of course I didn't know that, and it gave me the shock of my life."

Here Berry took out a note-book, turned to the page he wanted and bent the book open wide.

"You see," he explained, "the moment the coast was clear I wrote down what I'd heard. I was desperately afraid of forgetting : but the more I wrote down, the more began to come back.

" 'Fair does,' said Woking. 'Fair does. You'll admit I've studied your wishes in every particular : and now all I ask is that you should meet me halfway. Halfway House, Mr. Palk. I can't say fairer than that.'

" 'Fairer?' cries Casca. 'It was not fair in the least. Oh, no. You are to laugh in your sleeves and I am to 'ave all the dangers to carry the stuff.'

" 'But there *is* no danger,' said Woking. 'I've told you again and again. I'd tour in France for a year with the goods in my grip. And never know a bad night. But take them out I cannot. They're laying for me at the ports. And they had my picture at every door to this country before I'd been off the dock for twenty-four hours.'

" '*Mon Dieu*,' squeaked Casca. 'An' why 'ave you not tell me this? I 'ave no idea, of course. Ah, *mon Dieu*, I am lost. 'Ere I was making my friens with a well-known thief, telling all the worl' 'ow well we have been for 'ow long——'

" 'Now don't go up,' said Woking. 'I've not been watched. The French—they never do that. If America asked where I was, they'd say "somewhere in France". And that's as much as they know. But they *do* know that, because they've seen me come in and they haven't seen me go out. There's a ring-fence round this country—and that's a fact.'

"Well, Casca wailed and Woking kept picking him up. At last—

" 'It's all too easy,' said Woking. 'You get fed with the char-à-banc : so you let it go on without you and take your ease. After lunch, you guess you'll go for a drive. So you hire a car and drive through *ici* and on up to Halfway House. The driver's well known to the Customs—spends his life taking visitors up and down. But there shouldn't many on Friday. And there you are. After a stroll you go back. And the next day you jump a char-à-banc going in the opposite way.'

"There was a little silence, during which I perceived a wasps' nest six inches above my head. I'd thought that the flies seemed *distrait*. . . . I don't think they get on with wasps. And of course I was occupying the air-port of this particular nest. They swooped all round me to get in—millions of them. Jostling one another in the mouth. Must have been a rush-hour or something. I was digesting these very compelling circumstances and trying to work out, 'if four hornets can kill a horse, how many wasps does it take to do in a man?' when Casca picked up the ball.

"What he said is of no real import, but he gave me the clear impression of a man who is giving way. He let the rendezvous go and started to jib at the date. Woking was just beginning to speak of the boat he must catch, when I heard someone running like blazes the way I had come. The next moment they let out a yell.

" 'Monsieur, monsieur, where are you?'

"I can't pretend to reproduce in detail what then took place. For one thing, my brain was bending beneath the stress of remembering what I'd heard, and, for another, only a seismograph could ever have recorded such a frenzied blend of panic, incoherence and wrath. The chauffeur supplied the incoherence, Casca the panic and Woking the peremptory wrath. Of course I could guess what had happened, but the chauffeur kept howling about magic, Casca kept calling upon God, and Woking, who knows no French, kept alternately cursing them silly and demanding the truth. At last he wrung out of Casca that someone had taken the car and they blundered off through the greenwood back to the road. And none too soon for Arthur. Two less unobservant wasps had noticed my nose and were investigating that member with every circumstance of suspicion. Need I say I rejoined the flies, who were waiting six feet away?

"Well, there you are. I've told you as much as I heard. Unless the arrangements are altered, at Halfway House on Friday— to-morrow week, I assume—Casca is going to part with the stuff he stole. And that, after lunch. We know it all—every detail. The only question is, *Where is Halfway House?*

"It's plainly beyond the Customs. Woking as good as said so. Which means that it's outside France. You see, they mentioned no name. And that was sheer misfortune. But all the time Woking was talking he had the map in his hand. And no doubt he traced for Casca the route he desired him to take."

"Sure he said '*ici*'?" said Jonah.

"Positive," said Berry. "I thought some town's name was coming, and my ears were three times life-size. Why he didn't say 'here', I don't know : but Casca's English is so filthy that whenever he can, I suppose, he tries to jump into French. Oh, no, it's painfully clear. 'You drive through here,' he said, 'and on up to Halfway House.' And as he spoke, he was tracing the road on the map.

"Of course you see their game. Woking goes out of the country the day before. He's stopped at the Customs and searched, but he hasn't got any stuff so they pass him through. The next day he does Casca's stunt *from the opposite side*. Hires a car and drives up to Halfway House—to look at the view. And there's his old friend Casca, who's come up to do the same. . . .

"Well, as I say, there you are. Thanks to your dazzling foresight, we're practically home. Practically. But, unless there's a place called *Ici* . . ."

For what it was worth, there and then we looked at the *Guide Michelin*. Issy-l'Evêque was the only possible place : and that lay far from the frontier—more than a hundred miles.

"Let it go for the moment," said Jonah, "and I'll wind up the debate. My report is of very slight moment, and after the two we've heard it'll fall pretty flat, But it ties up one or two ends.

"When I saw the Lowland before me, I had the sense to pull up. Never mind what I thought had happened, because I was wrong. But I breasted that rise on my feet with my heart in my mouth.

"What did I see ? I saw a lorry at rest by the side of the road and, standing beside it, four figures, engaged in a furious alter-cation which was illustrated copiously by gestures of an alarming sort. That two were Casca and Woking, I saw at a glance, and, as you may well believe, I thought that the game was up. I had no doubt about it. Auntie Emma had had his way. I assumed, of course, that the lorry was hiding the Roquefort. It was big enough to have hidden a furniture van.

"Well, I've learned not to give up hope until the sentence upon you has been carried out : besides, I could see no reason for letting Casca know that we were around : so, before we did anything else, we got the two cars under cover—that is to say, out of sight. By Jove, it was as well we did so, for after devoting five more minutes to hatred and blindness of heart, to my amazement, the four clambered on to the lorry which started to pound towards us for all it was worth. Then for the first time I saw that the Roquefort was gone, and a wholly unreasonable hope began to lift up its head.

"We watched them go by. I'm glad to say Casca was sweating, and the chauffeur looked tired of life. But what hit me between the eyes was that Woking seemed full of cheer. And Casca, although he looked worried—well, he wasn't needing a stretcher to carry him in. . . . Then Berry came out of the wood and put us wise."

He put down his pipe and laid a hand on my arm.

"Well, of course, we went out after you. I was blinded with admiration for what you'd done : but, if I'd been there, I'd never have let you do it, for if Auntie Emma had caught you, he'd have cut up extremely rough."

"And Walker?" said I.

"Faked wire," said my cousin. "I saw it. It said. *Arriving Lalanne* 1.50 *please meet.* It was unsigned, but, as that's the way their guests seem to treat the Bluchers, Walker was sent for and told to be at the junction to meet the train. And, as Lalanne's forty miles off, he was gone from Loumy before we appeared on the scene. He was worried stiff about us, but all he could do was to tell his substitute to take the Roquefort and show him exactly the way which Woking wanted to go."

"But won't they get excited?" said Adèle. "What happened when Walker got back without any guests?"

"Happily, nothing," said Jonah. "The secret is safe. No one at Loumy will dream there was anything wrong. Even Walker, with all he knows, had never so much as attempted to do the sum. Of such is life at Loumy. Even when no one got out of the train at Lalanne, it never entered his head that the telegram was a fake. He simply assumed that the self-invited guests had found somewhere better to go. And if he suspected nothing, you may lay that nobody else will give the matter a thought.

"And now let's sum up. Our time here has not been wasted. We've ridden off Auntie Emma and we've won the information we came to get. I admit this will have to be construed : but there I think Susie may help. In any event, we're well over the biggest jump, and now I'm perfectly certain we're going to get home."

"All thanks to your training," said I.

"And your riding," said Jonah. "And Berry's. Never mind. It's what we all of us worked for, and now it's come off. And now I'm going to suggest that we don't discuss till to-morrow what Woking said. If once we start, we shan't be able to stop, and what we all of us need is a full night's rest. And then there's another thing. Auntie Emma went down to-day, but that doesn't mean that he's not going to try again. Woking's got to drive to the station. And so has Casca. And I think we should be in the background—just to see justice done. Of course he may leave them alone, because he may be uncertain which of the two has the pearls : and if he stopped the wrong one, the game would be up."

"That's right," said Piers. "That's why he struck to-day. It's the first time they've been together. Will Casca go to the station to see Woking off?"

"Not he," said Berry. "The theft of the Roquefort frightened him out of his life. He couldn't talk straight for sheer terror. His tongue was cleaving to the roof of his ugly mouth."

"I agree," said I. "Until he leaves Loumy, he'll never go out again. Of course by now he must know that the theft of the Roquefort had nothing to do with the pearls. No other conclusion will hold water. All the same, as Berry says, it gave him the shock of his life and—well, I don't know what his blood-pressure is, but I hardly think he'll court any more excitement after this afternoon."

"He clearly had the pearls on him," said Piers.

"That goes without saying," said Berry, stifling a yawn.

There was a little silence.

The faintest flavour of regret had stolen into our cup. The Padua pearls had been there—right under our hand : we might have had them—for the taking : had we been able to consult, we almost certainly should : but Berry had had no one to consult with, and to take a step which over and over again we had condemned in council was naturally more than he dared.

I adjusted the shade of a candle and lighted a cigarette.

The gentle glow of the candles upon the cloth was lending the parlour a comfort not always found in the *salon* ablaze with electric light. Behind Berry, the open window made a black square of darkness and ushered the cool, night air. Without, though I could not see it, a jolly orchard sloped to a hanging wood, and there some owl was crying to point a peace which once was a feature of the country, but now, before the drive of progress, is fast becoming extinct. This was absolute : and after the burden and heat of the restless day, made us a medicine rarer than any wine.

"I wish I'd been there," said Jill. "I'd love to have heard them talking. I don't mind wasps."

"Nor do I," said Berry. "The little dears. But I think it's a mistake to trespass upon a goodwill which my experience has shown to be curiously fugitive. Besides, I can't help feeling that you were better here. I don't say that your personal charms are not proof against slime. Indeed, I believe them to be invulnerable. But when you couldn't hear Casca, you'd have asked him to raise his voice."

"I shouldn't,"—indignantly.

"If you ask me," said I, "she'd have been so interested in the wasps' nest that she'd have missed nearly all that was said."

"I don't think I should," said Jill, leaning over to gaze at the book. "But I do love nests. I love the way they keep going in and out."

Berry shuddered.

"*Chacun à son goût*," he said. "Myself, I found that spectacle extremely sinister. Of course, for all I know, they may have been the same ones going in and out all the time. You know. Like a stage army. But that particular exercise suggested the presence of a lively fount of malevolence which was inexhaustible."

Adèle sat back in her chair and laced her delicate fingers behind her head.

"I do give you best," she said, "for writing it down. I should never had dreamed of doing that. Not until it was too late, I mean. I do think that was a brainwave."

"It shows," said Jonah, "a thoroughly practical mind."

"To be perfectly honest," said Berry, "that action was dictated by fear. It's bad enough to have to rack one's memory oneself : but the thought of having you five racking my memory for me for seven days was so unnerving that I lay in the midst of the bracken and fairly spilt it down." Here he leaned forward and picked up his precious book. "Not much to look at," he said, "but then the rarest editions seldom are. Of course my hands were slimy. And then again I used it to swat the flies. The moment I left the wasps' nest they picked me up. If I'd been decomposed they couldn't have shown more interest. They simply swarmed upon me, and all the time I was writing they tried to see what I said. Of course I corrected this impertinence. I killed about a quarter per cent. and you'll find them down." With the air of a verger, he pointed to an eloquent smear. "That's where Baldwin the Bestial came to a timely end. Here Percy the Persistent slipped up. And there I

delight to record that Oscar the Odious laid down his sodden life.
Hence the condition of the volume. All the same if it were put up
to auction, I guess that Auntie Emma would run it up. Let's send
it to him for Christmas. And the girls can contribute a book-
marker with an appropriate text. 'Pearls before slime', for
instance."

"I'll take it now," said a voice. "Sit perfectly still."

We all disobeyed the injunction—all, that is, except Berry, who
sat like a rock. The rest of us lifted our eyes or turned our heads,
to see, framed in the window behind my brother-in-law, the
shadowy form of the man we thought we had foiled.

I shall never forget that moment or the bitter chill of the iron
which seemed to have entered my soul. I cannot say I was dazed. I
was paralysed with horror at our appalling folly in letting the
enemy in.

As we had done to Casca, Auntie Emma had done to us. But
while Casca had made our way incredibly hard, we had as good as
strewn roses on Auntie Emma's path.

I have no defence to offer. Such, I suppose, is the way of the
amateur. But the fact remains that, engrossed in our efforts to slip
under Casca's guard, we had, like so many madmen, laid ourselves
needlessly open to the other's most deadly arm. At Nay we had been
very careful : we had looked to doors and windows before we had
opened our mouths. But at Mose we had dropped these precautions, and now, in the moment of triumph, our rival had struck.
The man whose tail we had twisted, over whom we were in the
very act of exulting, had quietly strolled into our presence and was
waiting there, in the shadows, to take up the prize we had strained
every nerve to secure.

The winnings of all our labour were bound in that little book.
The dangerous work in Paris, our efforts at Tours, the nightmare
week from which we had just emerged, Fluff's instinct and Susie's
wit, Jonah's brilliant strategy, Walker's goodwill—all these things
and others had gone to produce those pages, that rare dispatch.
And now, almost before we had read it, we had as good as pressed
it into the enemy's hand.

"Now isn't that nice?" said Berry. "We were just speaking of
you."

"I heard you," said Auntie Emma, and laughed.

I glanced about me.

The faintest of smiles hung on Adèle's proud face : two bright red spots were burning in Jill's fresh cheeks : Piers' sensitive nostrils were quivering like those of an eager horse.

"Did you ? Good," said Berry. "What colour would you like the book-marker? Black and green—like the Roquefort?"

"I guess I can smile," said the other. "Put your hands on the table, Mansel."

As Jonah obeyed, he cocked a leg over the sill.

"When last we saw you," said Berry, "you were running after a car. Not the Roquefort. Another make. I do hope the exercise was beneficial. What have you been doing since then?"

"I'll tell you," said Auntie Emma. "I've been letting some ——fools go out and get me some news."

"I see," said Berry. "I thought, perhaps you'd been getting together again. You know. Sitting on the step of a car, waiting for someone or other who doesn't arrive."

"They do—in the end," said Auntie Emma. He swung himself into the room. " 'Bringing their sheaves with them'."

Again he laughed. Then he came up to the table, keeping his right hand raised. For a second or so he stood between Berry and Jill. Then, with the quickest movement I ever saw made, he whipped the book from the cloth and stood as before. He had not so much as looked down, but his fingers never fumbled and his pistol hand was as steady as though his wrist were supported by some invisible wire.

As he stepped back to the window—

"Beautiful," said Berry. "I shouldn't like to sit next to you in a tram."

"Don't," said Auntie Emma. "Keep your distance. Take your insurance money and go right home. You've got in my way and I've passed it. But I shouldn't do it again. You've put those pearls on the market—a market where you can't deal. If you weren't ——fools, you'd know that. And I give you my word I'll have them as sure as I'm standing here. And God help the one that butts in. Or the two. Or the three. It won't faze me. You see, I've got a motto—'Let the dead bury their dead'."

"What a very charming sentiment," said Berry. "But it won't

faze us, either. Frightfulness never did. Besides, we've a foolish feeling that the pearls still belong to us. If somebody pinched your thimble—the one you keep for Epsom, I mean—and, when you asked for it back, said it had gone to some market in which you couldn't deal, you know I can't help feeling that—well, you'd argue the point."

With one leg over the sill—

"Not I," said Auntie Emma. "The knife don't argue with the butter. It takes what it wants—the same as I'm doing now. And if I were you I'd get a foolish feeling that I mean what I say. And there, maybe, Mansel'll help you. You saw his hands go flat when I spoke the word. If you don't believe me, come on. But the next one that gets in my way, I'll put him out."

"As you did to-day, for instance. And that's just what I said to the flies : but d'you think they cared? Never mind. See you at *Ici*. Now where would you say that was? I know it's where Baldwin went out, but I don't mean that. I mean, whereabouts on the map. Oh, and I knew there was something I wanted to ask you. If a hiccough and a half is no earthly, how many years can you get for——"

"Blow out the candles," said Jonah, and leaped for the door.

"No, no !" shrieked Jill, and I caught hold of his arm.

"Let him alone," I said. "He's bound to see you first and he'll have you cold."

My cousin drew in his breath. Then he put his hands in his pockets and lay back against the wall.

"Perhaps you're right," he said quietly. And then, "I'm very sorry. It's all my fault, of course. I must have been out of my mind to let him in."

"Rot," said Adèle. "If anyone is to blame it's me and Jill. We've had nothing whatever to do but hold the fort, and it might just have entered our heads that the ground-floor back was hardly the place to consult." She threw back her head and clapped her hands to her eyes. "Oh, I could weep to think that we——"

A stifled sob from the other side of the table told us that gray-eyed Jill was waiting upon no words. As Adèle flew to her side, I saw Berry open his mouth. Then he shut it again and rose to his feet.

When he had closed the window—

"Where's Carson?" he said.

"Asleep," said Jonah. "The man was on his last legs."

"Quite so," said Berry. "Well, let's adjourn, shall we? Before we do anything else."

Though no one answered him, we acted upon his advice. Our leaving of the room was tragic. The blow was not a knock-out, but Auntie Emma had hit us over the heart. Speech would have eased the situation, although there was nothing to be said : but even this was denied to us, until we should be out of earshot of all the world. In a silence big with gloom we passed upstairs to the Duchess of Padua's room. This gave on to the road. After a careful survey, we made fast the shutters and windows and shut the door.

Whilst I subscribed to these precautions, I found them futile. They had, of course, to be taken—as a matter of form : but now the stable was empty—the only horse that we had, had been stolen away. And when Berry, who had felt in the wardrobe and crawled underneath the bed, recommended that Piers should play sentry without the door, I know I suggested curtly that he should do so himself.

"I can't," said Berry. "I've got a statement to make. It's not altogether relevant, but it bears on the matter in hand. What's more, it's rather urgent. I'm sorry to be so trying, because I know how you feel—a little more than tired and less than kind. But at least he did no murder : he's bruised our hearts, of course : but these things are sent to try us. No Rose without a thorn. Piers, my lad, breathe through your nose, if you must, but go and do as I say."

In silence Piers crossed the room. As the door closed behind him—

"Well, you take it damned well," said Jonah. "I must confess if I'd picked a hatful of plums and then had to watch it lifted from, literally, under my nose, I don't think I should be handing out Moody and Sankey's balm."

A sob from his little sister suggested that the proffered specific had done her no manner of good.

"Now, not so fast," said Berry. "What's happened is most annoying."

" 'Annoying'?" we screamed.

"Well, provoking, then. I don't care which word you use. I repeat, it's been most provoking, but it might be so very much worse. Oh, incalculably. In fact—excuse me." He took out a handkerchief and carefully mopped his face. Then he indicated a flower which was printed upon the silk. " 'There is pansies, that's for thought.' But, believe me, there are some thoughts that make a man give at the knees."

I looked from him to Jonah, and then to Adèle. Both were frowning faintly and staring at Berry, as though he had lost his wits.

I swallowed.

"I don't understand you," I said.

"I'm not surprised," said Berry "I hardly comprehend myself. It's a mercy I'm still coherent. You see, I've had a great shock."

"Well, so have we all," said Jonah.

"Don't you believe it," said Berry. "Compared with what I've been through, you've been on the roundabout."

With an arm about Jill, Adèle averted her eyes. It was clear that she found this pleasantry out of time.

"Well, if that's the truth," she sighed, "you covered it up very well. The way you took the brute on was simply superb. I confess I couldn't think straight for mortification and rage."

"Fear," said Berry. "Pure funk. If I had stopped talking, I should have burst into tears."

"Rot," said everyone.

"Now don't contradict me," said Berry. "I'm—I'm over-wrought. One harsh look, and I shall scream and get into the wardrobe. I tell you, I'm all to bits. I must have a large beer presently. Several large beers. But first to the matter in hand." He swallowed violently. "You see—you see, it's like this. Auntie Emma—God bless him—has got the invaluable book. Well, that's a very painful reflection. But, you see, though he doesn't know it, the record which that book contains is not altogether complete. *Something else happened in the wood* which, as luck will have it, I didn't write down. It's not that it isn't important, because it is. But, mercifully, I didn't record it. And so, in spite of all, there is one item of news which so far is ours alone."

He stopped there and moistened his lips.

For the others I cannot answer : but I know that I was regarding him, saucer-eyed.

"Now when I say that, I meant it. Nobody knows this secret. *Not even Woking or Casca.* It's ours alone."

He stepped to the door and opened it half an inch.

"All clear, Piers?"

"Yes," said Piers.

"Good," said Berry. "Stay there until I call you. I shan't be long."

He shut the door and turned.

He took two steps towards us.

Then his hand went into a pocket and brought out the Padua pearls.

CHAPTER X

A Lesson in French

Adèle was the first to recover the power of speech.

"And—and you sat there," she breathed. "Sat there with the man behind you and pulled his leg."

"I had to," said Berry. "If I hadn't talked, I should have gone out of my mind. 'I'll have those pearls,' he said, 'as sure as I'm standing here.' And when he said it, he wasn't six inches away. Talk about burning my pocket, they damned well scorched my chest. If he'd touched me, he must have felt them. A pint and a half of filberts take up a lot of room. I've been waiting for one of you to ask me what was wrong with my coat."

What else was said I cannot remember, but I know that we all gave way and abandoned ourselves, like Mænads, to an ecstasy of delight. These rites were observed in silence, for our recent lesson had frightened us out of our lives : but the pearls were about Jill's shoulders and Jill was laughing and crying in Jonah's arms, and Adèle and Berry and I were dancing a *pas de trois* which would, I am sure, have found favour in Dionysus' eyes.

Then we had in Piers and told him the truth, while Jonah took his place in the passage and I kept asking myself if the thing was a dream. Then Carson was roused and came stumbling to hear the news and, when he was posted in the passage, Berry sat down on the bed and took up his tale.

"It's all due to the wasps," he said. "But for their nest, I should have lain in that gully till Casca and Co had had time to get back to the road. But, as I have told you, my trespasss had been remarked : the wasps that had found my nose were commenting audibly upon that organ in anything but favourable terms : and so I crawled into the bracken the moment that Casca and Woking entered the wood.

"Now Casca ran third. Mark that. The chauffeur and Woking were leading, and Casca ran third. That was to be expected : and I know it was so, because through the trees, I could see his white flannel bags. I was on my hands and knees, peering. All of a sudden I saw him falter and stop. Then, to my horror, the blackguard came pelting back.

"I fairly lay down on that ground. Thanks to the bracken, I must have been well out of sight : but I'd no idea where he was going and, for all I knew, I might be full in his path. You see, I'd made up my mind that Casca was doing a bunk. But there I was wrong.

"On the left of the path, by the clearing, was standing a hollow oak. Casca burst up to this, shoved a hand in his pocket, gave one frenzied look round—*and posted 'the pearls.* Dropped them clean into the tree." He produced a wash-leather bag. "Here's the wallet or satchel in which they lay. Then he squirted back up the path as hard as he could.

"Well, there you are. It doesn't want much working out. Convinced that the theft of the car was nothing less than a prelude to the theft of the pearls, Casca decided to offload. No doubt, as he passed it, he'd noticed the hollow tree, and at once it occurred to him that this would make an excellent safe. No one on earth would look there : and, when he was searched and found empty, the thieves *and* Woking would simply assume that he'd left the pearls at Loumy : and when the storm was over *and Woking was gone*, he could come back and collect them whenever he pleased.

"To tell you the truth, I think it was a very good plan, and I very much doubt if my brain would have worked so well. He didn't *like* leaving them there. Nobody would. And I'm not surprised that when he was up on the lorry he was wearing a worried look. But he knew in his heart they were safe—that only the flora and fauna had seen what he did. All the same, he'll be a shade *distrait*, until he goes back to collect them . . . until—he—goes—back. . . .

"And this is where I get off. I took the pearls out of the tree, because, to my mind, only a dangerous lunatic would have refrained. But I did it with open eyes. Before he leaves Loumy, Casca is going back. And, when he find the pearls gone, I can't help feeling he won't turn up at *Ici* to-morrow week."

There was a thoughtful silence.

My brother-in-law's conclusions seemed to me very sound.

The moment he found that the hollow tree was empty, Casca would realize that someone had seen what he did. He would know that somebody knew him for what he was—a common or garden thief. So far as he was concerned, Woking and Halfway House would, thereupon, cease to exist, and the rest of the stolen goods would lie in their safe-deposit for, perhaps, another three years.

"All or nothing," said Piers, swinging the gorgeous rope. "We must put them back in the oak. I can't take these things at the price of Daphne's bracelets and——"

"Which is absurd," said Adèle. "This isn't *roulette*. Supposing we can't place *Ici*. We've actually recovered the most important jewels. We can't possibly stake them again on the chance of winning the balance of what we lost."

"I entirely agree," said Berry. "In fact I flatly refuse to let them go back. Quite apart from locating *Ici*, in view of what happened this evening we should be out of our minds. Besides, I've suffered enough. I can bear the loss of the book. But I'm damned if I'm going to let you——"

"Let's get the thing clear," said I. "Of course we keep the pearls. But what we want to ensure is that, in spite of their loss, Casca will still go to *Ici* according to plan."

"You're mad," said Berry. "He won't be fit to travel for three or four months."

"Assume he survives," said I. "Of course he's lost the cream, but he's still got the other stuff. And Woking will be glad of those bracelets—any fence would. Only two things may stop Casca from going on. One is pride. He may be ashamed to confess that he's lost the pearls. And the other is fear."

"That's what'll stop him," said Jonah. "Stop him dead. The knowledge that somebody saw him deposit those pearls. Their loss will shock him—send him half out of his mind: but the knowledge that somebody knows him for what he is will turn his black heart to water, and he'll no more turn up at *Ici* than he'll go and give himself up. I don't want to harp upon this, but I tell you I've seen it before. That's why a fellow like Casca's so devilish hard to take. He is above suspicion. And the instant he thinks that he *isn't* above suspicion, he drops everything and stops dead."

"You mean," said Adèle, "that if, for instance, he'd simply lost the pearls—let them fall into a river or something like that, he'd still turn up at *Ici*, wherever that is?"

"I quite think he would," said Jonah. "He'd pitch some tale or other, and there might be a bit of a breeze. Woking would be very sticky. And he might refuse to purchase the other stuff. But if I were in Casca's place, I should try it on. Half a loaf, you know."

"Then the thing to do," said Adèle, "is to lock the safe. If we could do that, he wouldn't know they were gone."

"Quite so," said Berry. "The trouble is this isn't a fairy-tale. If it was, we'd go back to the wood, show every tree an empty beer-bottle, and when Casca rolled up he'd find himself in a forest of hollow oaks."

"What about a snake?" said Jill. "Couldn't we get a snake and put it in the tree?"

"The guardian of the pearls?" said Berry. "Yes, that's all right, but supposing the snake refuses to take it on. We can put it into the hole—at least, I can't, but somebody else can—but who says it's going to stay there? It isn't. The moment our back is turned it's going to get out. And how are we going to find one within twelve hours? I'll lay you Casca goes back as soon as he's wolfed his lunch. And in any event I'm not going to range the country, looking for snakes. It's contrary to my principles."

"How large was the hole?" said Peirs.

Berry shrugged his shoulders.

"About half a yard square," he said.

"And deep?"

"Good and deep," said Berry. "Very nearly the length of my arm."

"Then I've got it," said Piers excitedly. "The wasps' nest. We must put the wasps to sleep, dig out the nest and put it into the oak."

"By thunder!" cried Jonah. "The very thing." He glanced at his watch. "Eleven o'clock. We can do it. They won't be stirring till dawn. But first we must knock up a chemist to get the stuff." He stepped to the door. "Carson, both cars, please. And a pick and a couple of spades. And I'd like a pair of bellows. D'you think there are some in the house?"

"There's a pair in the kitchen, sir."

"Good," said Jonah. "We'll be along in five minutes." He

closed the door and surveyed us with shining eyes. "And now I may say that we are going to have some fun. Talk about locking the safe."

Berry lay back on the bed and closed his eyes.

"Well, I wish you luck," he said. "You can count me out of this show. I don't believe in dragooning a nest of wasps. If they'd wanted to dwell in the oak, the presumption is they'd have done so : and to forcibly remove thirty thousand armed and venomous swine is to my mind not so much tempting Providence as twisting that deity's tail."

"But they'll be anaesthetized," said Piers.

Berry sat up.

"I know," he said, "I know. Hence the bellows. I daresay some will succumb. But they can't all be built the same : and if only one per cent don't take—well, if three hundred wasps get down to it, they can make their influence felt. No, no. I don't mind coming along. I'll wait somewhere near the saw-mill. And if Auntie Emma should follow, I'll tell him the nature of your business. If he believes me, I'll bet he turns round and goes back."

"I'm sorry," said Jonah, "but we shall want you with us. You've got to show us the nest."

Berry started to his feet.

"Nonsense," he said. "You can't miss it, Straight down the drain, and it's the first on your right."

"The first what?" said Piers.

"The first nest, of course," said Berry.

"That's no earthly," said I. "They won't be moving now, and a bank like that has got any number of holes. We don't want to dig out some innocent water-rat."

In a silence big with laughter, my brother-in-law took a short turn.

"You see?" said Jonah. "You're indispensable."

With a gesture of patent desperation—

"You know, I think it's cruel," said Berry. "Mucking animals about like this."

Adèle and Piers dissolved into wails of mirth.

Jonah approached the dissentient and took his arm.

"Have you forgotten," he said, "the days when you were a child? Don't you remember Haycock, who used to take the wasps' nests and bring them round to the White Ladies for us to see?"

"Vividly," said Berry. "The first time he brought one was on my seventh birthday. I think I liked it best of all my presents— for nearly an hour. Then without any warning I was stung twelve several times."

"Exactly," said Jonah. "Young as I was, I still remember the noise. And why were you stung?"

"Ah," said Berry. "Why? Because I was present. That's why. I hadn't done them any harm. But I was available. That's why a wasp is so dangerous. He visits the sins of the——"

"You were stung," said Jonah, "because Haycock had only doped them. Byng, the second gardener, found him that night in the village and punched his head. On your own admission you played with the nest for an hour. And that at ten in the morning. Which shows they were out of action for ten or eleven hours." He turned to Jill. "Now you go to bed, my darling : you and Adèle." He whipped off his coat and began to unfasten his tie. "I think I'll wear your baubles under my shirt."

"Oh, let me keep them," said Jill.

"Not on your life," said her brother. "And to-morrow they go to Paris and into the Bank."

Adèle slid an arm round my neck.

"Do be careful," she said. "We shan't have an easy moment until you're back."

"I don't wonder," said Berry miserably. "Neither shall I."

"You needn't worry," said I, addressing my wife. "We can't go wrong with two cars. One covers the other, you see. Besides, we're five this time."

I kissed her slight fingers. Then I drew them down and into the pocket of my coat. As they closed about my pistol—

"I shan't want it," I breathed, "and I'm sure you won't. But I'd like to think you had it—just for to-night."

Adèle nodded intelligently. Then with her hands behind her she put up her mouth to be kissed. . . .

As Jonah slipped into his coat—

"Promise you won't hurt them," said Jill.

"They're very much more likely to hurt me," said Jonah, wriggling. "They must bruise your shoulders to blazes under a coat."

"Oh, they'll be all right," said his sister. "I mean the wasps."

Berry laughed hysterically.

"Same answer," he said brokenly. "Just the same—only more so."

Two minutes later we were again up on the road.

Looking back I am continually astonished less at the way in which Fortune played into our hands than at that in which Nature herself abetted our enterprise.

Indeed, the whole thing was so natural, and the pieces of the puzzle fell so perfectly into place that I cannot find it surprising that, when he regarded the picture, Casca de Palk saw no seams, but was fooled to the top of his bent.

What could be more natural than that wasps should make their home in a hollow tree? Or that, in his agitation, Casca should have failed to perceive that their nest was already there? Or that, when he found the safe "locked", it should never enter his head that the pearls were no longer inside?

For all that, when someone has done you a sum, it is easy enough to see that the answer is right, and I think that the greatest credit is due to Piers for unloosing so simply what, if it had not been unloosed, we should to this day have considered a Gordian knot.

Tired as we were, the comfortable reflections which I have just set down made us forget our fatigue, and, in spite of Berry's misgivings, long before dawn the nest had been safely dug out and lodged in the hollow oak. Considering the nature of the operation, our casualties were most slight. Jonah and Carson were each of them stung four times, I was stung twice, and Berry and Piers escaped. Our purpose having been effected, Berry proposed to withdraw, and when Jonah explained that the light of day was essential for us to remove all traces of what we had done, his strictures upon "Half hours with Nature" became so caustic that even Carson broke down and laughed till he cried.

At last the dawn came stealing over the hills.

Thanks to my cousin's care, we had made very little mess, and a heavy shower about five set upon our efforts the seal of complete success. When I took my leave of the spot, the oak was no longer silent : a fitful buzzing had begun to resound in the recess : and several wasps were crawling drunkenly over the rims of the hole. The trick had been done.

With sleep tugging at our eyelids we clambered into the cars to drive to *The Fisherman's Arms. . . .*

As we slid past the saw-mill, I lifted my head.

"Woking will leave for the station at half-past nine. I hope very much you don't mean to follow him up."

"I don't think it's worth it," said Jonah. "Now that he's got the book, Auntie Emma will almost certainly hold his hand. But I must leave for Paris this afternoon. You see, I'm not like Woking. I shan't sleep sound until I've got rid of these gems.'"

"You can't go alone."

"No," said Jonah. "I'd like you to come, but I think you ought to stay here. Piers had better come with me. And Carson, of course."

"And what about Casca?" said I. "Who's to witness the visit he pays to his safe?"

"If you ask me—no one," said Jonah. "You know I don't want to spoil sport, but I think it would be asking for trouble. We all ought to go and see it—lie about in the bracken and drink it in : but, if what we hope will happen in fact comes off, I know we should laugh so immoderately that Casca would certainly hear. I mean, I wouldn't trust myself. Not for a moment. There are degrees of mirth which no resolution can control. And then we should kick ourselves . . . What's more, to see it all, we should have to be very near : and what Berry said last night is perfectly true. The wasp has no sense of justice. Annoy him, and anyone who is available is for it. And I defy anyone to suffer, motionless and in silence, the malignant attention of a number of angry wasps. No, I'll write a line to Walker the moment we're in. Carson can catch him as he comes back from the station, and if you're not too tired, you might meet him to-night."

"Put it in the note," said I. "Half-past ten, if he can, at the usual place. But now look here. Casca will go to his safe, if not to-day, to-morrow : and, well, he'll come empty away. But don't you think he'll go back? I know it's a sticky business : but, after all, they are the Padua pearls."

"He can't," cried Jonah. "He's done. What can he do without assistance? And that he can't possibly seek. He's no idea how

to take wasps' nests. And, if he had, what could be more suspicious than going about the business—mark you, it must be by
night and he can't drive a car—and telling his chauffeur to wait
while he does the job? Oh, no. The safe is "locked" indefinitely.
If he isn't stung too badly, he may entertain a grim hope of
returning in six months' time. But I hope very much the wasps
will stick to the oak. Then we shall have blighted his life." He
laughed softly. "While I'm gone, will you think about *Ici*?"

"I don't suppose," said I, "I shall think about anything else.
Will you get some maps in Paris?"

"You bet I will," said Jonah. "And I'm going to try and see
Fluff. Did that wire go off to Susie?"

I nodded.

"I sent it myself."

And there, I think, I must have fallen asleep, for the next thing
that I remember was the flash of the morning sun on the walls of
the inn.

Walker pushed back his cap and accepted a cigarette.

"I tell you, sir," he said, "I never see such a thing. The
Captain's note had warned me that something queer was in the
wind, but all he said was that he wouldn't be surprised if after
lunch I took Monsieur de Palk for a run, and that, if I did and I
were to hear him holler, unless I was wishful to be stung, he
advised me to stay where I was. I couldn't think what he meant,
but, sure enough, the moment I was back from takin' the
American gent, an order came through for the Renault at two
o'clock. Pierre, of course, had gone off to fetch the Roquefort
'ome. I fairly put it across him for lettin' her go. I never did like
that chap: his eyes is too close for me. Still, he's bought it this
time, for no one believes she was stole the way he says: they
think he'd gone off and left her—any one would. And I think
he thinks it was Auntie Emma as stole it and did him down.

"Well, when I turned out, there was Monsieur de Palk at the
top o' the steps.

" 'D'you know the way we went yesterday?' he says.

" 'Yes, sir,' says I. 'The way Mr. Wokin' chose.'

" 'That's right,' says he. 'Well, you drive me that way again.
When that car was stole I dropped a letter I 'ad in the 'eart of a

wood. An' it's got an address I want. D'you know where the theft was done?'

" 'Thereabouts, sir,' says I. 'I don't know the actual place.'

" 'Well, I'll show you,' says he and gets into the car.

"Show me! He's got an eye for country—I don't think. Talk about blind leadin' the blind. . . . But of course I couldn't help him, if he couldn't help himself. Seven times he stopped me at different woods, but every time it wasn't the place he sought. You never see such a way as he worked himself up. These French! Each time he found he was wrong he carried on something awful, cursin' an' swearin' an' shoutin' an' showin' the whole of his teeth, an' to hear what he said about car-thieves would have done your 'eart good. I never seen a man sweat like he did— I don't know how much he lost. And I lost a bit myself. That's a heavy car. All the time it was 'Stop' and 'Go on' and 'Not too fast', and I never got so sick of a gear-box in all my life. But of course he hardly sat down. When he wasn't out of the car, he was standing up on his feet, a-hanging out of the window, directin' me where to go.

"After a while he starts shoutin' we're on the wrong road, but when I suggests we go back and Pierre bring him to-morrow, he stamps and raves like a madman and howls that this time to-morrow he'll have to be on the train.

" 'But I must 'ave that letter,' he yells. 'It's a most important letter—all about oil shares,' he says. 'I'll lose a fortune,' he screams, 'if it can't be found.'

"Well, after three solid hours we come to the place. I think it must have been right, for the moment he sees it he lets out a hell of a yell.

" 'Aretty,' he screams, 'aretty. This was it. I know this was it. I cannot make a mistake.'

"Of couse all his English is funny, but when he says that, I could hardly keep a straight face. However, I let him out and he started again. Prowlin' about an' peerin' an' snarlin' like any dog. At first I made sure he was wrong: and so did he, for he couldn't find the footpath, an' after five minutes' searchin' and all in vain he started in shoutin' again like as he was out of his mind. What with the heat and his state, his face was a mask of flies, and the way he went for them would have made a cat split its sides. I 'ad to laugh at last, for in tryin' to beat them off he fetched himself one on the nose. And then what's he do? Screams like a kid in a paddy an' chucks his hat on the ground an' spits on it. Well, I ask you, what good does that do? I tell you, they're funny, these French, when they gets worked up. . . .

"Well, I follows him along with the car and all of a sudden he comes acrost the path. . . .

"That was the medicine he needed for his complaint. You never see such a quick change. Throws up his arms an' smiles all over his face an' talks about perseverance an' how he was always right an' that when he got out before he knew he was wrong, but the letter was that important he couldn't take any chances an' so on. I says 'Yes' and 'Quite so' an' wonders what dirty work's coming an' whether he'll feel the same way before he's through. Then he wipes his face an' tells me to stay with the car.

" 'We don' want her stole again,' he says.

" 'I'll see to that, sir,' says I. 'I'd like to see anyone try while I'm around.'

" 'Well, don't you leave her,' he says. 'That other fellow's a liar. That's what he is. He says he didn't leave her: but if he didn't, why didn't he see the thief?'

"Well, I didn't argue the point, and off he goes down the path a-twirling his cane. . . .

"The road was quiet to-day. We'd met a bit of traffic, but now there wasn't a soul. And, after the doin' I'd had, I was thankful to stop the engine an' get down an' sit on the step. He hadn't said 'ow long he'd be, so I lighted a cigarette an' sat there smokin' all peaceful an' wondering what was to come.

"He must have been gone seven minutes when all of a sudden I heard a noise like a couple of garden cats in a first-class scrap. I give you my word it was lifelike. And then, with that for warnin', he started in. Talk about yells. . . . You'd have thought two men and three women were being killed. Without thinking, I started to run the way he had gone when all of a sudden I remembers the Captain's words. So I went on very careful and keeping a good look-out. All at once I see him coming. Running along like a mad thing all over the place. Twice he fouled some creeper and fell right down, but he'd found his feet in an instant an' come

on leapin' an' screamin' an' yellin' to beat the band. I didn't
fancy the job, but of course I 'ad to help him, but I thought I
might as well wait until he was clear of the wood, for I see the
wasps all round him and I liked the idea of the road if I had to
run.

"I give you my word, sir, he's paid a part of his debt. He
caught it good and proper. Of course he made more fuss than
half a dozen ordinary folk, and that was half the trouble. Oh,
more than half. D'you think he'd do as I told him an' drop his
cane? Kept slashing at the wasps like a madman, instead of
brushing them off. After he'd hit me four times, I managed to
catch the cane and throw it away. Then he screams blue murder
and tries his best to kick me and then he runs on to the heath
an' begins to roll.

" 'Get into the car,' I yells, 'and I'll drive you away.'

"But he was past all hearin' : he didn't know what he was
doing, and I thought he'd gone out of his mind.

"As soon as he sees me coming, he up and run as though I
was going to do him a mischief instead of help, and when I
stopped, he'd throw himself down and start in rolling again . . .
As for his row, I never would have believed one man could make
so much noise.

"I don't know how much he was stung. The servants say forty
times, but I don't know. But I chased him all over that 'eath till I
couldn't hardly stand up, and when at last I caught him he didn't
look scarcely human with what he'd done to himself.

"There was still a few wasps about, so I brushed them off, but
as for putting him straight—why, I didn't know where to begin,
an' then, if you please, as soon as he's got his breath, he up and
asks me why I hadn't come to his aid.

" 'That's a good one,' says I. 'I've been trying all I know for
a quarter of an hour.'

" 'But my cane,' he screams. 'You took away my weapon—the
only weapon I have.'

"And then he calls me an assassin.

"I couldn't believe my ears.

" 'Assassin?' says I.

" 'That's right,' he howls. 'You're an assassin, you are, and
I'll have you fired.'

" 'Assassins to you,' says I. 'Who fetched me four wipes with his cane and very near put out my eyes?'

" 'I wish I 'ad,' he screams. . . .

"Of course he wasn't himself. He was cryin' like any baby and he'd split his trousers in two and sweated right through his coat, while, as for his stings—well, his right hand had got the most. I could see that was all swollen. And then he'd got some in his head and he had to kneel down in the car because of his hinder parts. You see, his coat was short and his trousers tight and it seems the wasps had fair froze on to his seat.

"I hear the doctor says he'll be none the worse, but he's not to travel till Sunday because of the shock. No one knows how it happened or what he done. He says he never did nothing and the first he knew he was suddenly fell upon : but that's not the way of a wasp : besides, the Captain saw it coming, and he hasn't got second sight."

"I'll tell you one day," said I, and wiped my eyes. "D'you know if he found his letter?"

"I did inquire," said Walker, "but nobody knows. First he said he hadn't, and then he declared he had. When he said no, it seems as how Monsieur le Comte said he'd send me back, but then he swore he had it and hadn't understood what he said."

"Ah, well," said I, "it's a wicked world."

"I reckon he thought so," said Walker, "this afternoon."

"So perish all traitors," said I. "Can you be here again to-morrow, at half-past ten?"

"Certainly, sir. I daresay by then I'll know if he's going Sunday."

"So much the better," said I, "but I wasn't thinking of that. Major Pleydell will want to hear what happened this afternoon."

"But won't you be seeing him, sir?"

"I shall," said I, "but I'd rather you told him yourself. You see, it's a tale that wants telling. I couldn't do it justice—not in a hundred years. But you're a born *raconteur*, and that's a fact."

"It's all true," said Walker suspiciously.

Saturday and Sunday went by, and Monday came.

Jonah was back from Paris, and Casca was gone—according to Walker, "like Niobe, all tears" : and we sat still at Mose, because, to be honest, we knew not whither to go.

"You get fed with the char-à-banc : so you let it go on without you. . . . After lunch . . . you hire a car and drive through *Ici* and on up to Halfway House. The driver's well known to the Customs —spends his life taking visitors up and down."

A careful digestion of this statement revealed the following facts :—

(1) *Halfway House was some spot on the frontier itself between the Customs of France and those of some neighbouring State.*

There are, of course, many such places. Sometimes the rival guard-rooms stand cheek by jowl : sometimes they stand at either end of a bridge : and sometimes they stand ten miles or more apart, because the country between them is unfit for men to inhabit year in and year out.

(2) Ici *was probably the village in which the French Customs were lodged.*

(3) *The frontier in question was mountainous.*

"On up to Halfway House." "Taking visitors up and down." Besides, it is in the mountains that the guard-rooms stand back from a frontier that runs along snow-covered peaks.

(4) *Some regular autocar service was carrying tourists close to this very place and was using some town or village of which Halfway House lay within an easy drive.*

(5) *Halfway House was a place to which excursions were made.*

So far, so good. But all these things could be said of three several frontiers—those of Italy, Switzerland and Spain.

Now it seemed most certain that Woking was proposing to sail from the country which he could enter on leaving France.

That, then, ruled out the Swiss Frontier. But between the two which remained we could not choose.

If Woking was sailing from some Italian port, *Ici* was in the French Alps : but if he had made up his mind to sail from Spain, *Ici* was on the French slopes of the Pyrenees.

And that was as far as we could get.

The maps and guide-books my cousin had brought from Paris afforded a study which had, at first, seemed fruitful, but, rapidly losing its savour, soon developed into a maddening exercise, which provoked most bitter altercation and grew more and more depressing the deeper we dug. Often our text-books did not agree

together : more often still some vital information was unaccount-
ably withheld : and indeed the only fact upon which they all
insisted was that printed matter could only get us so far and without an acquaintance with the country which we were seeking to
explore our conclusions were bound to lack substance and might
be vain. And that was the devil. Of the Pyrenees we knew something, though little enough : but of the French Alps we knew
nothing—not so much as the name of a pass.

"But it mayn't be a pass," cried Berry. "At least not a pass
with a road."

"It must be," said Piers. "How else can Casca drive up?"

"And what about Woking?" said Berry. "Who says *he's* going
to drive up?" He dabbed at a map. "Here's a case in point. The
road runs up to the frontier, and there it ends : but a bridle-path
goes on and down to . . . down to . . ."

To find the name of the place he abruptly returned to the map,
unaware that Jonah was stooping to check his words. Their two
skulls met with a violent and sickening crack.

Before we could sympathize—

"There you are," screamed Berry, nursing his head. "You all
of you saw it. You all of you saw the assault. *I* was speaking. *I*
had control of the map. I only looked up to make you free of my
wisdom. And then that fish-faced——"

"I was stationary," said Jonah painfully. "If you looked where
you were going, these accidents wouldn't occur."

"Remove that man," said Berry, excitedly. "Take him away
and give him the rules of deportment. Explain that in polite
society no slow belly is permitted to . . ."

When peace had been made—

"What about this?" said Adèle.

With a delicate finger she followed a queer-looking line which
ran out of Modane.

"No earthly," said Berry, "The char-à-bancs don't go to
Modane. I suppose the road isn't dangerous enough. Any
way——"

"That doesn't matter," said I. "Why shouldn't Modane be
Ici? This road runs straight to the frontier."

"That's the Mont Cenis tunnel," said Piers.

"What did I say?" said Berry. "Now look at this. There's

Briançon—char-à-bancs swarm at Briançon."

"Then it can't be *Ici*," said I.

"Who said it was?" said Berry. "And do you mind shutting your head? It'll seem strange at first, but—well, it may save your life. I'm lower than the angels, you know. Not very much, but lower. And the way you interrupt is enough to make an archangel do grievous bodily harm. And now where was I? Oh, I know. Briançon. Well, that's where Casca gets off and takes his ease." He looked round defiantly. "Any one to object that? I'll do him in, if he does. I'm past the trifling stage." Adèle began to shake with laughter. "Well, then he orders a car and drives through Vachette—that's *Ici*, you blue-based fool—and on up to——"

"We did that last night," said Jonah. "It's Number Two on our list. If you remember. I told you that Hannibal went that way."

"I'm much obliged," said Berry. "And which way did Xerxes go? Not that it really matters, but Woking might have Persian ideas." He threw the map out of the window and got to his feet. "And this is where I withdraw. My skull has been injured : my sight has been permanently impaired : my faculty of conjecture has been outraged : my gorge has risen eight inches, and my bile ducts are choked. The only wonder is I haven't got ear-ache."

"My dear," said Adèle, "research is bound to be——"

" 'Research'?" screamed Berry. "This isn't research. Research is looking for a camel—needle in a bottle of hay. But we don't even know what we're trying to find. All we're doing is reducing the hopeless to the imbecile. You couldn't even do it by algebra. Fancy multiplying the frontier by a char-à-banc and dividing by an easy drive. I mean, consider the facts. We've found at least twelve places which answer Woking's description of Half-way House. And if we go on, we shall probably find twelve more. There are probably at least twelve others which we shall miss. So that's thirty-six different *Ici's* and Halvesway House." He expired violently. "Of course any fool can see that this is a case for finesse. We'd better approach Auntie Emma and pick his brains. Tell him that, if it comes off, we'll take the bracelets and he can stick to the pearls."

Adèle handed him a brochure.

"Just see if the char-à-bancs touch—well, it looks like Coutou," she said, "but it may be Soulou."

With starting eyes Berry accepted the tract.

"I expect it's Goo-goo," he said. "Where the monastery is."

"The Pyrenees," said Jill. "I'm sure it's the Pyrenees. He'd be stupid to go to Italy—miles away. But Tours is no distance from Spain."

"Nothing to that," said Piers. "If he left Tours at noon, he'd be in Turin next morning at eight o'clock. And——"

"Via Paris," said I.

"——from there to Genoa's only two hours and a half. Whereas if he sails from Spain—well, he won't get a boat before Vigo, and that's about twenty hours from the Pyrenees."

"But he's shy of Paris," said I. "For that reason I favour Spain."

"I know," said Jonah. "But when he's in Paris he won't have anything on him. I know which way I should go."

For the fiftieth time that morning he picked up the sailing list. . . .

For the fiftieth time that morning I looked at my watch. Eleven o'clock. I shut my eyes and, without thinking, began to murmur my calculations aloud.

"If Susie met Woking last night——"

"You've got the wrong page," said Berry. "We've done that bit. If a char-à-banc, holding forty souls and a driver, leaves Gavarnie speechless at a quarter to four, how many coffins would you order at St. Jean-de-Luz?"

"Sorry," said I. "But, unless and until we hear from Susie, I shan't be able to keep my eye on the ball. Half these calculations are useless. And to sit here——"

"Which half—" said Jonah, brutally.

I pulled myself together.

"If we don't get a wire to-morrow morning——"

"To-night," said Jonah, firmly. "If we don't get a wire to-night . . ."

"Oh, I can't bear it," said Berry. "Half the reason I entered that drain was to get out of going to Tours."

"Can't be helped," said Jonah. "It's simply a question of time. We can't go on sitting here : and if Susie can't worm out of

Woking which way he's going to take, we shall have to beat it for Tours and see for ourselves."

"He'll be all eyes," said Adèle.

"I know he will," said Jonah. "But tell me what else we can do."

Here the door opened, and Carson came in with a wire.

With trembling fingers I tore the paper apart.

Leaving Tours Wednesday for Spain.

At the critical moment Susie had done her bit.

Our excitement knew no bounds.

The guide-books and maps of The Alps were dashed aside, and, while the others were fighting for those of the Pyrenees, I snatched a clean pad of paper to set down roughly those passes which had seemed to us to answer the description of that we sought.

These were four in number—so far as we had made out : for, though, of course, there are many more ways than four which lead out of France into Spain, the others had all some feature which did not agree with what Berry had overheard.

Of these particular passes we knew not one.

Of three of the four we had never so much as heard, while we knew no more of the fourth than the mighty valley or basin which neighboured its foot. And this lay seventeen miles from the head of the pass.

As my wife looked over my shoulder to check my notes—

"We shall have to break up," said Jonah, "and each of us take one pass. The possibles now number four, and each of those four must be watched on Thursday next. I don't mean the passes themselves. We must watch the places at which the char-à-bancs stop : and whoever sees Casca alight must wire or go for the others to bring them in. I'll take Luchon : Boy'd better take——"

A piercing cry from Adèle cut the sentence in two.

"What on earth's the matter?" I said, looking up to her face.

With starting eyes, she pointed to the notes I had made.

I stared at the pad.

I had made a rude sketch of the pass whose approaches we knew : and because the names were familiar and time was short I had let initials stand for the villages' names.

"Well, what about it?" I said. "I don't see anything wrong. That's Eaux Bonnes. You know Eaux Bonnes—we've been there. That's where the char-à-banc stops."

"I know," said Adèle. "Go on."

"Well, that's Eaux Chaudes, where the Customs———"

"You haven't written 'Eaux Chaudes'."

For a moment I stared at the initials. Then I leaped to my feet and picked her up in my arms.

"E.C." I screamed. "She's got it. She's found it out."

The others were staring as though I were out of my mind. As Jonah reached for the pad—

"What on earth d'you mean?" said Berry. "Eaux Chaudes *may* be *Ici*—we all know that."

"He never said '*Ici*'," I roared. "He said 'E.C.' "

" 'He never said'—Oh, he's deranged," said Berry. "How very sad."

But Jonah was slamming the table, and Piers had seized Jill and was shouting and whirling her off her feet.

"What is it?" she cried. "Tell me. I don't understand."

"He thought he said '*Ici*'," yelled Piers. "But he didn't. He said 'E.C.' "

Jonah seized the pad and thrust it beneath Berry's nose.

"Read it," he shouted. "Read what's written down there."

"Not for worlds," said Berry, averting his eyes. "There's something wrong with that diptych. Everybody who sees it seems to go out of their mind. 'Not *Ici*, but *Ici*.' I mean, that's the sort of assertion that leads to a breach of the peace."

"E for Eaux," shrieked Adèle.

Berry began to look frightened.

"E for O," he repeated with a hand to his head.

"E for Emma," cried Piers.

"And C for Casca," cried Jonah. "Letter E, letter C. . . . Instinctively cautious, Woking mentioned no names. Instead, he used its initials to point out the place he meant. 'You drive through Eaux Chaudes and on up to Halfway House.' "

Berry sank down on a chair and closed his eyes.

Then he addressed my wife.

"My dear," he said, "such perception is not of this world. If you'll get me a bottle of beer, I'll drink your health."

CHAPTER XI

We Sail Very Close to the Wind

The sun was low the next day when we sighted the Pyrenees.

Although we had been heading straight for them, a swell in the foreground had masked them for mile after mile, and then, all at once, we must have surmounted the ridge, for there, some sixty miles off, lay the whole of the range.

We saw a rose-red screen some two miles high by two hundred and fifty long—a screen of unimaginable beauty, of dreamy spires and shadowy battlements, of peeping domes and keeps and galleried belvederes, rising and falling in a disarray so exquisite as to make architecture seem an art not so much lost as never yet acquired. Because it was midsummer, there was no snow upon the peaks: and, as the sun's glow left them, the rose faded and the softest shade of black I ever saw reigned in its stead. The change was magical. Before our eyes Mystery stole out of hiding, to climb this pinnacle and couch upon that ledge, till the range was full of secrets, and fairy-tale and legend sat on the heights.

"Superb," said Berry. "Box Hill isn't in it. Can we go on now?"

Adèle and Jonah and I ignored his remark.

"Why is it," said Adèle, "they're so perfect? They're not very high: there's no snow, and so far as grandeur goes, they can't compare with the Alps. And yet . . ."

"They're real," said I. "That's why. The eternal snows are unreal: they're a wonder, but not of the world: they don't belong to this world: they're 'stuff as dreams are made on', and the people who climb them go out of this world to do it: they enter another region—the upper air. But the Pyrenees are natural: they are a thing of beauty which common men and women can understand: there's nothing ethereal about them: they are a wonder of *our* world. Edelweiss grows on the Alps: but daffodils and irises blow on the Pyrenees."

"We will now sing," said Berry, "hymn number four million and forty-four, 'Now the gorge is rising'."

Adèle buried her face in my sleeve.

"I'm not laughing, Boy," she quavered.

But Jonah's shoulders were shaking, and Carson had a hand to his mouth.

"My dear," said I, "I bought it. To detain a mountebank when hungry is simply to press the button marked 'Poisonous gas'."

"Is it indeed?" said Berry. "Well, here's another adage. 'Cast not your slush before friends, lest they rub your nose in it'."

Before I could counter this insult—

"Oh, look," said Adèle, pointing. "The first of the pastorals."

Round the next bend was streaming a flock of goats. It spread all over the highway and over the bullock-walk, a casual, stiff-necked company, marching with an air of independence, not so much scornful as selfish, caring for nothing but the thought upon which it was phlegmatically intent. A small kid was strutting in front, like any mascot, and the herd and his dog were in rear. The man was playing on his panpipes to pass the time, and the primitive ripple of notes went echoing down the ages and into the golden world.

As they drew near—

"I do hope Jill saw them," said Adèle. The Lowland, with Jill and Piers, was somewhere ahead. "They're really straight out of Hans Andersen. And don't say that kid in front isn't pretending to lead them, because I know he is. Look at his self-conscious face."

Berry uncovered and gave his head to the breeze.

Then he touched Adèle on the arm and pointed to the brown tide now flowing about the sides of the car.

"Why is it," he said, "they're so perfect? They're not very high—at least, I've known higher. And yet . . ." Dramatically he flung out an arm. "Because they're real. That's why. There's nothing ethereal about them. Flies may——"

Here I delight to record that a passing goat took his headgear out of his hand.

The next two minutes were crowded.

With tears running down our cheeks, Adèle and Jonah and I stood up in the car, while Berry and Carson, thigh-deep in apprehensive goats, sought to locate and recover what had been a good-looking hat.

We Sail Very Close to the Wind

Most animals, when pursued, will drop their spoil. Not so the goat. While displaying all the symptoms of panic fear, the flock could see no reason for resigning its lawful prey. Before Berry's ravening eyes, the hat was inspected, passed, dropped, trodden upon, picked up, disputed, carried up a bank and finally discarded on the bullock-walk as having been proved and found wanting—a thing of no interest or value to any goat. More. Ere the goat-herd could restore it to Berry, the flock, once more collected, was proceeding with a sober air of detachment which had to be seen to be believed. The incident was closed.

"Well, I did enjoy that," said Jonah, wiping his eyes. "Haven't laughed so much for a long time."

"Thank you," said Berry. "It's very nice to know that. I'm only sorry I wasn't mauled. Then, I suppose, you'd have burst a blood vessel. Of course, personally, the spectacle of bereavement and insult has never appealed to me." Hat in hand, he entered the car and sank into his seat. "And now would it be in order for us to proceed? Or shall we wait for the bears? You never know. They might like the look of my trousers."

As Jonah let in the clutch—

"But you offered it them," wailed Adèle. "You stretched out your arm, and they thought——"

"I see," said Berry. "They thought a pearl-gray Homburg, warm from the head, was being presented to them by a complete stranger to mark his appreciation of their pollution of the air. Well, if you knew as much about goats as I do, you'd know it was sheer bestial malevolence. Compared with the goat, the skunk is a philanthropist, and the mule an artless and charitable trump. Never mind. Assume you're right. When I pointed out their mistake, what did they do? They feigned alarm : they pretended to run before me—but they retained the hat. They passed it to one another. They mouthed it. They spurned it with their filthy cloven hooves. Finally they left it, with every circumstance of contempt, not on the highway, but in the mire. And you talk of pastorals."

"It was Nemesis," said I. "I commended the beauty of Nature, and you derided my words. She took appropriate action."

"That's right," said Berry. "Be blasphemous. And if I should presently assault you, remember that I thought you asked for it, will you? And in any event, that I'm only an instrument of Fate. And now let's change the subject, shall I?" He pointed to the side of the way. "What a very beautiful dunghill that is. Straight out of Samuel Johnson."

Half an hour later we came to the outskirts of Pau. There the Lowland was waiting, and after a moment's parley we stole through the cool, dim streets to a quiet hotel.

By one consent we were early abroad the next day. We had, of course, plenty of time, but a natural impatience to survey the scene upon which the last act of our drama was to be set had carried us over the foothills by half-past nine.

For once we were all in the Rolls, while Carson was driving the Lowland and following close behind.

As we swept over a saddle—

"The valley of Laruns," said I. "In five minutes' time we shall strike the char-à-banc route."

We sang down a winding hill and bore to the left, to see before us the whole of the mighty valley, some twelve miles long, at the opposite end of which lay the foot of the pass.

The day was perfect and promised to grow very hot, but even at this height the air was as cool as though it had passed through water, and every breath we drew was so refreshing that breathing became a sheer pleasure, like the drinking of wine.

Not a cloud was fretting the fathomless blue of the sky, against which the mountains about us were lifting their lovely heads. Although those flanking the valley were but the spurs of the range and, therefore, not near so high as those to which we should come, their lively grandeur was arresting, and a man that had no business might well have sat at their feet and studied their luxuriant detail from first to last.

On either side a living, breathing tapestry of gray and green, softer and richer than any silk or wool, hung down from heaven, an arras charged with every kind of beauty, with sparkling lawns and groves and falling water, with immemorial cliffs and elegant, hanging woods, with smiling slopes and beckoning bridle-paths, with elfin sheep and even a toy of a village, clustered about a steeple, lying in a fold of the hilltops, more than a thousand feet above our road.

The car sped on.

We swung to the right and over the bustling torrent which measured the valley's length. Then we turned to the left, and before we had covered a mile we saw a char-à-banc coming to prove the truth of my words.

I must confess that I watched it with a quickening pulse. There was no doubt about it. We were approaching Philippi.

As the leviathan went by—

"We're getting warm,' said Jonah. "That's the char-à-banc service which Woking told Casca to use—as far as Eaux Bonnes. And that one's just come from Eaux Bonnes, only going the opposite way."

"That's right," said Piers. "If he's up to time, he'll pass where we're sitting now about five o'clock."

"But I don't understand," cried Jill. "Why should he pass here at five?"

"Not five, dear," said Berry, helpfully. "He passes at sweet seventeen. He dines at nineteen and a half and he ought to be fast asleep before twenty to twenty-two. The next day at fourteen-fifteen—of course, this is summer-time. Thirteen for twelve, like when you buy sponge-cakes."

Jill looked round dazedly.

"What on earth does he mean?" she said.

"Darling," said Adèle, uncertainly, "before he opened his mouth I had the times clear in my head. Now I'm completely confused. He's done it on purpose, of course. The moment anyone talks about sixteen o'clock, my brain becomes paralysed."

"And it is so simple," said Berry. "You've only got to remember that sixteen is eight o'clock, and that'll give you——"

"It isn't," said Piers. "It's four."

After a spasm of mental arithmetic—

"I mean four," said Berry, shamelessly. "Well, once you've got that into your head . . ."

As the outburst of indignation died down, Jonah drew to the side of the road and threw out the clutch.

Then he looked across Piers to me.

"Just state the case, will you?" he said.

I shut my eyes.

"And you might leave out the scenery, will you?" said Berry.

"There's nothing the matter with our eyes, and it's too soon after breakfast for home-made Turkish delight."

"To-day," said I, "is Wednesday."

"Oh, he's been looking at the almanac," said Berry. "Never mind. Have you all got that down?"

"Wednesday," I repeated. "Last night Casca left Paris for Biarritz—to visit his aunt."

"On his mother's side?" said Berry.

"Be quiet," said everyone.

"He's just about getting there now."

"Where?" said Berry.

"To Biarritz, of course. And to-morrow morning—Thursday —he'll take his seat in a char-à-banc going to Carcassonne. Well, the char-à-banc comes this way. It passes this actual spot about five in the afternoon : and just about half an hour later it reaches Eaux Bonnes. That's as far as it goes that day, so everyone in it gets out and puts up at some hotel. The next morning—Friday —at eight the char-à-banc resumes its journey to Carcassonne : but Casca doesn't go with it. He 'lets it go on without him and takes his ease.'

"Now for Woking. Woking leaves Tours to-night for Spain, and to-morrow evening he'll sleep at a place called Jaca which lies just over the mountains, just about sixty-five miles from where we are now.

"So to-morrow evening Casca and Woking will both of them be at their posts. Casca will be at Eaux Bonnes and Woking will be at Jaca, each of which is within an easy drive of the Franco-Spanish frontier and the spot they call Halfway House."

"We have, therefore," said Jonah, "two days in which to reconnoitre the way which Casca will go—the road 'through Eaux Chaudes and on up to Halfway House'—and, what is just as important, the environs of Halfway House. Until we've had a look at the country, we cannot make any plans, and, if we're to beat Auntie Emma, we've got quite a lot to make."

"If you ask me," said Berry, "Auntie Emma won't be on in this act."

"Why?" said I.

"Because he'll never place *Ici*—not in a million years."

"He hasn't got to," said I. "He'll simply shadow Casca as far as Eaux Bonnes. And there the guide-book we gave him will do the rest."

"In that case," said Berry, "we may as well go right home. If Auntie Emma tracks Casca as far as Eaux Bonnes, he won't waste any time over *Ici* or Halfway House. He'll simply go into his room between twelve and two, put the icy blast up Casca and come out again with the stuff. I mean to say, Loumy was a bulwark all right : but a country hotel full of tourists . . ."

"If I thought you were right," said Jonah, "I'd do it myself. But it's all Donegal to a divot that the moment that Casca gets in, he hands the stuff in at the office and has it put into the safe."

"What if he does?" said Berry. "I can guess what sort of safes they keep at Eaux Bonnes. If you showed them a pair of pliers, they'd probably melt."

"Quite so," said Jonah. "But that sort of thing takes time. You cannot possibly rush at a job like that. Before you start in, you must know the ways of the house—what the night-porter's doing and where the manager sleeps. Without that knowledge, Auntie Emma would never begin. And he won't have time to get it. Neither, for that matter, shall we. There are several hotels in Eaux Bonnes, and till Casca gets out of the bus we shan't have the faintest idea which he's going to choose."

Berry sighed.

"Well, you can't complain," he said "You seem to know everything else. Where do we strike?"

"That depends upon Auntie Emma. I'd very much rather we struck at Halfway House. Otherwise, there'll be the devil to pay. Casca's chauffeur, you see. Talk about publicity. We should have to call in the police in self-defence. But if we can wait till he's actually out of the car, we've only got to stroll up and show him our hand."

"Exactly," said Berry. "If. If not—well, the dead bury their dead, don't they? In fact, the drive from Eaux Bonnes to Half-way House promises to be most exhilarating. Fancy a running fight for twenty-one miles." He raised his eyes to heaven and took a deep breath. "As for Casca's chauffeur, I should think he'd lecture about it to the day of his death. Of course if he sticks to his job, that won't be very long."

Jonah frowned. Then he let in the clutch.

"It's a very good thing," he said, "to be first in the field."

Half an hour later we whipped up a long zigzag, plunged into fragrant woods, sailed round a curling shelf and into Eaux Bonnes.

From there we drove to Eaux Chaudes.

Here, sure enough, were the Customs—and little else.

As we entered its shadowy street, an official stepped out of a doorway and held up his hand.

I, who was driving now, brought the car to rest.

"We're going for a picnic," I said.

"You're not going to Spain?"

"No," said I.

"Very well," said the man, and stood back.

I pointed over my shoulder.

"That's our chauffeur behind. He has only the luncheon-basket."

"Very well."

And that was all.

As we passed on, I could not help wondering how much stolen property went this way. The thing was too easy.

As far as Eaux Chaudes our road had been cut like a shelf on the side of a gorge, with a torrent thundering below us and cliffs giving back its music on either side : but now we left the chasm and, crossing the troubled water, began to ascend more sharply the flank of a mountain itself.

Our way was now most handsome, now striding through hanging forest, now scaling some sunlit spur, now riding upon the shoulder of some complacent giant and all the time commanding majestic prospects, the finest of which was that of the *Pic du Midi*, the darling of all the range. There was no mistaking this peak, for, apart from its exquisite shape, it stands in the midst of, and yet aloof from its peers, and the fantastic impression that they have agreed together to give it pride of place is most compelling.

We passed the hamlet of Gabas before the scenery changed.

A miles from that huddle of houses, we joined again the scurrying, turbulent water which we had left, and almost at once this led us into a valley which seemed to be shut at both ends. The mountains about it had now lost much of their height and gave it the strange appearance of a gigantic trough—a place of pastures and avalanches, desolate, no doubt, in winter, but now a blithesome pleasance, a lazy smiling cloister, where the road, no longer dominant, toiled slowly and obediently upward as best it could.

We were not yet above the tree-line, but were plainly nearing that verge, and I afterwards learned that the way here is closed in winter because no manner of labour can keep it clear. That I can well believe, for we crossed the tracks of six or seven avalanches, and the havoc which these had wrought was still to be seen. Boulders and mouldering tree-trunks lay scattered along their tracks, and more than once the debris so overhung the road-way that I was quite glad not to loiter beneath the shadow of such inexorable wrath.

By my cousin's wish, however, we made no haste, and it was nearly midday before we reached the frontier at the top of the pass.

The frontier was marked by a stone, and here the road bellied out so that several cars could stand waiting without obstructing the way. The spot was open : all about us was heath and moor, and the mountains seemed to stand back from this honest stretch of upland which rose and fell for two or three miles each way. As such, it was deceptive, for there was a lot of dead ground and we very soon saw that a man who cared to go strolling could disappear ten times over before he had walked half a mile.

It was, therefore, a first-class place for Casca and Woking to make their monstrous exchange. A score of dips and depressions were ready to hand, and since any one could be entered from any side, no one but the fowls of the air would so much at witness their meeting, far less the actual business which they were to do.

The slopes of the *Pic du Midi* were now on our right, and we seemed to have passed the mountain, which lately had risen before us and had stood to our left.

I suppose we were early. Be that as it may, we had the world to ourselves. Far in the distance a herd of cattle was feeding upon the hills, but, except for this, the landscape was wholly deserted and only the road suggested that man had been there before.

As we stood looking about us—

"Ideal," said Jonah. "For Casca and Woking, I mean. And it

looks as if it might suit us down to the ground. But I'm not quite sure about that, so I'm going to see."

With that, he told Carson to put out the luncheon-basket and turn the Lowland about. Then he took his seat in the latter and waved his hand.

"Have a good look round," he said. "And if you get hungry, don't wait after half-past one. I hope to be back by then, but I might be late."

Before we could put a question, he was gone the way we had come.

There was a moment's silence. Then—

"Half-past one," screamed Berry. "He's being humorous. I broke my fast this morning at seven o'clock."

"Business first," said I. I pointed to a neighbouring crag. "Just pop up there, while the rest of us go to ground. If we're out of your sight when you get there, blow your nose."

"No, you hide first" said Berry. "Then when I hiccough twice, you come out and look. I'll try and not make it too hard. But before we begin, just flick that luncheon-basket into the shade of those rocks. I'm just going to count the beer."

It was easy to perceive the nature of the game he was proposing to play, and his private possession and almost immediate production of an implement which he called a 'life-preserver' and most people call a 'beer-opener' suggested that his enumeration of the bottles at present reposing in the Rolls was to be anything but superficial.

"Greedy beast." said Jill, indignantly. "There's poor Jonah——"

"Well, he should have waited," said Berry. "Where's the rush? This place is at our disposal for another forty-eight hours. I always consider impatience one of the deadly sins. That and inconsideration. Stand by with a glass, someone."

"This is indecent," said Adèle. "Can't you wait even five minutes?"

"Easily," said Berry. "But I'm not going to. Life promises to be short. In three days' time I may be sitting in some Elysian Field with a bottle of nectar and nothing to open it with." As though appalled by this reflection, he seized a bottle of beer and ripped off its cap. "Now then, look sharp with that chalice. This stuff has caught it from Jonah. It's not going to wait."

With a haste which was by no means disinterested, I opened the luncheon-basket and sought for a glass : but before I could reach him, the froth had welled out of the bottle and was coursing down over his fingers and falling on to the turf.

Berry regarded it affectionately.

" 'I sometimes think'," he said, " 'that never blows so *green* The *Grass* as where some' beer was spilt." He drank and looked pleasedly round. "You know, this place is familiar. I probably passed here as Charlemagne, on my way to champion chivalry or show some haughty burghers the flat of the sword. Possibly you were among my camp-followers, or charged with the sparkling duty of preparing my frugal lunch. Now isn't that just like History? Always repeating itself."

Here he refilled his glass, held it up to the sunlight and drank again.

"You're getting mixed up," said Adèle. "Charlemagne was Charles the Great, not Charles the Gross."

"Eschew irreverence," said Berry. "If Solomon had seen your mouth, he'd have had to be helped home : but as soon as he'd got his wind, he'd have sat right down and added another chapter to his Song. So you mustn't abuse it. Those little lips were never made my ears to scandalize. And now I feel so much better that I can wait for my lunch. Not too long, of course. That would be dangerous."

With that, he gave me the bottle and Piers the glass. Then he withdrew to the shade and lay down on his back.

Piers and I shared what was left of the beer. Then he and his wife went down to the laughing water, while Adèle set her arm in mine and urged me towards a hillock which seemed to command the scene.

She did not speak, and, if I did, she only nodded and smiled, but when we were up, she sat down and pulled off her hat and pushed back her beautiful hair. Then she looked up and patted the turf by her side.

I sat down obediently.

For a little while we sat in silence.

Then she touched my arm and pointed to Halfway House.

"I brought us here," she said quietly. "Don't let that memory

curse me as long as I live. . . . I want you and Berry and Jonah
to go in and win. Now that we've got so far, it'll be simply cruel
if you can't. But if—if anything happened to you or to either of
them, it'd break my heart. I don't think twice about Berry's
'weather forecasts'—if he didn't prophesy evil, I should be
alarmed. And I don't pretend to know how far a man like Auntie
Emma will really go. I imagine that half he said was the purest
bluff. For that reason I haven't told Daphne what happened
last Thursday night. All the same, you won't forget that he doesn't
know that the pearls are no longer for sale. . . . And if in the heat
of the moment, he—he did see red . . . I mean, my darling, I
don't want to cramp your style. I wouldn't spoil sport for the
world, for that's what it is. The pearls were different—they are
historical gems : but what do Daphne and I care about our
jewels? The play's the thing, and has been from first to last. It's
been glorious to take on Casca. . . and Bethgelert . . . and Auntie
Emma, and beat the lot at their own rotten game. But that game
must be worth the candle. If it is, well and good. . . . Of that you
must be the judge. And now I've done. But please don't forget
that I trust you. Of Piers I say nothing : I know you'll find some
excuse to put him out of the way. But I'm very fond of Berry and
Jonah, and I—I set quite a value on every hair of your head."

If I made no reply, I think I may be forgiven : but I know I
put her hand to my lips and counted myself very lucky to have
such a wife.

So for a little we sat looking over the world.

Below us the Duchess of Padua was leaning, bare-legged,
against a boulder, with her rosy feet in the stream, directing the
building of a dam, while the Duke, knee-deep in the water, was
piling the stones.

Two hours went by before we saw Jonah again : and when we
did he was walking over the moor.

"Hullo. Where's the Lowland?" said Piers.

My cousin pointed over his shouder.

"Three to four miles off," he said, "on another road. It's pretty
rough—been used for hauling timber : but that's neither here nor
there. It joins this road by Gabas, and it offers a simply perfect
line of retreat. Assume we outpace Auntie Emma, and assume we

are present when Casca and Woking join up. Well, we take the stuff—that's easy : but what about getting away? With Auntie Emma waiting round one of those bends, with his car clean across the road and a pistol in each of his hands? Talk about running the gauntlet. We wouldn't stand an earthly. Nobody would. But now we've got a way out." He pointed to the *Pic du Midi.* "When we've done the trick, we just stroll over the heather, get into the cars and drive home. And when I say home, I mean home. I hope we shall sleep at Bordeaux on Friday night."

I filled a glass and put it into his hand.

"You say 'the cars'. We can't follow Casca on foot."

"I know," said Jonah, accepting a plate which was laden with galantine. "We hire a car for that jaunt. On Friday morning Piers and Jill and Adèle must take the Rolls and the Lowland to where the Lowland is now. She's just beyond that shoulder where the rock comes down in two leaps. They can take some glasses with them and sit up there and watch the whole of the show. We others must come up with Casca——"

"And Auntie Emma," said Berry.

"I imagine so," said Jonah. "Most of the way."

"Quite so," said Berry. "Quite so. 'Most of the way'. Whereabouts would you put the graveyard—the cemetery which he foreshadowed on Thursday night?"

"I hope very much," said Jonah, "it won't appear on our map."

"But if it should," said Berry.

"Then here," said Jonah. "Here, up at Halfway House. That's as obvious as if it were signed and sealed. Don't think I'm boasting—I've only just perceived it. But I'm really rather ashamed of not having seen it before."

With that, he put into his mouth a morsel which precluded all possibility of replying to the question which we naturally asked with one voice.

Impatiently we watched its reduction. . . .

"I've got it," said Adèle. "I see why. Of course Auntie Emma won't strike before Halfway House."

"Why not?" said I, staring.

"Because two birds in the hand are very much better than one. *Woking will be stuffed full of bonds* . . . bearer bonds . . . the price which Bethgelert has authorized him to pay. I guess they're a far bigger scoop than the jewels themselves. But if Auntie Emma waits and we don't get in his way he's every chance in the world of getting them both."

There was an admiring silence. Then—

"He will be glad to see us, won't he?" said Berry. "Fancy getting between Auntie Emma and sixty thousand quid. I mean, if you jogged my elbow when I was just going to pick up three thousand a year, I should be quite rude about it. And if I'd already warned you off. . . ."

"It wants working out," said I. "Happily we've plenty of time."

"And there you're wrong," said Berry. "No amount of calculation can alter the cardinal facts. We're out to pinch his cake, and he knows it. The moment, therefore, he sees us, he'll—well, he'll take off his coat. More. Unless he eliminates us, he won't get his cake. The inference is obvious."

"We shall have to fool him," said I. "If you were to make up like Casca and leave while Casca's at lunch——"

"Yes, that would be fun," said Berry with a hysterical laugh. "A decoys B. And when B overtakes A and discovers the fraud, what should A do? Start reading the burial service?"

"Must you follow Casca?" said Jill. "Why not come up here beforehand and sit down and wait?"

"I'll tell you," said Jonah. "First, Casca mayn't ever get here. He might have a smash or something halfway up : in which case Auntie Emma would rob him at once. Secondly, somehow or other, Auntie Emma simply must not be permitted to get so far." He pushed his plate to one side and lighted a cigarette. "At least, that's the way I see it. I may think differently tomorrow, but I don't think I shall. And now, who'll walk to the Lowland and take Carson a spot of lunch?"

"Nothing I should have liked better," said Berry, hastily. "Unfortunately——"

"Quite all right," said Jonah. "I'd rather you stayed. I want you to help me examine some avalanche-tracks."

In a silence big with laughter, Berry lay back on the turf.

"I see," he said. "We—we shall have to be careful there, shan't we?"

"Very careful," said Jonah. "Some of those boulders weigh forty or fifty tons. Dislodge one of them, and——"

"Quite so," said Berry. "And your friends just cut your name on one of the tons. Of course, it saves a lot of trouble." He sat up there and expired. "You know, your mind's diseased. You simply can't conceive an operation which doesn't invite a sudden and violent death. Whether it's useful or not doesn't seem to enter your head. Fancy inspecting an avalanche. And to-morrow, I suppose, I shall have to find a bear and take its temperature."

With his words we heard the sound of an engine, and almost at once two cars appeared, toiling, on the Spanish side of the pass. They made their way to the frontier, and there they stopped. As their occupants were alighting a third car arrived from France. . . .

Here I may say that before we left two of the cars had gone and another four had arrived. None of them crossed the frontier, and the tourists they brought did no more than stroll to and fro, or make their way to some eminence not too far off. This with an air of disappointment, while some were plainly disgusted to find no line of demarcation running over the hills. I confess I understood their grievance. The verge of two great countries deserves some dignity. I should have felt the better for a second Hadrian's Wall.

It was Piers and I that walked over the moor to the Lowland, and, if the journey was hot, we were more than repaid. The road on which Carson was waiting, to the end of which he had come, lay very much lower than ours : we, therefore, descended steadily most of the way and had passed below the tree-line before we rounded a spur to see the car standing below us in a bower which might have survived from Paradise Lost.

On one side the moor rose sharply by leaps and bounds : on the other the delicate foliage of beechwoods was masking the gray of a cliff. At the head of the dingle a torrent curled out of hiding to water its length, and the grandeur of the *Pic du Midi* was piled at its farther end. The spot was ablaze with sunshine, yet seemed most cool : and the vivid green of the natural lawns by the water, the fluting of birds in the beeches, and the ceaseless, sturdy song of the torrent itself issued an invitation which will go into no words that I know.

Naiad and Dryad might well have been glad of such a place:
there Artemis might have rested and found no fault in it: had
Horace been with us, and the bottle which Piers was bearing
been full of old wine, the world would have been the richer by
another inimitable ode.

When Carson had eaten, we drove the way he had come, to
emerge half a mile above Gabas upon the frontier road. Before
we had been there ten minutes, the Rolls glided round a corner
and came to rest.

"Find your way all right?" said Jonah. "No casting about?"

"None," said I. "But what a peach of a place."

"Is it, indeed?" said Berry. "Well, to-morrow I'll go and—and
watch it, and you can smell round the avalanches. They're very
interesting."

"If you could have seen him," wailed Jill. "He was frightened
to death."

"I don't deny it," said Berry. "The avalanche-tracks have a
gradient of one in one, and when you approach a tree-trunk
which half a dozen toadstools are holding back, it's enough to
quicken the action of anyone's pulse."

Jonah slid to the seat by his side.

"Let Piers come on with Carson, and you come and drive.
I cannot drive and look round on a road like this."

I took my seat at the wheel. . . .

It was half-past five by the time we had passed Eaux Chaudes
and nearly six before we came to the cross roads, one of which
led to Eaux Bonnes and the other to Pau.

"Which way?" said I, feeling the brake.

"It's early yet," said my cousin. "Just run us up to Eaux
Bonnes."

We were halfway up the zigzag when I saw the mass of a char-
à-banc toiling ahead.

"Hullo," said Jonah. "They're late. They should have been in
at Eaux Bonnes by half-past five." He slewed himself round in
his seat. "There you are, Jilly. This time to-morrow Casca will
be on that mammoth—or, rather, a sister-ship. If you like to hide
up on that bank, you shall see him go by."

"Someone," said I, "ought to watch him alight at Eaux Bonnes.
Just to be sure he's turned up."

"You might do that," said Jonah. "If you take the Lowland, you needn't get out of the car."

I nodded.

We were now on the heels of the monster, and Jonah leaned out of the Rolls to see if the road was clear for me to go by.

"Right oh," he said. "Let her go."

What then took place happened so swiftly as far to outrun my pen.

As I pulled out, I sounded the electric horn.

This had a startling note, and a man in the back of the char-à-banc turned his head.

Now why I should have glanced up I shall never know. But I did. For a fraction of a second we looked one another in the face. Then he averted his eyes.

For another fraction of a second I sought to remember where I had seen him before.

And then I had stopped the Rolls dead, and the road was all blurred before me, and every nerve in my body was tingling with shock.

The face was the face of the "watery-eyed wallah" into whose arms Berry and I had blundered that night at Tours.

As somehow I brought the car to the side of the road—

"What is it?" cried Jonah. "What is it?"

"There's a f-fellow there," I stammered, "that was shadowing Casca at Tours."

"My God," said Jonah, half rising. "Then Casca——"

"——is there," I cried. "*There in that char-à-banc*. He must be. How else could that fellow have got here, except by following him?"

"Then he's early," cried Berry. "He——"

"No," I cried, writhing. "*We're late*. We should never have banked on Friday. The last thing you heard in the wood was Casca just beginning to jib at the date. But what you didn't hear was Woking give way on that point."

As the char-à-banc rounded a corner and passed out of sight—

"Quite right," said Jonah, weakly. "We don't deserve to be here. But, oh my God, what a shave!" He wiped the sweat from his brow. Then he shot a glance over his shoulder. "Will you take the Lowland on and watch him get out? Quick as you can. I mean, I may be wrong, but I'll lay a pony that Auntie Emma's behind. And if we could get under cover . . ."

"There's a track on your left," said I, "two hundred yards on."

My cousin nodded.

As I fell into the highway—

"Tell Piers to lie down in the bushes and watch this road."

With that, he was gone, and I ran back to the Lowland, ten paces behind. . . .

Eaux Bonnes has no main street, but most of the village is built about a great *place* on the slope of a hill. In the midst of this *place* is a garden of turf and tall trees—a pleasant place for idlers and children, as a summer evening will prove. But though the garden is long, it is none too wide, and anyone sitting in a car on the roadway which runs to its right may very well watch what is happening on the roadway which runs to its left.

So it was that I saw Casca, though he never saw me.

The man looked pale and uneasy, as well he might, and stood staring helplessly round in an obvious attempt to determine at which of the several hotels he should pass the night. All this assurance was gone, and when somebody bumped against him, I saw him start as a felon in dread of arrest.

There was no point in waiting, and so I released the brake, and the Lowland began to move. . . .

As we slid out of the *place*, another car met and passed us, perhaps fifteen feet away.

I think its principal occupant saw me before I saw him : but neither of us made any attempt to hide.

So, for the second time that evening, my eyes met those of a man I had seen before.

I cannot pretend his air was friendly. In fact, if I am to be honest, there was that in his face which made my blood run cold.

Jonah drove home as only Jonah can drive. I cannot believe that that particular stretch has ever been covered so fast, and I do not think one of us there remembers a chain of that run. Hardly a word was spoken. The way in which Chance had checked us on the very brink of the pit—surely the most ghastly of pitfalls that ever six imbeciles dug—was enough and more than enough to tie up our tongues. For myself, when I thought of our folly and the ignominious fiasco which we had been spared, the palms of my hands grew hot : and for most of that drive, to my shame, I thought about nothing else. My cousin has more control. And the look on his face declared that his brain was slaving to find out some plan of action—to settle the shape of the battle which we must now give to-morrow, soon after lunch.

As we entered the lounge of the hotel, an elderly, kind-looking Frenchman rose to his feet and bowed low to Jill and Adèle.

Then he spoke very fast and humbly, giving his name and standing, and praying us to hold him excused.

To-morrow was a day of collection, of collecting money for some institution or other which cared for poor children and sent them away to the sea. He asked for no subscription : he asked for help. They had sore need of helpers, of attractive lady-helpers, who would carry collecting-boxes and solicit a contribution from whomsoever they met. He had seen *Mesdames* that morning, and at once he had known that if they would lend their services, these would be of more value than thousands of francs.

He spread out reverent hands.

"They will not refuse you, *Mesdames*. I could not refuse you myself. And so your way is easy. Ask me to spare you, and I can do nothing else."

"I'm dreadfully sorry," said Adèle. "But we're going into the mountains. We've promised——"

"Go where you will, *Madame*. I do not care. If only you will take a box with you and ask everybody you meet——"

"I accept for them," said Jonah. He smiled and put out a hand. "Give me the boxes, sir. I've seen them do it before and you're perfectly right. They may not see many people, but those they do will give them whatever they ask."

As a man in a dream, I saw two tin boxes produced and pressed upon Jill and Adèle. They received them dazedly, while the old fellow bowed and beamed, and Jonah made up for their silence by talking French like a native and discussing the art of collection as though he had begged for his living for twenty years.

At last the play was over, and we passed upstairs to our rooms.

As the door closed behind us—

"Am I dreaming?" said Berry. "Or did I see and hear you deceive an elderly man with a nose on his wart—I mean, a wart on his nose?"

"I didn't deceive him," said Jonah.

"I see," said Berry. "And who, may I ask, are you proposing to touch? I can't see myself asking Auntie Emma to help to send poor children off to the sea."

My cousin sank into a chair.

"Can't you?" he said. "I can."

I think that we were still staring, when Piers came into the room.

CHAPTER XII

Enter Hortense

We had to wait two full hours before Jonah disclosed his plan. Most of that time was employed in purchasing rope and crow-bars and other such gear, and in finding and testing and hiring a fast, open car. There was no time to argue—we all knew that: we simply did as he bade us and trusted in him.

When we were alone together, he put a wire into my hand.

"From Fluff," he said quietly. "Probably came this morning, and ought to have come last night."

A.E. left here last night full strength I should watch out he doesn't half want what he wants and he's laid for an accident.

"An accident?" said I, frowning.

"An accident," said Jonah. "Fluff's using the word in a very special sense. When one of that crowd has the misfortune to commit murder, they are said to have 'met with an accident'."

I gave him back the paper in silence.

There was nothing to be said.

A letter from Daphne, which Adèle read to me whilst I was washing my hands, made better hearing.

. . . It's just as well somebody's here. The first thing this morning a wire from Casca arrives. "Would it be convenient to you to receive me at end of July?" A blind, of course. He wants to be sure that we're here. I replied at once, "Only too delighted." I may say that your letters are maddening. I'm perfectly sure you suppress twice as much as you tell. Mind none of you take any risks. It isn't good enough. . . .

At last we had dinner—upstairs: and at last the waiters with-drew.

"Crowbars?" said Adèle. "Why crowbars?"

"To break open the collecting-boxes," said Berry. "To get back the couple of francs we put in as decoys."

As we turned to Jonah, there fell a knock on the door.

"It's only Carson," said my cousin, and cried "Come in."

Carson entered quietly and stood to the door.

"And now," said everyone.

Jonah sat back in his chair.

"To-morrow," he said, "after lunch, Casca and Woking are meeting at Halfway House. I hope that we shall be present : but it's no good our being present if Auntie Emma is there. . . . Well, we can't prevent him from starting, but I think perhaps we can manage to stop him *en route*. Now he can't be stopped until after he's passed the by-road which leads to the dell. If he's stopped before that, he'll be on our line of retreat, and that's unthinkable. So he's got to be stopped after Gabas—that's where the by-road begins. And Gabas is just nine miles from Halfway House.

"I propose to call in Nature to do the trick.

"There's an avalanche-track just five miles from Halfway House, where the trunk of a tree is suspended some twenty feet up. I don't know what's holding it back, but it's little enough. If that trunk is released and guided, it ought to be able to fall clean across the road. I should say it weighs four or five tons, and as the way's narrow just there, once it's in place, no car will be able to pass till a breakdown gang has put in a good day's work.

"Now for the question of escort.

"Casca must be escorted all the way from Eaux Bonnes. I think we're agreed upon that. Auntie Emma is doubtless proposing to wait until Halfway House, but any one of a score of things might happen to make him change his mind and rob Casca *en route*. Hence the car we've just hired. That car will contain the escort. Now you can't escort from a distance—that's common sense. It follows that somehow or other the hired car must follow Casca's—lie between him and Auntie Emma, and keep its place.

"The point is how to do this without arousing the suspicions either of Auntie Emma or Casca himself.

"Well, that's where the collecting-boxes come in. Charity may cover sins, but I hope to-morrow it'll put the eye off the ball.

"Boy must drive the hired car, supported by Berry and Piers. They'll be dressed as attractive women, made up, of course, to the forelock, as is the fashion to-day, and shaking their boxes and shrieking to beat the band. The boxes, of course, are their permits to misbehave. The Lowland will bring up the rear—behind Auntie Emma, of course—to give him a ball to keep his eye on, something to watch.

"So we go up the pass.

"The Rolls is waiting in the dingle : Carson and I are waiting at the avalanche-track : Woking, I hope, will be waiting at Half-way House.

"At Gabas the Lowland falls back and, when out of sight of Auntie Emma, takes the by-road to the dingle and joins the Rolls.

"Then comes the critical period.

"Carson and I will manage that tree-trunk all right, but it's bound to take us longer than shooting a bolt. I mean, we can't time it to a hair. Yet we must hold our hand until after the hired car has passed. A gap must, therefore, exist—at least a hundred yards long—between the hired car and Auntie Emma when you come to the avalanche-track. That, of course, is a matter of driving : there are ways and means of keeping a fellow back.

"The rest is simple.

"As the hired car goes by, the trunk falls across the road. Then Carson and I 'join the ladies', and we drive in Casca's wake up to Halfway House. Auntie Emma will probably follow as best he can : but five miles of that sort of going will find him out. In fact by the time he gets there, we ought to be well across country and nearing the Rolls."

There was a pregnant silence.

Then—

"Make a lovely film, wouldn't it?" said Berry. "Oh, and what about my moustache?"

"I know," said Jonah. "I'm sorry. I'd take your place if I could. But I know my limitations. I simply could not get away with a show like that. Then, again, I want to be in the back-ground, in case anything misfires." He got to his feet and started to fill a pipe. "I admit the plan's full of holes. That escort duty is going to be no joke. But I can't think of anything better—and we're up against Time."

"To be perfectly honest," said Berry, "I think it's a wonderful show." We warmly agreed. "Slightly melodramatic in parts, and there are one or two hiatus which are going to be the devil to fill.

But on the whole it's superb—and most artistic. I should think the interview between Casca and Auntie Emma at Halfway House will be almost historical."

"More," cried Piers. "Casca will be stopped by the tree-trunk on his way back. Unless he can wangle a lift, he'll have to walk home."

"Sixteen miles," said Berry, and covered his face. "Who says that the wicked flourish?"

"Jill and I in the Lowland?" said Adèle.

"That's right," said Jonah. "I don't much like that bit, but it can't be helped. So long as you keep your distance he'll never see who's inside."

I looked at the Duke of Padua.

"Piers," I said, "will make a wonderful girl."

"The *jeune fille*," said Berry. "And you and I are the toughs. Hortense and Toto from Biarritz—out on the loose. And now I begin to see daylight. The worse you appear to drive, the less Auntie Emma will suspect. But I won't wear high-heeled shoes."

"No need," said I. "We shan't get out of the car before Halfway House."

"Are you sure he won't know you?" said Jill. "I mean——"

"What, painted and powdered and hatted? Not on your life. Besides, he'll be watching the Lowland from first to last."

"It all depends," said I, "on the pace at which Casca goes. If he goes a good lick, we're all right. But if he goes slow, Auntie Emma will be on our tail the whole of the way."

"What if he is?" said Berry. "By the time I've done with the skin-food I'll lay I could give him a date and he'd write it down. But I can't dress here. We must take a room at Louvie."

"That's an idea," said Jonah. "Breakfast at Louvie-Juzon at ten o'clock."

Louvie-Juzon lay close to the mountains. Its fine old inn was flanking the road we must use. We had passed it twice already and had marked its generous gateway and the shade of the court beyond.

"And my costume?" said Berry. "My perfumes and *lingerie?* Hortense can't shop in Louvie. No *grande cocotte*——"

"Adèle and Jill," said Jonah, "must buy the clothes. We shall be otherwise engaged. They must buy all you'll need and settle the bill. Then they take the Lowland and meet you three at Louvie at eleven o'clock."

" 'Otherwise engaged'." said Berry. "I suppose that means a night in the mountains surveying the road to ruin without any lights. I'm sorry, but——"

"I'm sorry for everyone," said Jonah. "But tree-trunks weighing five tons require quite a lot of coaxing before they'll do what you want. Carson, you'd better get to bed. I shall want the Rolls and the hired car at half-past four."

From six to nine the next morning we laboured like men possessed, to bring the trunk to the angle my cousin required. Apart from the heavy labour and the furious rate at which we worked, the exercise was a nightmare, for the boulders which hung above us were threatening every instant to resume their headlong course : and though, looking back, I imagine the danger was less than it seemed, at the time each stroke of the pick might have been a challenge to Nature to unleash those shocking forces which were actually crouching to spring. At last, however, it was over, a mass of rubble had been shifted and the trunk had been moved and roped to neighbouring trees. Cut the left-hand ropes, and the baulk must swing out and pivot, as a gate on its hinge, to leave the bank and crash down full in the road. There it was bound to settle because of the ropes which were playing the part of hinges and holding its other end.

That we were not disturbed at our labour offers no room for surprise. The road beyond Gabas is little used but by tourists, and none would have climbed so far before nine o'clock. Indeed, we saw no one but shepherds, and they were far down in the valley and did not see us.

All the tools but two crowbars were then put into the Rolls, and since, when the trunk had settled, my cousin proposed, if he could, to remove the ropes, there would, we hoped, be nothing to show that Nature had been provoked or abetted to block the road.

Jonah and Carson remained at the avalanche-track. This was inconvenient, but could not be helped, for, had they returned with us to Louvie, we could not have spared the time to drive them back to their post. It seemed just as well, however, that someone should be in waiting not far from Halfway House. Casca might possibly be early. . . .

"And don't forget," said Jonah, "that I'm in reserve. If there's a hitch of sorts—well, Casca's bound to come by here to get up to Halfway House. We can see the road for two miles, so we can't be surprised. If he comes up alone, I shall stop him and take the stuff : then I shall make for the Rolls. But I don't think that's at all likely. And now you'd better be moving—time's getting on. My confidence in you is unbounded : but, whatever you do, lead by a hundred yards when you get to this spot. That means a short seven seconds. I don't mind Auntie Emma's fouling the trunk but I don't want the trunk to foul him. The world would be the cleaner, but people might begin to ask questions : and that's the last thing we want."

I drove the Rolls back to the by-road and so to the pretty dingle where she was to stay. Piers and Berry followed me in the hired car. Swiftly we hid the tools in a cleft of a rock, and when I had locked the Rolls, we washed in the shining water as best we could.

I shall never forget the moments we snatched from that frantic morning to spend in that perfect place. All the peaceful charm of Arcadia tugged at the heart, and strife and haste and scheming seemed empty and hollow things. The place was an eclogue, breathing a sunny counsel we could not take, and, as I entered the hired car and took my seat at the wheel, I could not help wondering what would have been our fortune before we saw it again. Then I started the engine, and we made our way back to the world.

Twenty minutes later we were approaching Eaux Chaudes.

When we had passed in the dawn, the Customs had slept : but now an officer stopped us and asked if we came from Spain. I told him no : that we had gone by very early and meant to come back.

"Did you not pass yesterday?"

"Quite right," said I. "You see, we're exploring the mountains, and as we're leaving the district we want to make the most of our time."

The man hesitated.

"Are you going to Laruns, Monsieur?"

"We're going through Laruns," I said.

"I have to go there on duty. Will Monsieur give me a lift?"

"With pleasure," said I, and opened the door by my side.

He cried to some comrade or other that he was leaving at once, and as soon as the other appeared, he entered the car.

He was a pleasant fellow and talked or laughed all the time, and when we left him at Laruns, he could not thank us enough.

"I shall see you again," he said. "You have said you are coming back. And I think I know what you are doing up there towards Spain." He winked elaborately. "These early jaunts to the hilltops. And presently the ladies will arrive. Is it not so? That you do not want an audience I well understand."

Wishing I had Jonah's address—

"I assure you," said I, "we are only——"

"If you ask me," said he, "you are making a scene for a film."

For an instant I stared at the man. Then I allowed a smile to spread over my face.

"I won't say you're wrong," said I. "But keep it quiet."

"I knew I was right," he said jubilantly.

Half an hour later we sat down to breakfast at Louvie, with one eye, so to speak, on the clock, and the other on the ribbon of road by which the Lowland must come.

When we had passed three cars and none of them stopped, I began to feel less conscious of my ridiculous state.

I was wearing a coat and skirt of printed *crêpe de chine*, with a scarf of the same material now floating over my shoulder and now disputing with the flaps of my white silk blouse. My head was extremely hot in a white felt *cloche*, while the impression that I was naked from the waist downwards was as persistent as it was unreasonable.

For the hundredth time I put my skirt over my knees, wondered why women do not die of exposure and tried to believe that things like myself had been seen off the music-hall stage. The driving mirror, however, was not encouraging. Had I been soliciting alms, I cannot believe that I should have had a good day.

Which brings me to Piers.

As I had said, he made a peach of a girl. His smart little dress of black silk, with cuffs and a long, low collar of rose *georgette*, his broad-brimmed black-and-white hat and his rhinestone brooch served to set off his delicate boyish face, while his obvious shyness and the way in which he cast down his eyes bespoke to the life the blushing *ingénue*.

He had reason to blush.

By his side Hortense, florid, exuberant and profuse, was illustrating a stream of high-pitched commentary with a flurry of gesticulation which out-Frenched France herself.

I can never do justice to her looks.

A lemon-coloured dress, surmounted by a bolero of apple-green lace, made the most of her ample lines : a fold of black satin ribbon across her brow was tied in a luxuriant bow over one ear : and a green straw hat with a brim about half an inch wide completed as daring a headgear as ever I saw.

Compared with her face, however, these things were of no account.

Her superb, but vivid complexion, her ripe and voluptuous lips, the wicked darkness of her eyes—above all, the flood of vivacious expressions which chased one another like lightning over her countenance made a kaleidoscopic disguise which I doubt if my sister herself would have perceived.

We were all made up, of course, and all wore gloves and handbags, while a decent dust-rug concealed my companions' legs : but though, I suppose, I passed muster and Piers was sure to be found a good-looking girl, Hortense was quite distracting in her appeal to the eye.

And ear.

As we came to Laruns—

"Toto, *chérie*," she squealed, "go slowly through the village : we may get off. Yvonne, *ma petite*, sit up and brandish your box. Whoever gives us twenty-five francs can squeeze my hand—through the glove, of course, until dark."

But I was taking no chances.

To the frantic rattling of coins, we fled down the village streets, while Hortense waved and giggled and drew excited cheers from a char-à-banc full of tourists drawn up by a kerb.

"For God's sake," cried Piers, "don't do it. My nerve'll go. Boy, do argue with him. It's simply shouting for trouble to——"

"*Mais, comme elle est mignonne,*" raved Hortense. "You know,

I just dote on that pleading, die-of-shame look. It's simply bung in the picture. Toto, love, stop when you can : I want a spot of powder behind the ears."

It was now about half-past twelve, and we were approaching the road which Casca must take. It seemed unlikely that he would start before two, but once we were in position, he could start whenever he pleased.

The road which led up to Eaux Bonnes might have been built for the ambush we meant to make. As I have said, it was a zigzag. We could, therefore, lie just out of sight round one of its bends, and as soon as we heard a car coming I had only to start my engine and let in my clutch to appear to have been descending and be ready to leap in pursuit the instant it passed. But, to gain this commanding position, we had to go up and then turn. And if, whilst we were climbing, Casca should chance to come down . . .

As we came to the cross roads, I turned to wave to the Lowland a furlong behind. A slim arm waved in reply, and we swept out of view. The Lowland was to come no further, but to take up the chase the moment it saw us go by.

For the next ten minutes, even Hortense was subdued. Once we heard the horn of a car coming down, and each second seemed a minute until it rounded a corner to prove a delivery-van. And then at last we were up, and could see Eaux Bonnes close above us between the leaves of the trees.

I turned the car about as fast as I could. Then I slid round the first bend and into the shade, for such was the heat of the sun that if we had to endure it we should soon have been literally unmasked.

As I slewed myself around for Piers to powder my face—

"So far, so good," breathed Hortense. "Of course we may be too late : but unless he went off in the morning, I don't think we are. He won't get a local chauffeur to miss his lunch."

This seemed common sense, and I made up my mind not to worry till half past two : but I might have known that waiting to take the plunge is a racking business and offers a field of fear which few can ignore.

We smoked, we listened, we disputed in undertones, and each time we heard a car coming, I started the engine and sat with my foot on the clutch : but with every alarm our nerves became more ragged, and when an hour had gone by—and seventeen cars—I must confess that I hardly knew how to sit still.

At last—

"How long do we wait here?" said Hortense. "I mean, if he doesn't turn up? Not that I mind, of course, but I've only got enough powder for another two hours."

"We may be wrong," said Piers. "It mayn't be to-day. Casca arrived last night, but they may be meeting to-morrow, as Berry heard Woking arrange."

Before this appalling suggestion I felt rather dazed. Life seemed suddenly valueless. As for the jewels . . . Looking at myself in the mirror, I decided that once I had put off my motley, nothing this side of Death would induce me to wear it again.

"Well, that's done it," said Hortense. "I've no nightdress. And I don't think this *bandeau* will get through another day. Never mind. We'll start over again. To-morrow I shall wear my crushed hogshead-brown with the broken-bottle-green *toque*. Oh, and my oil-silk undies. What if——"

"Car coming," said Piers. "Two cars."

As I started the engine—

"I'll lay two to one on," breathed Hortense. "Stand by with that safe."

The next moment two cars went by—the first closed, the second open. And in the second was seated Casca de Palk.

We were in his wake in an instant, thanks to the fall of the road.

"And that's that," said Hortense. "You saw who was in the first car?"

"Who?" I cried. "Who?"

"The watery-eyed wallah, with two little friends."

Before I could think—

"And here's Auntie Emma," said Piers, mirror in hand.

"How far behind?"

"Half a furlong," said Piers. "And travelling fast. I think I should close up on Casca."

As we swung round a bend—

"And here," said Hortense, "are the darlings we left at Laruns. *Just in time to mislead Auntie Emma.* But what a superb bit of luck! Now let yourself go, Yvonne. Squeal and wriggle and whisper and laugh like hell."

The recognition was mutual—and cordial in the extreme. We passed the char-à-banc amid a storm of blown kisses and squeaks and yells.

"*Vive l'amour*," shrieked Hortense. "Yvonne, my child, that was perfect. If A.E. had any suspicions we've killed them dead."

This I believe was a fact. When he saw us between him and Casca, the man may well have wondered if we were indeed what we seemed : but the char-à-banc made us a touchstone—and we had passed the test.

To maintain the illusion, I took the next corner too wide, corrected my mistake with great violence and flung Hortense into a corner and Yvonne into her lap. But while their squeals of alarm were commendably realistic, I was too much concerned to relish the delicate touch.

By splitting his forces, Auntie Emma had put in peril the whole of our plan. Had he learned our design, he could hardly have countered it better, for even if everything went as we had desired, three of his gang would precede us to Halfway House. And once they were there, unless we were to give battle we might as well throw up the sponge. Yet even to try to stop them was out of my power. To do so, we should have to pass Casca. That was not to be thought of this side of the avalanche-track : and afterwards how could we pass him—with Jonah and Carson as large as life beside us to proclaim the doom which awaited him if he went on?

With a frightful effort I thrust this menacing prospect out of my mind. The present was sufficiently crowded, and all our wit was needed if the barrier up above Gabas was ever to fall into place.

Three things stood out, as the three worst jumps stand out of a wicked course.

The deception I hoped we had established had to be maintained for twelve miles.

The Customs had to be passed without any hitch.

The gap of a hundred yards had to be made.

Now the maintenance of the deception depended almost entirely upon Hortense and Yvonne. It depended upon their performance—and Auntie Emma was sitting in the very first row of the stalls. I determined to do what I could to help them out. . . .

As we came to the cross roads, I made as if to turn off to Laruns and Pau. Quick as a flash, Hortense gave a shriek of protest, and I wrenched the wheel round to miss the wall by an inch.

I hope I may be forgiven for the way that I drove that day. I swerved, I strayed over the road, I squeezed such cars as we met, while the noise which I made with my gears might have wakened the dead. And though I am sure Auntie Emma would gladly have passed us, he never once sounded his horn and I think he soon made up his mind that, so long as we kept close to Casca, it was not worth his while to take such a risk.

"The Lowland's behind," said Piers.

"That'll do," said Hortense. "Don't look in that mirror too often, but think about something else. I should like to dilate upon Casca : but that would be wrong. Was ever a man so escorted? And he's not the faintest idea. Never mind. Let's talk of old days at the convent." He laughed idiotically. "Toto, do you remember when we put the slugs in the Aunt Inferior's shoes?"

But my mind was on the Customs.

I had no fear that Casca would be delayed. His driver was certainly known, as Woking had said he would be. But we might be stopped and questioned, and if we were held for more than two or three seconds, Auntie Emma would be waiting behind us and able to hear what was said.

The nearer we came to *Ici*, the blacker the outlook grew.

My French was fair, but my voice at close quarters would not have fooled a child. Nor, for the matter of that, would that of Hortense. We could not, therefore, attempt to mislead the Customs as to our sex. And when they knew we were men, what would they do? The best we could hope for was that they would subscribe to the jest—with Auntie Emma waiting but twelve feet away. . . .

Then I saw a familiar figure, plodding along up the gradient, with his cap on the back of his head.

In a flash I had come alongside and had opened my door.

"In you get, my friend," said I, "and we'll give you a lift. Quick!"

As the Custom-Officer mounted the step, I let the car go.

"You see," said I, "you were right. You said that the ladies would come—and here they are."

The fellow shot one look round. Then he collapsed in his seat and laughed and laughed till the tears ran over his cheeks.

"*Mon Dieu*," he gasped. "It is better than any play. That fat one behind——"

"'Not angles, but angels'," simpered Hortense. "But, you know, you should see me at night. Then I'm really immense. And when I'm trying—well, Molyneux and Paquin have had a row about me."

I touched our passenger's arm.

"Listen," I said. "That man in the car behind us thinks that we really are women. I want him to think so. I beg you—don't give us away."

"But how should I, Monsieur?'

"You might, when he stops at the Customs. Tell your pals if you like, but wait till he's gone. I hope they won't keep us waiting."

"You need not stop, Monsieur. I say it. Drop me and drive straight on. But, *mon Dieu*, he is funny, that fat one. I think he would make any film."

"Call me Hortense," giggled Berry. "Oh, and put this franc into my box, or I'll bite your neck."

The contribution was made amid an explosion of mirth.

As we entered the street of Eaux Chaudes, I saw Casca leaving the Customs and the closed car a few yards before him gathering speed.

As we came to the guard-room, our friend stood up in the car : then he opened his door and set a foot on the step.

"*Au revoir*," said I.

"A thousand thanks—Madame."

"That's the style," said I, with a foot on the brake.

The next moment he was out and saluting, his colleague had stepped to one side, and we were through the Customs and leaving Eaux Chaudes.

"Luck all the way," said Hortense. "It's our day out."

Now how long elapsed before Auntie Emma was suffered to proceed, I do not know : but as the minutes went by, and he did not appear, I began not unnaturally to wonder whether indeed he was going to play into our hands. The road here was very winding, but some of its reaches were fully two hundred yards long. It follows that for the moment we led him by double the distance which Jonah required. If only the man were content to allow us this lead. . . .

Six miles to the avalanche-track.

I pressed as close up to Casca as ever I dared.

The latter sat dull and listless and seldom moved. He never looked about him and never turned round. But now and again I saw him wipe his forehead, or, at least, put a hand to his head.

I found myself wondering what tale he was going to pitch Woking about the pearls. . . .

As Gabas slid into the foreground . . .

"Auntie Emma coming," said Piers.

I smothered an oath.

"How far behind?"

"He's out of sight now. About a furlong, I think. Oh, less. I can see him again. He's coming up fast."

"That'll do," said Hortense. "We've got to get right with Gabas. There are the lads of the village. Lift up their hearts."

Once again the boxes were flaunted, while Hortense yelped incoherence and Yvonne giggled and squealed.

Answering shouts and laughter followed us out of the hamlet and up the hill.

"Don't drive too well, Toto."

"Sit tight," said I.

Again I misjudged a turn and brought us round with one wheel up on the bank. Then I shaved a convenient lorry and swerved to avoid a chicken as though it had been a bath.

As we passed the mouth of the by-road, I strove to marshal my wits.

Not quite four miles to go, and I was right up on Casca and leading Auntie Emma by sixty yards.

I could not think what to do.

When a mile had gone by—

"Fifty or sixty," said Piers. "Not more than that."

I could not get on any further : I dared not fall back. Wilful obstruction was the last thing I wanted to try. And yet I must make the distance that Jonah required.

Regardless of my complexion, I dashed the sweat from my eyes. . . .

"What about slowing up?" said Hortense.

"I daren't," said I. "I may lose the lead that I've got."

"It isn't enough," said Piers.

"Don't I know it?" I snapped. "But what the hell can I do?"

Another mile passed . . . And another . . . But, as though he could read my thoughts, the sweep in the car behind us kept sixty paces behind.

We seemed to be rushing on failure. All the signs of impending misfortune began to appear. Their rôles forgotten, Hortense and Yvonne sat silent, biting their lips. And I was not driving like Toto. . . . With a shock I realized that I had not been driving like Toto for more than three miles. It was, I think, the horror of this realization that suddenly cut the knot.

Directly ahead, the road rose up very sharply and curled to the left.

"Stand by," I cried over my shoulder, and put down my foot.

I took the corner almost abreast of Casca. Then I brought us up all standing and threw out the clutch.

In a flash we were running backwards and gathering speed. . . .

My spurt had won twenty yards, and as we swung back round the bend, I saw Auntie Emma below us as yet some fifty yards off.

What were his feelings I neither know nor care. But even before he saw us, the screams which Hortense was letting must surely have curdled his blood.

I steered to hit him amidships. And, to save his life the driver, sitting beside him, drove his car into the ditch.

As I missed him by inches, I jammed on my excellent brakes. . . .

And then I was in first—second, and putting the car at the hill like a bull at a gate.

Before our furious victim was out of his car, once again we were round the corner and out of his sight.

Hortense was yelling like a madman.

"Gone away!" she screeched. "Gone away!" and flung her arms round my neck.

Two minutes later, perhaps, the tree-trunk crashed into place.

The portcullis was down.

"I'd like him to see us," said Jonah. "I don't want him making a cast to see where the Lowland has gone. His car wasn't smashed?"

"Oh, no," said I. "He ought to be up any minute."

"Here he comes, sir," said Carson.

"Then let her go," said my cousin. "We may as well get out of range."

I let in the clutch. . . .

To Auntie Emma's demeanour I cannot speak, but Jonah stood up in the car and waved his hat, while Piers blew kisses and Berry, supported by Carson, stood up on the seat and made a whole series of gestures which were as derisive as they were unmistakably masculine.

As we rounded a bend—

"And now for his friends," said Jonah. "Unless we can——"

Behind us two shots rang out, to echo around the great valley and gradually lose themselves in the tops of the neighbouring hills.

We were well out of sight of the tree-trunk, so if Auntie Emma had fired, he had not fired upon us.

"That's a signal," said Jonah. "He's calling the other car."

We tore round another bend to prove the truth of his words.

A mile ahead, the closed car in front of Casca had come to rest. For one dreadful moment I thought that its occupants were going to hold Casca up. Then the latter's driver scraped by, and the closed car began to slide back towards a patch of greensward which would give it the room to turn.

"What could be better?" said Jonah. "Carson, they mustn't see us. Sit down on the floor."

With that, he leaned down till his head was between his knees and began to tell me exactly what I was to do. . . .

As we approached it, the car was still sliding back, but, since the road was so narrow, it stopped to let us go by.

Instead of passing, however, I drove up directly behind, and, as Jonah and Carson descended, I stopped and sounded my horn.

A man leaned out of the window on the off side.

"Why don't you go on?" he blared. "There's buckets of room."

Then he turned to see Jonah standing upon the near side.

"Put up your hands," said my cousin. "I've got you cold."

The driver took his foot from the brake, but Carson had scotched his wheel, so the car stood still.

Whilst I drove slowly on, Carson stopped the engine, opened the bonnet and took the contact-breaker away. Then he took their arms—two pistols, while Jonah addressed the thieves.

"I've a message for your leader," he said. "It's very short, but pregnant. And here it is. . . . 'The knife doesn't argue with the butter. It takes what it wants.' Just tell him that, will you? I think he'll know what I mean."

Then he and Carson rejoined us and we drove up to Halfway House.

"Well, Casca," said Berry. "How nice to see you again! Mr. Woking, I'm charmed to meet you. In fact, we all are. We've been looking forward to this for more than a month. No, I shouldn't move. My cousin has got you covered. Just take his pistol, Carson. . . ." The weapon was deftly removed. "And now for the jewels. Casca, you'd better produce them. None of us want to touch your filthy carcase. . . . Go on, you blackguard."

The order was not obeyed.

Casca who had never stopped shaking from the moment he heard Berry's voice had lost control of his limbs.

His face was wet and gray, and its lines, now very obvious, seemed to be blue. His jaw had dropped, and he was dribbling. Though his eyes were wide and staring, he did not appear to see, but might have been some gross image of "Abject Fear".

It was Carson who brought out the wallet and gave it to me.

"Sit down, Mr. Woking," said Berry. "I believe the grass to be dry."

With bulging eyes, the latter did as he said.

I opened the wallet.

Within were six wash-leather bags.

As fast as I could I opened them, one by one, and called out the contents to Piers who checked them off on a list.

At length—

"That's the lot," said Piers, and sat back on his heels.

"Then, what's this?" said I, and took up the last of the bags.

It was a fine rope of pearls, fully as long as the Padua rope and just as lovely to look at in every way. Had we not known that the

Padua pearls were in Paris, that these were not they would never have entered our heads.

"False," said Jonah quietly. "It's a copy he's just had made. It isn't exact, of course : but it's near enough for his purpose—the dirty dog." He looked at Woking. "I guess you'd have paid on these."

As a man in a dream, Woking stared at the speaker and then at the rope.

"Not—not real ?" he stammered.

"These," said Jonah, "are not the Padua pearls. They're not the pearls you valued at Loumy." Woking looked ready to faint. "You'd have found it out at New York, but would you have found it out here ?"

Woking put a hand to his head.

"But——"

"Answer the question," barked Berry. "Would you have paid on these pearls, or would you not ?"

Woking moistened his lips.

"I—I guess I should, sir."

"Then thank your stars," said Berry, "that we've butted in." He pointed to Casca. "That full-marks skunk would have stung you for—Which reminds me. What were you going to pay for this little lot ? You needn't worry. We don't belong to your set. And if you behave yourself, we're going to let you go—bearer bonds and all. But you'd better answer our questions, or else we might change our minds. What was the price—the total ?"

There was a moment's silence, only broken by the click of the jewels which Piers and Carson were putting back in their bags.

Then—

"Two hundred thousand dollars," said Woking between his teeth.

But he was not looking at Berry. His eyes, now burning bright, were on Casca de Palk.

The latter began to whimper—a dreadful noise.

"Cigarette-case, cuff-links and studs," said I. "These things belong to you." I flung them down on the ground. "The underwriters will learn that I have returned them to you."

The whimper grew more pronounced.

"Stop that noise," said Berry, "and listen to me. You thought we should never suspect you because we had made you our friend. But we knew it was you that had robbed us before we called in the police. And ever since then we've had our hands upon you. Paris, Tours, Dinard, Loumy, Eaux Bonnes. We took the pearls at Loumy five minutes after you'd put them into the oak : and lest you should find the tree empty, we put the wasps' nest there. Perhaps that'll show you that we've been behind the curtain from first to last. Consequently, we know *everything*.

"Very well. If I had my way, I'd lodge you in jail to-night. But, instead of that, we're going to give you a run. The police will be told all we know in three days' time. That's the start we give you. If you want hard labour for life you'll let it go."

With a choking cry the snivelling wretch went down on his bended knees.

Having passed sentence, Berry applied the lash.

"You're a dirty piece of work, Casca. As dirty a piece of work as ever I saw. You're rotten—crawling, right through. Braggart and cur and coward, you broke our bread and betrayed us : you basked in our ladies' favour and robbed them whilst they were asleep. You doped their wine, Casca. You doped your hostesses' wine. And while they slept, you stripped them of all they had. In a word, you're not fit to live. But I wouldn't kill you for worlds, for, the moment the police get going, you're going to pass under the shadow that gives no rest. Of course you may outwit them : but until a warrant is quashed, it lies on the file. And lying low isn't really much of a life. Disguises, cheap lodgings, strange towns. Afraid to post a letter : afraid to go out before dark. In fact, of the two, I believe I should choose hard labour. But you may think otherwise—in which case your three days' start will help you. But after that you're an outlaw : and if ever I see you again I'll give you in charge."

Blubbering incoherence, Casca fell flat on his face and, crawling like any reptile, essayed to kiss Berry's foot.

Had it not been revolting, the scene would have been absurd.

My brother-in-law, stern and majestic, looked exactly like one of the elder sisters in a *Cinderella* pantomime, while Casca might have been Caliban, pleading with Prospero, in a production of *The Tempest* in modern dress.

I felt rather sorry for Woking.

For one thing, it seemed unlikely that his eyes would ever go back. By such continued protrusion the muscles must have been stretched. For another, his brain was jibbing, not so much reluctant as unable to adopt the fantastic report which his eyes and his ears had been rendering since we appeared. Finally, he was hideously uneasy. His turn was obviously coming. Besides, he had upon his person two hundred thousand dollars worth of bonds. The grass upon which he sat might have been redhot.

Berry stepped back from Casca and turned to Bethgelert's man.

"While deploring your profession, Mr. Woking, we bear you no particular grudge. We shall therefore omit your name from our report to the police. 'An emissary', we shall say, 'of Beth-gelert, the notorious American fence.' " Woking blinked very hard. "And now I'll give you a tip. As soon as we've done with you, I should leave this place. If you don't, you'll be joined by Auntie Emma." Woking started violently. "Yes, I thought it more than likely you'd know his name. And, as no doubt you surmise, he is not coming here to pick flowers.

"He'd be here now, but for us. In fact you hadn't an earthly —he's travelling five men strong."

In manifest agitation Woking got to his feet.

Berry continued imperturbably.

"Of course he'd have taken your money, and, remembering where we are, I think it more than likely that he would have taken your life. So, all things considered, I think you owe us a lot. In return, I'll ask you a favour." He produced his collecting-box. "The Duke of Padua and I are asking for money to-day. Believe me, in a very good cause. To send poor children away for a week at the sea. We haven't done very well—we've had such a lot to think of. But perhaps you will give us something— whatever you like."

The strangest expression came into Woking's face. For an instant I thought that the fellow was going to burst into tears. Instead, he took out a note-case and out of its depths he produced two hundred-dollar bills.

"I guess I can spare that," he muttered.

"I guess you can," said Berry, taking the notes. "And now I should spurt for Jaca. Good afternoon."

Woking hesitated.

"Can I have a look at those pearls?"

I threw them across.

For a moment he examined them closely. Then he let fall the rope and sprang at Casca de Palk.

Unnoticed by us, the latter had got to his feet, but before the sudden onslaught he crumpled and measured his length, with Woking cleaving to his body, like any wild beast.

The latter, I think, would have killed him : he had his man by the throat. Carson and I dragged him off : but it took us all we knew to make him let go.

As we flung him back on the heather—

"When we want your assistance," said Berry, "we'll let you know. And now clear out. Let me be frank, Mr. Woking. We don't care a damn about you : but we don't mean Auntie Emma to get your bonds. And if you're not gone in two minutes, as sure as I live, we'll burn them before your eyes."

Woking picked himself up.

Then he took a deep breath.

"I'm through with Europe," he said. "It isn't safe."

He hesitated there and looked round, as though searching for words. But the scene was too much for his tongue, and the old, bewildered look came into his face.

"Well, you beat it," he said helplessly.

Then he clapped his hat on his head and turned to make for his car.

Before two minutes had passed, the sullen drone of its engine had faded away.

Now all that I have related took place in a fold of the ground out of sight of the road : and since we had left the hired car below the last crest of the pass, neither Casca's nor Woking's chauffeurs had seen us at all. If other cars or people were present at Halfway House, I neither saw nor heard them, and from what I afterwards learned I believe we had the place to ourselves.

I saw Jonah glance at his watch.

"I must have ten minutes," said Berry. "Give me pencil and paper, someone. My Muse must not be denied." He looked round desperately. "What can I write on?"

"The bonnet of the car," said I.

"On the near side, then," said Jonah. "Carson is going to take the magneto away. But we must be quick. They won't be here just yet, but I don't want to run."

With that, he strolled to a bend from which he could watch the road, while the rest of us made for the car which had served us so well. And there, on its step, I confess I was glad to sit down, while Piers stood by to help Carson, and Berry sprawled over a wing and wrote his note.

Auntie Emma, Esq.

Dear Sir,

    It is our hope that you will accept these pearls as a souvenir of to-day. They may not be what they seem, but they are by no means valueless, and, should you ever decide to part with them, any but the most grasping receiver would offer you twenty pounds. The originals were in my pocket that night at *The Fisherman's Arms*. But you preferred to take the book. There is no accounting for tastes, but I cannot help feeling that though any document of my making is, as you will agree, a precious thing, in these degenerate days the Padua pearls would, except among connoisseurs, command a higher price.

    Upon careful consideration I fear that you have found us obstructive. You have never actually said so, but that night at *The Fisherman's Arms* I gathered that that was what was in your mind : and I have an uneasy feeling that nothing has occurred since then to cause you to alter your opinion. But though we have twice encouraged you to take walking exercise when you had proposed to be driven, reference to almost any medical man will disclose that from a health point of view the two methods of progression are quite incomparable. To-day, for instance, your pores must have acted with a freedom which they have seldom known—with the direct result that after a good night's rest you will almost certainly be able to kick yourself and so gratify an inclination which many feel, but few—such is their physical condition—are privileged to indulge.

    Let me commend to your good offices a fat and dishevelled Frenchman you will find hereabouts. He has lately suffered a bereavement and will appreciate your condolence. You should get on together. He shares, for instance, your affection for other people's jewels and had recently arranged to sell a parcel of these to an American for forty thousand pounds. The deal, however, fell through. Forty thousand pounds in bearer bonds.

Finally—good-bye.

I shall always remember our day at Loumy together and the little conundrums which we exchanged. And to-day's been even better. In a word, it's been an immense pleasure to us all to beat you all ends up at your rotten game.

And now I must go and change.

Yours faithfully,
Berry Pleydell.

This note we put with the pearls and the contact-breaker on the seat of the hired car.

Two minutes later we started across the heather *en route* for the dell.

As we dropped out of sight of the road, I turned to see if Casca was where we had last seen him, supine on the ground.

The blackguard was sitting up, arranging his tie.

When he saw us looking, he deliberately turned his back, like a naughty child.

"Oh, the pet," said Berry. "And if we took a step towards him, he'd run for his life."

With that, he dropped the coil of rope he was bearing, let out a yell and began to run towards Casca, waving his arms.

The latter gave one look round. And then he was up on his feet and plunging over the heather as hard as he could.

But he was not built for such country, and before he had gone thirty paces he took the toss of his life . . .

It is my pleasure to record that when he arose he seemed dissatisfied with his state.

As Berry rejoined us—

"Pure negligence," he said shortly. "He didn't look where he was going. And there you are. Cows will be cows."

With tears running down his cheeks—

"To you the glory," said Jonah. "And now pick up your string

235

and we'll make for that ridge. If we're over that in ten minutes, that ought to do."

"Quite so," said Berry. "Can I have a drink at Louvie? Or must I wait till Bordeaux?"

"That depends," said Jonah, "on what Adèle has to say."

From the moment we crossed the ridge, only Adèle and Jill were in a position to see what was happening at Halfway House. They were lying high up on a shoulder above the dell. So for nearly an hour we knew nothing of what was toward. But since they made us no signal, we knew there was nothing to fear. And, as we caught sight of the Rolls, they began to descend. Before we had put off our corruption, they had joined us on the bank of the stream.

"Still there?" said Jonah.

"Only Casca and his chauffeur," said Adèle. "The others have taken his car and gone down into Spain."

Half an hour at Louvie-Juzon refreshed us in mind as in body, for there in an old-world parlour Adèle took up her report.

"They arrived about five minutes after you'd crossed the ridge. Auntie Emma was easily first, but he looked all in. He fell upon the pearls like a madman, but from the way he scrumpled it up, I don't think he liked Berry's note. When the others arrived, he fairly put it across them. Of course they couldn't argue : it was all they could do to stand up : and when one of them answered him back, Auntie Emma slung the pearls in his face and he just fell down. Then they started to look for Casca. . . .

"They didn't have far to go, for Casca was being cleaned. I don't know what you'd done to him, but he seemed as mad as a hornet about some state he was in and the chauffeur was trying to clean him up with petrol out of his tank. Then Auntie Emma came up, and Casca sagged at the knees.

"For what it was worth, they searched him : and when the search was over they knocked him down. Then they hauled him up and started to ask him questions, and each time he gave the wrong answer they shook him by the scruff of his neck. From his frenzied protests I fancy he told them the truth. But that didn't help him. The truth was ugly and so the answer was wrong and he got it in the neck. Presently they obviously asked him which way you'd gone, and when Casca pointed to the *Pic du Midi*, I thought he was going to be murdered before my eyes. So did Casca. Auntie Emma took out a pistol and shoved it against his chest, and Casca shut his eyes and screamed blue murder until he took it away.

"At last they let him go, and two of them ran for the hired car, while the others got into Casca's and started her up. When the chauffeur demurred, Auntie Emma showed him his pistol, and he backed straight into Casca who was sitting in a state of collapse. I think he trod on his hand, for Casca wrapped himself round him and tried to bite his leg.

"By now Auntie Emma was moving, but the others came tearing after to say the hired car wouldn't start. After a furious altercation Auntie Emma took them aboard and then the five went rocketing down into Spain.

"So Casca and his chauffeur were left.

"I must say they were awfully funny. Casca sat on the ground nursing his hand and rocking himself to and fro and waving away the chauffeur, who kept showing him some bright object which must, I think, have been the cap of the petrol-tank. Then he showed it to him once too often, and Casca snatched it away and flung it across the road. Then they had a stand-up row. . . . Time and again they came to the edge of battle, each, I suppose, unjustly upbraiding the other for what he had failed to do. Seven times they parted, and seven times one or the other shouted some obvious insult sufficiently biting to bring them together again. But at last they agreed to join forces, and when I came down they were trying to turn the car."

"That's right," said Jonah. "To coast down as far as they can. With luck they should get to the tree-trunk."

"I don't think they will," said Adèle. "Casca's idea of helping was very crude."

"He never helped at all," cried Jill. "The chauffeur had to leave him to take the wheel, and the moment he left him Casca sat down on the step."

"The old Adam," sighed Berry. "I've done the same thing myself. Never mind. He's a great time coming. I've no doubt they took all his money, and that's a hell of a jar when you've only got three days to cover your tracks."

237

"D'you think he'll believe," said Piers, "that we mean to inform the police?"

"We must," said Jonah. "He knows that as well as we. We told them the jewels were taken, and we must tell them they're found. And if we don't, the underwriters will. Oh, he'll disappear all right. We can refuse to prosecute—but Casca will never know that. He may suspect it : but the only way to make sure is to come back and see."

"Exit Maimie," said Berry. "You know I can hardly believe that we're back as we were. Fancy not having to get up at dawn to-morrow and lie in some beerless arbour to wait on some bandit's whim."

"I hate to say it," said Jonah, "but from Bordeaux to Havre is over four hundred miles. If we're to do that to-morrow we ought to be off by eight."

"What's eight o'clock?" said Berry. "For the last three weeks I haven't slept after four. I tell you this early rising's got on my nerves. I took a bath last night and when I got out I couldn't remember whether I was getting up or going to bed. Never mind. It's been well worth it. If Auntie Emma had beat us, I should never have slept again."

"Then let's get on," said Jonah. "I know he went down into Spain, but he might come back. And we've been caught bending once in a wayside inn."

The allusion brought us all to our feet— as well it might.

Five minutes later we were once more upon the road.

*   *   *   *   *

"My darling," cried Daphne, "where on earth's your moustache?"

"That," said her husband, "depends upon the drainage at Louvie-Juzon. If it's by septic tank——"

"It was shot away," said I, picking up the Marquis Lecco. I lowered my voice. "Who's that man over there with a spare room under his nose?"

"Belly bein' funny," said the Marquis, and hid his face in my coat.

We had been ashore but two hours and had driven straight from the quay to our Hampshire home.

Enter Hortense

As though to hail our entry, the New Forest was *en fête*. Pride of the morning had turned the yellow roads brown, silvered the floods of bracken, darkened the weathered jackets of sentinel oaks : thicket and greensward glittered, and hedgerows flashed, and the fine, fresh air was stuffed with those matchless perfumes which only the earth of England can ever brew.

Our breakfast-table maintained the brilliant argument. Diamonds and emeralds sprawled on the white linen cloth, the Marquis was arranging our cuff-links in one long chain and out of our four cigarette-cases the Lady Elaine was making a miniature pavement of winking gold.

"Toast," said Berry, taking the two last pieces that stood in the rack. "I'm glad to get back to toast. And a loaf of brown bread that isn't like potter's clay."

"Tea," said Adèle. "Real tea."

She drank luxuriously.

I raised my cup.

"To you and Jill," said I. "You've had a rotten time, and you've stuck it damned well. Waiting, watching, packing, clearing out at a moment's notice, meals at all hours. . . ."

"I enjoyed every minute," said Adèle. "And now, as if I'd suffered, I have my reward."

She picked up her great-grandmother's necklace and clasped it about her sweet neck.

"That," said Berry, "is life. Man goes out and sweats blood and brings his spoils and lays them at woman's feet. Why? God knows. And now let's apportion the credit."

"We can't," said Piers. "It's indivisible. I admit I didn't do much, but you and Jonah and Boy . . .

"And Fluff and Susie," said I. "By thunder, they did their bit."

"And Adèle," said Berry. "Be fair. But for that brown-eyed siren you call your wife——"

"I'll divide it," said Jill, "because I'm the only one who's done nothing at all. Jonah comes first because he found out it was Casca and——"

"Yes, and who got the pearls?" said Berry. "Recovered them single-handed in the sweat of his trunk? Why, but for me——"

"That was a fluke," said Jill. "Besides, it was Jonah that——"

"Fluke?" screamed Berry. "Fluke? Oh, give me strength. And

here's ingratitude. I suppose it was a fluke that I won the information you'd all been trying to snaffle for over six weeks."

"And wrote it down for Auntie Emma," said Piers.

"Oh, the venomous suckling," said Berry. "That's what I get for finding his rotten beads."

When order had been restored—

"Listen," said I. "I'll put it all into a book."

"That's right," said Berry. "I'll help you. And the public shall judge."

"Real names?" said Jonah.

"Why not," said I. "If Casca sues me for libel, I'll take him on."

Upon consideration we altered two or three names. Blucher and Loumy, for instance, are substitutes : and so are Woking and Nay. But as Fluff and his wife have made their home in New Zealand, we let the nickname stand.

THE END